CH00949984

Never
The Twain

A dark blend of Gothic romance and murder

Jane Fenwick

CIP catalogue record for this title is available from the British Library.
ISBN 978-1-9161957-0-7

Cover design by Charlotte Mouncey
Cover illustration Whitby Abbey Terrace 1861
courtesy of Frances Elizabeth Wynne

Printed by Amazon

www.janefenwick.co.uk

About The Author

Jane Fenwick lives in the market town of Settle in Yorkshire, England. She studied education at Sheffield University gaining a B.Ed (Hons) in 1989 and going on to teach primary age range children. Jane decided to try her hand at penning a novel rather than writing school reports as she has always been an avid reader, especially enjoying historical and crime fiction. She decided to combine her love of both genres to write her first historical crime novel *Never the Twain*. Jane has always been a lover of antiques, particularly art nouveau and art deco ceramics and turned this hobby into a business opening an antiques and collectables shop in Settle. However her time as a dealer was short lived; she spent far too much time in the sale rooms buying items that ended up in her home rather than the shop! Animal welfare is a cause close to Jane's heart and she has been vegetarian since the age of fourteen. For the last twenty years she has been trustee of an animal charity which rescues and re-homes cats, dogs and all manner of creatures looking for a forever home. Of course several of these have been "adopted" by Jane! Although she lives in the Yorkshire Dales Jane is particularly drawn to the North East Coast which she knows well; often visiting Whitby, Sandsend and Alnmouth for research purposes. When she isn't walking on Sandsend beach with her dog Scout, a Patterdale "Terrorist" she is to be found in her favourite coffee shop gazing out to sea and dreaming up her next plot. Jane is currently writing a historical saga series again set on the North East coast beginning in 1765. The first two books are being edited at the moment; *My Constant Lady* and *The Turning Tides*. Look out for *My Constant Lady* in 2020.

Late 19th Century London
Prologue

Come in out of the cold. The foyer is warm and welcoming is it not? Were the girls under the arches troublesome? Covent Garden isn't what it used to be. Some of those whores once trod the boards, before their looks deserted them, life can be cruel don't you think?

Inside, the gaslight is low for a reason. It hides a multitude of sins. The red velvet curtains are moth eaten and the paint is peeling on the gilded pillars and posts, but in this light everything looks grand, it feels opulent, inviting?

The foyer is thronged. The audience fligged up in their finery, mill about deciding who is al à mode and who has remodelled last year's best. Men in their frock coats, cloaks and toppers deposited in the cloakroom, puff on their cigars. The ladies rustle in silk and taffeta. They preen and prink while fans waft away the smoke; musky cologne masks body odour – well almost. All classes are assembled here tonight, from the high brow to the low born.

The coarser element of the audience guzzle hot meat pies,

flakes of buttery pastry fall to the carpet for the mice to nibble later. The lad over by ticket seller is a well known slanger, so watch out or your carriage fare home will be gone.

There is a general feeling of anticipation; opening nights are always nerve jangling events. Something could go wrong: a missed entrance, a prop failure, someone could forget their lines and need prompting.

The performance is about to start. Come, take your seat. Stalls, dress circle, a box perhaps? I hope your eyes are becoming accustomed to the limelight, it seems to cast deep shadows don't you think? Are you wondering what lurks there? Do not worry – it is not a ghost story although I hope some may find the tale a little haunting. The performance has some scenes, which the more nervous of you, may find distressing. It all depends on your point of view. If you are a lady, some scenes may shock. If you are a gentleman you may be titillated before you find yourself heeding a warning. Then again, if you are in the cheap seats, well, who knows what you will make of it, you probably only came in out of the rain. I must warn you all however, be you Lord, Lady or commoner, the first act is, perhaps a little, shall we say, unpleasant for mixed company; for those of you unused to the labours of the child bed that is. But bear with, it is soon over.

You will, no doubt, all take a different moral from the story – each to their own. Come what may, the main protagonists have learned their lines but there has been little rehearsal and I anticipate a lot of improvisation. The show as they say must go on. I will provide you with the asides just in case you were too tight to buy a programme and lose the plot.

Now you are settled in your seat I hope you are full of expectancy while you wait for the first act to begin. There is no intermission, so if you need to go, you had better go now before curtain up. Are those chocolates? I hope you won't be bothersome and rattle the wrappers.

The stage is set, the cast assembled, the curtain is about to rise. In the wings the cast prepares to make their entrance. It is yet to be seen whether they receive a standing ovation. That is for you to decide. Let the show commence.

Act 1
Whitby 1873
1

The clock on the mantel shelf ticks on. The labour is twenty six hours long and the birthing pains are at last coming quicker. She bears down, puffs out her cheeks and wishes it would end. Elizabeth Buchanan's delicate frame stiffens; her body is not built for endurance. The vice like grip abates. She tries to recover her equilibrium ready for the final assault.

'One more push and it shall be over,' the midwife encourages her. Elizabeth waits for the swell to rise again, her body responds as if of its own volition. The child enters, centre stage, takes her first breath and cries. Elizabeth sinks back exhausted. There is to be an interval, but not a long one.

The midwife quickly and expertly cuts the cord, gives the child a cursory wipe with a scrap of linen, then wraps her in a blanket and lays her in the bassinet.

'Come now Elizabeth, take a sip of brandy wine, you need to gather your strength again.'

The clock chimes midnight. Elizabeth lifts her head, wets her parched lips and feels the liquor burn her throat.

'I am so fagged,' Elizabeth says knowing the performance is not yet over.

The midwife moves to the bottom of the bed and prepares by placing a clean towel over the soiled sheets. Elizabeth feels the next painful swell rack her body, straining and panting she pushes hard. Beads of perspiration, for ladies do not sweat, break out over her hair, head and neck. Another push, another breath and another baby comes wailing into the world. She is swiftly dealt with and placed next to her sleeping sister. Sharing the limelight will soon become familiar to the girls.

'Well now, let's get you sorted.' Mrs O'Leary bundles up the bloodied soilings and sets to tending to Elizabeth's needs with care and attention.

'Two bonny girls,' she mutters as she removes the afterbirth, 'twin bright stars to light up the stage no doubt. 'Tis a pity it was not one of each.'

Elizabeth lays still, eyes closed – she is spent. The births have been arduous. Too tired to heed the prattling of the midwife, she lays wrung out and dishevelled, sleep is all she craves. As she drifts into a blissful state her shoulders are lifted and bolstered with soft, downy pillows, Elizabeth slumps back. Two bundles are placed in her arms. She rallies a little as she looks at her twin daughters for the very first time. Both babies sleep contentedly as though their debut has been too much for them.

Elizabeth smiles winsomely. 'Which one opened the show?'

'Her in the lemon blanket.' The midwife stops her work, looks down on the sleeping babes and smiles, 'I knew I would get in a muddle so devised a plan before we started.' The midwife looks suitably smug. 'Ain't that funny they are twins but they have different birthdays! I noticed the clock strike twelve. Miss Lemon-drop here was born just afore midnight and the other came five minutes after.' Elizabeth is too tired to think about it, then suddenly says, 'But not just different days, different months surely? For yesterday was the last day of April and so today is the first of May; their birthdays are in different months!'

The midwife chuckles, 'Would you believe it, twins born a month apart! I never knowed such a thing afore an' I've delivered twins more than once.'

The midwife continues to chatter on. Elizabeth is absorbed with the new arrivals. The translucent skin under their eyes has a bluish tinge. Fine, fair hair and lashes – they are like tiny china dolls, each face identical, so small but perfect.

'April and May,' she tells them. 'You could have no other names.' Elizabeth stares in wonder at the twin likeness of her daughters but does not see understudies; their celebrity will be of a different kind.

♣

Elizabeth Buchanan is an actress and a beauty. She has pale, blonde hair and ocean-blue eyes that have never had dark circles under them, until now that is.

Elizabeth will worry about them when she has rested and looks in the mirror. She needn't; she will quickly regain her looks. You have not seen her at her best. She is usually better prepared than when you first met her, disarranged after giving birth to babies she does not want.

No amount of rehearsal could have prepared her for the role of Mother. It is a face change she has not sought, she prefers not to play farce and this is certainly no comedy. A tragedy perhaps? The part she is playing is certainly against type.

Although Whitby born and bred Elizabeth has spent most of her time away from the North East harbour town, performing on the London stage. Sometimes she goes to Glasgow if the part warrants it, but she is in demand and can pick and choose her roles. She likes to stay in the metropolis where she has many admirers.

One such admirer has given her more than flowers, fine dinners and jewellery. He has now given her twin daughters. They are not as welcome as the gifts she can exchange at the pawn broker. Elizabeth has never, not even for a second, contemplated keeping the babies. Her career, which she has worked hard for, would be compromised, one baby would have been difficult enough, but two is unthinkable.

The father, minor aristocracy and married, is somewhat shocked at the news his mistress is with child. It is not what he would have expected from Elizabeth. Despite her attempts to rid herself of the problem, attempts that have always worked in the past, she soon realised she was going to be indisposed for some time as the mistake refused to be dislodged.

The father has made some monetary recompense before leaving for the continent with his wife and sons; twin sons. Therefore, when in the seventh month of her pregnancy, Elizabeth was told two heart beats could be detected, she was not surprised. Dismayed but not astonished. The cast list is to grow and Elizabeth is reluctant to share the stage with anyone, especially children. The old adage "never work with children and animals" is one she has adhered to all her life; she does not intend to be a stock character now, held back by the unwanted brats.

♠

'My instinct to return to Whitby for my confinement is the right one,' Elizabeth had told her maid. 'I do not want to be viewed while my waist thickens and my ankles swell. Elspeth watched as her mistress turned and assessed herself in the looking glass.

The father had now jumped ship – Elspeth suspected her mistress did not want to be seen by any replacement who might offer his protection.

'For the first time in my life as an actress I see the benefit of "resting".' Elizabeth patted a curl.

Having secured a house on fashionable West Cliff Crescent she settled to await the births. She was not a happily expectant mother; she was a prisoner waiting to be condemned. The grey of the cold North Sea matched her gloom, without adoration she wilted like a picked bluebell.

'This last month I have grown enormous.' she curled her lip, 'It is tedious and tiring.' She fanned herself as she lay on the velvet chaise.

'It will soon all be over, you are the type of woman who likes company and male company at that, there is none to be had in your condition; come take a stroll with me, it will be a distraction – you grow exceedingly listless.' Elspeth stands but Elizabeth refuses to budge.

'It will take more than a walk around this dreary town to distract me! I miss the friends who normally flock to my elegant parties and dinners, they are conspicuous by their absence are they not? The few female friends I have avoid me as though being with child is a highly contagious disease!'

Her usual self confidence has fled along with her waistline. Elizabeth's looks and figure are her bread and butter, without them she cannot hope to find stage roles or a man of means to keep her in the manner she has grown used to expecting.

'I so look forward to the day when, my figure back as it should be, I can once again return to my former life of merriment and men, parties and admiration. When I am back centre stage and applauded, back treading the boards where I belong I will be bright and cheerful again Elspeth, you will see.'

The day cannot come soon enough for Elspeth; she has heard the same speech daily for the past six weeks.

Elizabeth's only support, if support is the right term, at this trying time is Mrs Jansen. She is fair and of Dutch descent, having landed on these shores on the arm of a seafaring man who, almost at once, abandoned her. She too is an actress – of sorts. However, the salon is her theatre, the bedroom her stage.

Having no other means of support she has kept herself, like many before her, by selling the only asset she has; herself. She could never consider the role of fishwife, gutting herring would turn her stomach. In a sea port where prostitution was a lucrative profession she soon became popular in the art of pleasing men. She learned quickly to be discerning. This was the way to make money enough to live and not simply to survive. Velda Jansen never intended to stand against the damp walls of Whitby on wet and windy nights. If she was going to sell her body, and she knew of no other way to make her living, she was at least going to lie down on the job.

Nowadays in elegant and comfortable surroundings her "gentlemen" relax and take their pick of the most beautiful girls in the North East. Her establishment caters for all tastes and predilections – at a price of course as she never tires of telling her gentlemen, "Beautiful, clean girls do not come cheap."

Now she sits, tall and imposing, on Elizabeth's gold brocade sofa. In her late thirties she is still beautiful, her bone structure has seen to that.

'So there now, not one but two daughters, one would, I am sure have been an encumbrance but two!' The trace of a Dutch accent is still to be detected.

'Yes double the trouble I am afraid.' Elizabeth sips her tea and looks at the beautiful creature sitting by the Madam's side. She looks barely sixteen and is slender with a pale elegance; to Elizabeth she has a vacuous look about her but then she thinks, men do not pay the girl for her conversation.

'Would you care for one of these luscious chocolates,

my dear? My beau sent them to me from France, so thoughtful.' She hands the box of violet creams to Velda. 'He knows they are my absolute favourites.'

The man she refers to is long gone, the chocolates she has ordered herself from a prestigious shop in London. She is keeping up appearances.

Velda's long fingers plunge into the box, she takes one before handing the confectionery to the vacant girl, whose eyes suddenly light up. 'You shouldn't eat those if you want to keep your figure my dear,' Velda says spitefully as she hands the beribboned box back to Elizabeth.

'I never put on weight, dearest one,' the actress smiles. 'I am the same size now as I was before the birth. My waist has just snapped back into shape.' She helps herself to another. Elizabeth closes her eyes, an enraptured look on her face and bites into the fondant. Velda knows the theatricals are for her benefit.

'What will you do with the twins, my dear? You cannot take them with you. I presume you have an engagement for the season in town?'

'Of course not! Next month I return to play at the Adelphi. The girls shall stay here in Whitby. I cannot wait to get back to the lights and the laughter, I have been much frustrated here in this tedious place and much missed I dare say.'

Elizabeth is her own self-publicist. She has had to be.

Mrs Jansen bristles at her adopted town being thus described and at Elizabeth's vanity. Whitby has been the making of the Madam, she has grown rich from the oldest profession in the world and thanks God daily for the seemingly never ending procession of rich, horny, men who spend handsomely at her brothel.

The constant stream of clients, with needs to be met, has made Whitby attractive to her: another tide another ship, another crew with urges to be serviced. Whaling and ship building put money in men's pockets and Mrs Jansen knows how to pick those pockets.

Each morning her girls promenade about the town, chaperoned by the lady herself, advertising their presence to every newly docked frigate or schooner, cutter or lugger. Dressed in bright ribbons and lace, the girls might be mistaken for the daughters of the newly rich merchants, but on closer inspection one might detect a swaying of the hips no lady of breeding would exhibit.

Elizabeth wipes her delicate fingers on her napkin and sighs, 'My sister is to take the twins, to all intents and purposes they will be her children. She has none of her own and will be recompensed for her troubles so all is happily arranged to everyone's satisfaction.'

The beautiful creature with the empty head twists a curl in her finger idly and looks about her. Her attention span is short.

'Your sister who is landlady at The Angel Inn?' Velda knows the sister well. The Madam regularly sends girls to the tavern's rooms, if the men are prepared to pay extra.

'In time your daughters will be a useful source of free labour I am sure,' the Madam says encouragingly. Elizabeth turns the tables.

'How is business Velda dear?

'Could not be better! My select bevy of beauties are educated in ways I know will suit my clients. No other bawdy house on the East coast has girls so willing and beguiling, so accommodating and so talented.' Mrs Jansen smiles at the girl by her side. 'I look after my charges as if they are well bred ladies at a finishing school, except on my curriculum there are more useful skills to be learnt; skills which earn me good money.'

She uses her elbow to rouse the girl. 'Don't slouch my dear, God gave you a back bone for a reason.'

'I am pleased you are doing well.' Elizabeth could not care less.

'My gentlemen know my girls are talented and clean. After all, most of my gentlemen are married men, or about to be, and no one wants to give the clap as a wedding gift.' She sips her tea and arches an eyebrow. 'The unchaperoned fiancée is as rare as hen's teeth and married ladies are not always compliant in the bedroom. Men will always have needs and I, or rather my girls, see to those needs with the utmost discretion and care – for a price.'

'Indeed, I am glad to hear it.'

'Mine is the only establishment where the well-heeled will venture, if, that is, they can gain admittance.' Mrs Jansen smiles knowingly. 'While their wives and sisters take the medicinal spa waters at the Chalybeate Springs along the cliff top, their husbands and brothers sample a tonic of a different sort.'

The girl yawns; she has heard it all before.

Elizabeth smiles: 'You have done well for yourself, you have made your little bordello quite the toast of Whitby.'

From humble beginnings on 'Grope Lane', Velda has moved up, quite literally, in the world. From the squalor of the East Cliff alleyways and ginnels of Whitby

Harbour, she has worked her way upwards via the inns and taverns to a high class establishment on West Cliff. Here, far above the blubber house, coaching inn and fish market she has built up a clientele and a stable of girls that is renowned.

Velda bristles. 'My gentlemen are members of a selective club. We have titled gentlemen on our books. Of course some men are just passing through the port and in that case exceptions can be made, but generally they are either introduced by a member or, and this rarely happens, they must impress me with the size of their purse or cut of their jib. My girls are too precious to squander on some mid-ship man with little coin and no prospects.' Velda adds proudly 'I do not admit just any scurvy sailor.' Velda Jansen only ever thinks in the long term, never the short.

'Other exceptions can be made if, for instance, the young son of a gentleman member arrives without tin to be "blooded".' She laughs and waves a lace handkerchief as if batting away a fly. 'I have been known to allow him entrance, knowing that when he comes of age some of his inheritance will swell my coffers, I am a business woman after all.'

Elizabeth nods. 'And a shrewd one my dear, all seems well arranged as you say.' Velda makes ready to leave and nudges the girl beside her.

Has she nodded off? Who can blame her? Her night time encounters are tiresome as most of her clients are old and expect her to do all the work.

'In the meantime if you are able, and I am sure your funds must be dwindling, I could send you a gentleman or two to keep your spirits up. I should only send someone who would be entertaining, you understand. I have always the need of a good looking woman of experience, you only have to say the word.' Mrs Jansen smiles condescendingly as she plays with her ring infested fingers.

'That is most kind my dear, but I am not sure your provincial gentlemen can afford a celebrity like me.'

Elizabeth delivers the line with all the assurance of a professional.

'Soon I will be gone, my labours but an unpleasant interlude. My twin daughters set aside to allow me to continue my rise to the top.'

Velda Jansen smiles and kisses her friend's perfect, pink cheeks as she leaves.

2
Whitby 1890

The next time we meet April and May they have grown into beautiful young ladies, well not ladies exactly. They are about to endure a change of circumstance.

Over the years April and May see their birth mother rarely. An annual visit to the spa town is arranged so Elizabeth can take the waters and visit her "nieces" and sister. The twins at seventeen are not easy to place – if one saw them out and about the streets of Whitby they would not be taken for the daughters of the landlady of a coaching inn. They have been raised higher than their station.

They turn heads in their matching outfits. Their identical looks, blonde curls and dainty manners mark them out as they go about in the town. Many a sailor has his ardour roused as they trip along the lanes and ginnels, side stepping slimy fish guts with their dainty slippers.

They have received an education, clothes and accoutrements from a quarterly allowance supplied by the efforts of their birth mother, and whichever oblivious suitor she was in thrall to at the time.

April and May are a cut above the acquaintances of their adoptive mother. They are cuckoos in the nest. Yet still they are not quite ladies, their clothes and style being just that little bit too flashy, a smidgen too gaudy for Whitby; theatrical perhaps? Definitely showy. Neither are they of the mercantile class, having no father's profession to mark them. They take after their thespian mother in mode, manner and demeanour. Eyes are drawn to them wherever they go, they have potential.

Potential for what I hear you ask? Have you not been paying attention?

In the intervening years, Elizabeth's career has grown and her popularity with the aristocracy along with it. She is sought after at all the fashionable London hotspots. Protectors have come and gone and now, in her early thirties, if she is to be believed, Elizabeth's acting career has begun to stall for the first time.

As luck has it, she has managed to draw the attention of a Lord, who, having kept her as his mistress for the last four years and having lost his young wife in the child bed is keen to take Elizabeth as his wife. He is exceedingly old and in need of a companion to service him without the need to trouble himself beyond his own estate. Marriage is an unfamiliar concept to Elizabeth as it has never presented itself for her consideration before.

'I know most Lords do not marry their mistress so I am keen to secure this starring role before it slips between my fingers,' she tells Elspeth.

Desperate more like! She knows at her advanced age such

an opportunity may never come her way again.

'You need the security now more than ever. You are beginning to be upstaged by younger girls, with less talent and more front.' Elspeth says less than tactfully.

You will no doubt be forming a picture of Elizabeth. Self interest you will see is paramount to her. Before you judge, ask yourself what you would do in her circumstances. She may not have provided her twins with love and attention, but she has provided them with a home and an education. It is more than some in her situation would have done. Most mistakes go over the harbour wall at the dead of night.

So it is a bitter blow when Elizabeth receives the news that her sister has died! Suddenly and without due concern for what is going to happen to the twins she has cared for since their birth. Elizabeth is vexed. She is just about to be married. The supporting cast in this ensemble has gone, stage right, the timing could not be worse. Now, after seventeen years, the twins are once again a headache to their mother.

Her brother-in-law left the company several years ago, when the twins were toddlers so he cannot be of use.

'My soft hearted sister has shied away from the twins wenching at the inn. She has preferred to pay for labour while two able girls sat idle!' At the time Elizabeth had concurred, she did not see it as any of her business. Now she sees the error.

'They are spoilt – their soft hands untarnished. Educated, pretty, but not fit for work, they are now miscast', she tells Elspeth emphatically. 'The coaching inn can no longer contain them.'

'Perhaps they could come to London?'

By the time Elizabeth's train steams into Whitby Railway Station they have no permanent roof over their beautiful, identical heads.

Elizabeth is plunged into despair. 'What am I to do? My marriage is imminent I cannot present my aged, future husband with a wedding gift of two nubile and attractive girls.' She looks pleadingly at Elspeth.

The long suffering maid can see the comparison might prove the undoing of her mistress but knows better than to say so. She sees trouble ahead.

'Nor can I send them away to school,' Elizabeth bemoans, 'they are already educated way above their station, to continue down that path would not only be costly, but foolish. Besides, now I am to be married my income from the stage will disappear.'

Elspeth thinks also as her future spouse is, naturally, blissfully unaware Elizabeth has children in the first place, he can hardly be asked to pay for their upkeep.

Elizabeth can think of only one solution.

♦

April and May know their lives are about to change when their Aunt Elizabeth arrives at The Angel Inn for the first time that year. True, their mother, her sister, has died two months ago but as she had not come for the funeral they are concerned when she arrives and asks to see them in one of the inn's private rooms. They are concerned, but happy to see their Aunt as they are beginning to wonder what will become of them.

They have hopes that will soon be dashed.

'You both look radiant my dears.'

Elizabeth has rehearsed her lines on the journey north no doubt.

'Your looks have not been affected by the loss of your dear Mama I am pleased to see. You must feel so lonely here now without her guiding hand and influence?'

The girls tell of their mother's last weeks and become tearful and melodramatic.

Elizabeth listens impatiently to what she has already read in a long letter the twins were thoughtful enough to write and feels the audition needs to progress quicker and so she pushes on.

'Yes, yes. Very sad. Both of you have had a good education but must realise that you cannot stay under this roof now it is under new management. You are obviously too well bred and too precious to stay in such an establishment.'

Both girls smile happily. They want their aunt's visit to effect some change as they, too, feel the disparity in their surroundings. They are both keen to go to London to live with their famous aunt and there, hopefully, meet rich, handsome husbands. Or, if their Aunt Elizabeth thinks they are capable, they might even become actresses themselves. After all, it is in the blood; how hard can it be? They are good looking, with trim waists and bright blonde hair. They already look the part.

Elizabeth says, 'As you are aware I am soon to have a change of circumstance and expect to be "sur le continent" after my marriage. I expect to be gone for many months. Therefore I have devised a plan whereby you both might be placed in employment that would afford you a lifestyle. I need to know before I go abroad that you will be cared for, I owe it to my darling sister.'

The twins watch as Elizabeth dabs the corner of her eye with flimsy French lace. 'I have spoken to a lady here in Whitby, an old acquaintance of mine, and brokered an apprenticeship – of sorts.'

The twins' faces drop. They do not want to stay in the spa town. They had hoped to see the sights of London and be admired by more than randy whalers and fishermen.

'An apprenticeship Aunt, here in Whitby – to learn to do what?' May, always the most forthright of the sisters, can hardly keep the disappointment from her voice. When April and May are told what their training will lead to they can barely comprehend it.

♣

It is a bright and breezy day when the twins take up residence in their new abode, high up on the West Cliff overlooking the spangly sea. It is two weeks since they learned of their fate from their charming, but determined Aunt Elizabeth.

When she had told them what had been arranged for them, they could scarce believe it. Even now, two weeks later, they are still finding it hard to come to terms with their destiny. April, always the most sensitive of the twins, has been inconsolable.

Aunt Elizabeth has explained all the advantages of such positions. She has made it appear like the best solution in the world for their predicament. She has brooked no argument when May suggests they should come to London to live with their aunt. Elizabeth makes it perfectly clear this is not going to happen; under any circumstances. What has been offered to them is going to happen, make no bones about it, there has been little debate. It is a case of take what is on offer or fend for themselves, alone, in the cold, wide world.

From the moment the twins know their misfortune they are resigned; double crossed and angry with their only living relative, but reconciled to their fate. April and May have soon come to see they must submit to this new life.

They are to become, what is the correct nomenclature? Concubines, courtesans, paramours, ladies of pleasure? If we are being kind, certainly. If not then whores, prostitutes, ladies of ill repute, harlots, trollops, tarts? The list is endless. Whatever the title, at least they are to be placed in a renowned establishment. It is this, or earn their living as working girls in much the same way but in much reduced circumstances – on the docks of Whitby Harbour.

'But we could get employment as governesses or even shop girls, surely we could manage? We have been schooled,' April says wringing her hands in frustration.

May, ever the more pragmatic is not so sure. 'We could, quite possibly or one of us at least could but where should we live? Since Mama died everything has changed; we do not even have shelter now.' She strokes her sister's hair to try to comfort her. 'The money needed to keep body and soul alive would be hard to earn as shop girls, we are not equipped. We should need introductions or references to be companions or governesses. Who is to do that for us? We have only each other. We have talked of this endlessly dearest and I can see no other way as yet. Yes, we could become shop girls and live in some squalid little hovel but should you be happy living from hand to mouth, for I should not! Let us succumb to the inevitable for the time being and set about a plan. At least we will have a roof over our heads. We are not in immediate danger of losing our virtue if Aunt Elizabeth and Mrs Jansen are to be believed. We have six months to come up with a way to escape this, this abomination and I for one do not mean to be sold to the highest bidder on my eighteenth birthday. We must keep our wits about us, accept the roof that is being offered, and make plans for our escape. Then we can arrange our own lives to suit ourselves, though how, I have yet to see.'

April knows her sister is right but continues to try to think of a plan to avoid the new life that is being prescribed. She does not want the part that is being offered and intends to resist the demeaning role.

♠

Velda Jansen smiles as she shows the girls into her private sitting room and pours tea into translucent china cups. For some minutes she makes polite conversation about the weather and the girls' health, all the while her eyes roam over the twins admiringly. They will most certainly be an asset to her establishment. Twins, such a novelty for her "gentlemen", will be in much demand she thinks.

The girls have fine, almost classical features, rosebud lips and glorious, silky blonde hair. And they are young; young and untouched. She is keen to discern any differences in the girls' appearance and scrutinises them closely. She can find none. They are like the proverbial "peas in a pod".

'Your erm, aunt,' Mrs Jansen remembers the relationship just in time, 'has been solicitous on your behalf my dears. She has arranged for you to join my prestigious establishment as apprentices, as it were. You will, until the age of eighteen be kept chaste, free from any contact of an intimate nature, if you understand my meaning; I could not have inexperienced girls on my books. My gentlemen would not like it I can assure you. Over the next six months you will be instructed in the art of pleasing men, there is *much* to learn. You will watch and study. It is a wonderful opportunity for you both. During this time you will of course, be expected to work in other ways to earn your keep, I am not a charity you understand.' She smoothes the silk of her dress, her sharp eye notices one of the twins flinch but for the life of her she has not a clue which one.

'The ways in which you will be expected to earn your living initially, will be by way of welcoming my guests. Acting as hostesses in the reception room, making my gentlemen welcome. That is, you will engage in flirtatious talk, flatter egos, and most importantly, encourage the clients to spend money. Act the coquette; with your pedigree I am sure you can perform. Warm the men up as it were, before the main event.'

A fruity laugh escapes her painted lips. 'Encourage them to partake of wines and spirits and to buy them for you too.' Mrs Jansen is warming to her theme. 'You will be given lessons in how best to sweet talk them into being parted from their coin, but I am sure such pretty creatures as you two will need little instruction.'

She smiles at the girls who remain impassive. 'You will

also be taught dance and the art of tableau. I, personally, will teach you how to look your best and give you lessons in deportment. I want to dangle you both, as it were, like delicious fruits for my gentlemen to admire so that by the time you are ripe they will be most keen to pluck you – secure one or other of you.' Or both together she thinks.

'That, of course, is your uniqueness. Identical twins, both beautiful, both virgins.'

Mrs Jansen hands a plate of biscuits which are refused. 'In the meantime you will have every comfort, all your needs will be taken care of just as though I was your dear Mama, may she rest in peace. You will from this day forward, receive my utmost care and protection.'

April and May sit listening to this discourse but do not speak. Their identical faces show the same vapid expression.

'You will eat the best food, be provided with the latest fashions and live under my roof. You will share a pretty little room together so you do not feel alone.' She simpers and waits for the twins to thank her. They do not. She continues, 'All I ask in return my dears is your loyalty and your promise as ladies that you will undertake your studies with due diligence. At eighteen you will both be launched.'

Velda smiles to herself. What she has planned for their eighteenth birthdays will set a bidding frenzy for the twins' maidenheads, the like of which no brothel has witnessed before. Velda Jansen is a business woman and she means to reap the reward of her investment.

'Now, let me show you to your room and you can unpack and settle yourselves in. Perhaps you would like to get to know some of my girls. They will show you the ropes I am sure. Stella, my most experienced girl, will be invaluable to you both I am certain.'

3

Captain Edward Driscoll has taken delivery of his latest ship and is enjoying the hospitality of his shipbuilder, William Vaughan. The two men are relaxing having eaten a good dinner at Mr Vaughan's mansion house on Royal Crescent. They are enjoying a crusted port and courtesy of the captain, smoking fine Virginia tobacco. The captain's family fortune has been made from its import in the last century. His business still involves, amongst other things, importing tobacco into Port Glasgow.

'You plan to sail her back to Scotland late next week after my painters have inscribed her name?' Vaughan asks.

'I do, I just need another night to think on it. I am certain she shall be named "The Two Brothers" but then I change my mind and think to call her 'The Edward and Alistair'. One of my ships is named after our sister, Effie Claire. I like to continue the tradition of using family names that my father started.'

'Let me know at your earliest convenience then my

painter can get started, we do not want a shoddy paint job ruining such a magnificent ship.' He passes the port which Edward refuses. He generally does not over imbibe especially when doing business.

'You tell me you are a single man, I was wondering if you are open to some sport with the ladies?' He winks at Edward who smiles back at the shipbuilder.

'What had you in mind, a tour of the harbour brothels?'

'Nothing so sordid my friend; just along West Cliff is an establishment where all needs are catered for in very pleasant surroundings. The girls are attractive and are checked regularly against diseases, which the harbour whores most certainly are not. I can introduce you as the Madam there is very particular about whom she admits. We could take a walk down and see if anyone takes our fancy.'

Our Leading man has made his entrance; the young one not the old codger. Edward Driscoll is a heart throb and no mistake. Is yours all-a-flutter?

The two men stroll along West cliff, the blustery winds buffeting them about. Captain Driscoll does not usually frequent brothels as he has no need of them. Although a handsome man he has found his money is the biggest draw where the ladies in his circle are concerned.

As he is wealthy, filthy rich in fact, he never has a shortage of women to keep him warm on chilly, Scottish nights.

The two men are shown into a ground floor room, lavish in its decoration. To Edward's discerning eye it is a vulgar stage set. Three or four other men sit on sofas talking to the young "ladies". Two young women, dressed identically, are sitting on a window seat talking quietly together. Mrs Jansen introduces them.

'Gentlemen, here are April and May to whet your appetites as it were,' she smiles saucily, 'They are going to be my brightest stars and next week they will be launched. It is to be a grand event. Please ask the girls about it and avail yourselves of wines or spirits, I am sure you will find something to your taste. The twins will look after you both, I shall leave you to become acquainted.' She nods to them and after making a circuit of the room, makes her exit.

Captain Driscoll looks searchingly at April and then at May. Next he looks at William Vaughan with an ironically raised eyebrow.

'Good evening ladies, I hope you are both well,' he says returning his gaze to the twins. I imagine most men begin with an exclamation about the fact that you are identical, or some such speech. I should imagine it is tedious in the extreme to begin every conversation in the same vein?'

'Certainly it is sir, it is a refreshing change not to begin a discourse with the self same explanation as we endure every evening,' May says. 'This is my sister April and I am May, can we offer either of you refreshment?'

Both men decline, having just dined and taken their fill of port.

The twins are reading from Mrs Jansen's script. Unbeknown to Captain Driscoll the girls have been given a list of suitable topics for conversation, all of them lead to bawdiness.

It is a role they have been forced to perfect for the pleasure of the old, unappealing men who usually grace the bawdy house. For the past few months they have each practised a monologue, a speech written to tease and stimulate the men, who with their foul, boozy breath, leer and paw the twins' peach soft skin.

Captain Driscoll addresses April. 'I should imagine you cannot be above seventeen years of age, how do you come to be here at such tender ages? Have you no guardians to look out for you, is there no other profession you would rather do?'

April gives a version of how they had found themselves at the brothel. She does so in a quiet voice so as not to be overheard by Stella, Mrs Jansen's head girl – her eyes and ears. Stella misses nothing and reports all.

April explains 'We have hopes of escaping this place to take employment as companions or some other reputable profession.' Edward can see the young girl in a different role, given the right clothes.

'So the plan is to auction you off to the highest bidder, your virtue and the fact you are twins being the main draw?' He looks at Vaughan and shakes his head. 'What say you William? I hope you do not think me a hypocrite, but when I have paid for women in the past, which has been infrequent, I had thought they should at least be old enough and wise enough to sell themselves of their own free will, it smacks of the cattle market does it not, this bartering?'

Mr Vaughan agrees but adds distractedly, 'It is as you say, but I am sure the young ladies do not complain. After all, I expect this life is preferable and more comfortable to a life on the streets.' Edward shakes his head in disbelief at his associate's cavalier attitude.

'Do you have learning April?' Edward sees that the sisters both have ladylike qualities; they seem out of place in this tawdry place.

'We both do sir, we went to school until last year. We both read, write and can do arithmetic. We studied music, history and geography.'

'April my dear, I hope Stella cannot hear this discourse; it is definitely not on our list of appropriate conversation.'

Edward laughs. 'You are given guidance on what to say! I am sorry April you were saying.'

'I was just going to say in addition we can sing and sew of course.'

'I am sure your discerning eye can see Captain that we are miscast here.' May says: 'We have accomplishments but sadly, no one to protect us.' He sees she looks downcast and being soft hearted he feels for the poor girls and their predicament.

♥

Tonight it makes a pleasant change, May thinks, to have someone worth making the effort for. She would not give Mr Vaughan a second glance but Captain Driscoll is the most handsome man she has ever seen. He has a distinguished look about him: a lazy, languid smile and twinkling eyes – eyes which she notices, do not undress them like most of the drabs they entertain. He reeks of money.

She thinks, if he took one of them for his mistress, he would, she is sure, prove to be their saviour. He is just the sort of rich, young man they have been looking for this past six months.

Mr Vaughan, being an older gentleman, is looking about him. He wants an experienced, real woman, not these young things who have not yet learned the tricks of their trade. He is hoping to spy Clara his favourite whore who he has spent time with on many occasions.

May begins to flirt, this one cannot get away – the six months is almost up. Edward shakes his head in disbelief when May tells him they can also ride.

She is not being pert!

'And yet with all your attainments you have both ended up here, in a bawdy house! It is scandalous.' His outburst is interrupted by Alfred, announcing a dance is to take place in the Red Room for the edification of the gentlemen.

Alfred, one of the stewards, a bully boy who, when he is not announcing, keeps his eye out for trouble. I say eye, as he only has the one! A patch gives him a piratical look. He was a whaler in a previous life and had his eye taken out after a drunken brawl when he beat a stevedore to death with his bare hands. He never has to lift a beefy finger here as his mere presence is a deterrent. But I digress.

♦

William Vaughan excusing himself rises. 'I think Clara might be one of the dancers, she is a particular favourite of mine. If she is, I will make myself known to her before someone else does.' Four or five other men have entered the room since their arrival and he does not want to miss out on her company.

Clara has talents Vaughan admires; abilities that feed his vicious predilections. He is never brutal you understand, but is another one who is handy with his fists.

Captain Driscoll remains seated and looks as if he is about to call it a night and leave the brothel. May knows if he leaves without spending money on wine or women, the Madam will blame them.

'Are you certain you would not like to view The Ladies sir? Mrs Jansen has the most wonderful girls, I am sure one of them would be to your taste.' She hates to offer him up, but what else can she do? She smiles seductively. She has practised the look, under Stella's direction, by looking in the mirror. She has perfected it.

Much to May's chagrin, the captain looks to April and smiles his languid, white toothed smile. 'I have always been of the nature that can wait for the best if I have to – so no thank you Miss May.' He stretches out his long legs. 'I am used to the finer things in life and seldom have to put up with second best. I thank you, but I have been spoilt by the company of you both tonight and so, I will venture out into the cold night with just your smiles to keep me warm.' Again it is April to whom he addresses this remark, a lingering look making her cheeks glow. May watches as he leaves and is frustrated.

♣

The following night, Captain Driscoll arrives at the door of Mrs Jansen's establishment. He is alone. He is recognised and shown in. He sweeps the salon with an intent look until he sees the twins. He hears the tinkle of May's laugh as they sit together with three men, lechers all, drooling and old enough to be their grandfathers. Edward scowls as he sits and watches as the men fawn over the twins. One strokes a finger down April's arm then lays his sweaty palm on her thigh and squeezes her leg. The thought of one of these men robbing this sweet girl of her virtue, makes him angry – and jealous. His feelings are confused you see, he is rankled. He has no appetite for this charade now, he feels the outrage on her behalf.

Stella has seen the captain enter and has been despatched by the Madam to make sure that tonight, the famously rich captain puts his hand in his silk-lined pocket.

'Good evening sir, Captain Driscoll is it not? Would you like company? I have a hatred of seeing such a handsome man as you sitting alone. May I get you something to drink?'

Edward sees what a raven haired beauty Stella is, as she slides beside him onto the sofa. She sits close. He smells her scent, honey and vanilla, and appreciates the swell of her pale breasts as they quiver in time to the beat of her pulse. He watches as her dark eyes cover him shamelessly, leaving him in no doubt as to what is on her mind. She is, he thinks, the sort of woman who knows how to please a man by guile.

In the usual course of events the encounter would have had only one outcome; he would have taken her – she is his type. Tonight he gazes at her half heartedly because since meeting April he sees no other woman will satisfy him. He has thought about the demure young woman often during the day. She has aroused his curiosity.

'Good evening,' he says, 'I will not take a drink at present thank you.'

'I was watching you last night captain and hoped

you would ask to join me, but then you left without satisfaction, I hoped you would come back soon.' The woman leans in closer and places her hand on his arm. 'I would wager there are strong muscles beneath,' she says as she squeezes the biceps beneath the fine wool of his jacket. He suspects this woman knows how to part men from their money, flattery rarely fails but to Edward this girl seems coarse in comparison to April.

♥

The captain is distracted, but not by her. Stella can tell. She is used to men being appreciative of her charms and is put out that she cannot hold his attention.

Stella is a rare thing indeed as she is a whore who enjoys her work. She likes to be looked at and desired but most of all she likes to be renowned for being able to please any man. She has been pleasing men for the Madam for five long years. She enjoys privileges no other whore can demand because her inventiveness and skill tempt men to return to her time and time again. Stella knows Mrs Jansen admires her. She trusts her – almost.

Using her wiles to advance herself, Stella makes it her mission to be the most sought after whore in the brothel. She is ambitious. Stella's speciality is her acting skills; she can be the bawdy kitchen wench or the innocent maid. She is the consummate artiste and the landowning gentry are particularly keen to pay when she acts shy and demure then becomes unleashed.

Yet lately she has lost interest in the play acting, she is bored by it. She looks for a different challenge, like any actress she needs stimulation if she is to give her best performance. She is able to handle any character requested of her given the right incentive. There is no act she will not submit to, no part she cannot play.

The captain, she thinks, could be her slave, she his concubine, he could be her pet, she his mistress. She could be submissive, he the aggressor she could be his mistress, he her lover...her mind has wandered from the task at hand. She smiles at Edward and sets about charming him with an experience borne of necessity. She wants to make him want her. It is her due.

A different tack is needed. She needs to rise to the challenge and, she tells herself archly, so does he. She flatters and flirts to raise the flaccid and does her utmost to persuade him upstairs, yet he is resolute and slack and staying where he is. She sees how he watches the twins like a cat watches a mouse. She knows he is waiting for the three men to move off, and then he will pounce for the kill. Stella does not have to wait long.

'Will you excuse me,' he says not waiting for an answer and moves off to where the twins sit. Stella is left alone and furious – she has never failed before.

'Good evening Miss April, Miss May.' He has correctly identified each twin. The discomfiture Stella felt is now passed to the twins as they have been warned by the Madam to encourage him to buy the overpriced, watered down liquor. They have seen that Stella has been unable to persuade him, so what hope have they?

♦

Knowing the Madam may walk in at any moment May, always the most assured of the twins decides on a way to make him pay; she does not relish the thought of a tongue lashing. She begins a delicate coughing. 'Please excuse me, I seem to have a tickle in my throat sir.' she coughs delicately again.

'Should you take a drink perhaps?' He lifts his arm to get the attention of the bar man; the twins visibly relax. When he has ordered drinks for them both he lounges back in his chair and smiles at April.

'I see now I have not been playing by the rules, I should have ordered drinks before should I not? I am unused to brothels and do not know the etiquette I hope you did not get into trouble on my account last night?'

May replies, 'We may have done if tonight Mrs Jansen's coffers had not been filled! We are supposed to ply gentlemen with drinks before they go upstairs. They are very expensive I think as she likes to make a good profit.'

April looks about her, an anxious look on her face. 'May that is indiscreet, if you were to be overheard we would be in trouble,' she whispers.

Edward laughs. 'I try not to drink after the port, I find it is easy to over indulge and wake up with a sore head. I have a business to run and need my head clear, not sozzled. I will try to remember in future to buy drinks for you ladies, and then the Madam will have nothing to complain of.'

He begins to talk about his business and his home port of Glasgow where he tells them he has just built a fine new house in the city. May showing a keen interest asks, 'Is your wife with you here in Whitby? Does she take the waters at the spa while you are about your business captain?'

'I do not have wife,' he looks pointedly at April as he makes the statement, 'My brother and I shared the family home by the port until recently, and then my sister and I moved to George Square. Effie Claire is enjoying being further in town, she likes to meet with her friends and shop and do whatever it is young girls do. She is just sixteen.'

The night grows late and the captain shows no inclination to go upstairs. May suspects he is smitten by the shy, modest, April and is irritated. 'You seem incongruous in this place – given a different wardrobe both of you could pass as ladies.' May smiles shyly, trying to imitate her sister. It is all to no purpose as once again the captain leaves without availing himself of one of Mrs Jansen's lovelies.

♣

On the third night Captain Driscoll makes a bee line for the twins the moment he enters the salon. The Madam watches from the sidelines anxious he is wasting her time. Three nights and no whore!

It is early and a quiet night, the twins are alone. This time he orders champagne and Mrs Jansen is hopeful at last she is finally going to see the colour of his money. She sends Stella with the tray and strict instructions. 'You know what you have to do – arouse him one way or another – he must be horny as hell by now!'

'I will have him even if it kills me!' Stella says through gritted teeth. The Madam smiles, confident Stella will get her man. 'And make sure he pays dearly. Do not forget what I said, he has wasted enough of my time.'

She watches as her best whore bends low over the table and places glasses and the bottle so the captain gets an eyeful of her assets, but to Mrs Jansen's surprise he barely notices as he pours the champagne.

Not to be deterred, Mrs Jansen lingers and moves closer to listen in.

'There will be entertainment shortly, Captain Driscoll,' Stella says breathlessly. 'I do hope you will come up and see me perform, I shall look out for you especially. I am sure you will see something to make you want to stay a little longer this evening. I must warn you however, my dancing makes men stupid when they gaze upon me. Sadly most men tend to promise what they cannot deliver. I need a real man to satisfy me and inflame my passions, I suspect you would not disappoint.'

The Madam could not have done it better herself. 'I adore being desired but sometimes these old men do not possess the skills they boast of, I need a man who can give satisfaction.' She licks her lips.

Stella is shameless! Do you blame her for trying her luck? Faint heart and all that... What's the betting the Madam has told her how outrageously rich he is. He is wealthy, under thirty and good looking, what more could a whore ask for. It is about time she got out of this place she thinks. She feels she has earned the right to be the mistress of this young, virile, moneyed man. He is the answer to her prayers. If ever she said any prayers that is; she mostly utters oaths.

The conversation is interrupted when Alfred announces the show will be starting shortly. Stella winks at the captain as she moves off.

This time the twins get up to leave as they are to be part of the troupe tonight. Mrs Jansen shoos them off irritably. She knows they have been rehearsing their parts all week but April is timid and cannot act her part without blushing. The Madam hopes some poor sop will find it becoming. May, on the other hand clearly takes after her mother, she can at least see the girl has some talent, some artistry?

The Madam watches as the captain follows the other men to a large room on the first floor decorated lavishly in crimson and gold.

'This way Captain Driscoll I have saved the best seat in the house for you.' He is shown to a seat, front and centre. The Madam has been assured of his extreme wealth by Mr Vaughan and she means to see some of it and sooner rather than later.

For the previous two nights he has left the brothel without availing himself of any of her girls... perhaps he has other inclinations? In that case she thinks, he might see something else that takes his fancy tonight. She hopes this is not the case; she would dearly like him to bid for the twins. He could up the bidding considerably.

The Madam licks her lips in anticipation. Nothing makes her happier than the thought of making money and she intends to make vast amounts from the beautiful twins.

♠

Edward had thought not to come upstairs – he is apprehensive about what he might see. He hopes April will not be diminished. He has never been to such an

41

establishment before where pre-coital entertainment is offered; he cannot imagine the performance will be tasteful.

You will see that the handsome young captain is holding a torch for April. What he sees in her, rather than her twin, is known to him and him alone. Either way he is clearly enamoured. On the one hand he desires her, like any other punter, yet on the other he feels a brotherly concern and a need to protect her. Men! They want it all ways.

A dais serves as a stage and is set as a Greek temple. Three girls wearing flimsy, sea green outfits cradle baskets of grapes in their arms and bite seductively at the fruit. The men in the audience settle themselves as music wafts through the room from behind a screen. Girls, bare legged, wearing tiny togas sway onto the platform carrying urns.

It is not subtle you will no doubt notice. All is designed to distract and titillate. Who would believe this is Whitby in late spring? Down on the docks whale blubber is being rendered, stinking the town out something awful. Here, oil of roses scents the stuffy air. Scantily clad whores flaunt bare breasts as though there is not a Force nine threatened outside.

Two young men, muscled and oiled are naked to the waist and wear towels that barely cover their manhood. Remember Mrs Jansen is catering for all tastes. The men begin to fill a bath tub with jugs of water while the gyrating girls throw rose petals, dancing elegantly about the stage in time to the music.

From behind a screen Edward sees more girls emerge, April and May are amongst them. The twins, much to Stella's annoyance, wear diaphanous, pale peach togas.

Slips of chiffon trail from their hands. At first they are lit from behind and their slender forms can be seen in silhouette as they separate themselves from the group. They move forward, the lighting making them appear naked until they come down from the platform and recline languidly on cushions and look brazenly at the audience.

At least May looks brazen; April just looks ill-at-ease and keeps her eyes lowered. She has not the theatrical skills of her twin. She would prefer to be anywhere else in the world at this moment. Poor girl, she was not brought up for this life. May, on the other hand, glances at Edward with a becoming look that she hopes says, "Rescue Me".

Edward shoots a glance at his fellow guests and sees the lecherous looks as they search every inch of the twins' bare shoulders, arms and legs. The men, perspiring profusely, look on slack jawed. There are murmurs and leering. Edward is torn, should he stay to watch, a voyeur like all the others, or leave?

He is a red blooded man remember, he has needs. The lovely April has beguiled him with her charms. Why not avail himself of a sneak peek?

Meanwhile, Stella, raven-black hair cascading down her slender back, steps out into the limelight and begins to move to centre stage, hips sashaying provocatively. With the help of the two muscle bound men, she unfasten the clips at the shoulders of her pale, transparent dress. Her long white limbs, her ample bosom and her Mound of Venus are exposed as the silky sheath slips to the ground. Both men stroke her arms, her hair, her bottom, until she grabs one of them by the hair aggressively and kisses him full on the mouth, biting his lip hard.

Thomas has irritated her earlier; she is now paying him back. He gets above himself sometimes and she intends to keep him in his place. The audience are enthralled. Thomas's lip is bleeding, the man glares at Stella and pinches her arse – hard. The audience are delighted. Stella smiles on, promising herself she will have her revenge on the little fag.

She steps gracefully into the bath tub, but not before snatching away the men's towels to show them standing to attention. The troupe continues to dance and sway and pour more water into the tub as the music plays on. From the bath, Stella points and stretches an elegant foot into the air and sponges it sensually, her head thrown back, a look of ecstasy on her face.

She is muttering under her breath, she will kill Thomas later; the water is barely lukewarm – again.

April and May rise and dance towards each other wrapping and entwining their arms about each other's slim waists. The grey bewigged man beside Edward groans lustily. Edward watches as April moves about the stage never far away from her sister now, it is designed so the men see how alike they are and make the same comment that men always make when seeing the likeness for the first time.

I said it is not subtle; Drury Lane eat your heart out. The audience however, appreciate it well enough. Mrs Jansen knows her girls will be thronged before the curtain falls; the till will be ringing – there will be relief all round.

April has poise but her face is impassive. It seems to Edward as though her body is there but her mind is elsewhere. He has an urge to leap onto the stage, cover her lithe body with his jacket and rescue her from this shameful display.

In contrast a smiling May flutters her lashes, her rosebud lips look as if they wait to be kissed. Her almond shaped eyes linger on Edward provokingly, imploring him to bid for her.

The twins move down from the stage towards the audience and sway and strew more petals. They sweep by and the men see the perspiration between their breasts, it glistens and drips tiny rivulets of dampness down to their bellies. As they move the transparency of their artfully arranged dresses drape about the contours of their young bodies. The slightest movement seems to set the flimsy fabric slipping off a shoulder, as if by accident, cunningly exposing a breast, which is coyly recovered only to be uncovered again, almost at once. The audience is openly excited now.

April and May only just manage to regain the stage as two of the more agile old duffers reach out to possess them.

Edward is unsure what happens next. Once April has left the stage he stands and is jeered at by the men behind him: 'You make a better door than a window!' He is blocking their view. He makes his way to the lobby. He asks to see Mrs Jansen urgently.

4

May sees her reflection in the looking glass. She sighs knowing the inevitable will now happen; next week she will be a virgin no more. Her sweet, innocent sister will also suffer the same fate.

After six months at the brothel all their escape plans have ended in failure – failures that have brought them sanctions imposed by the furious Madam.

Mrs Jansen has a lot at stake in this venture. She is not going to let the twins ruin her plans.

Knowing her honour will be lost May hopes at least it will be the man who has been so attentive over the last four nights who will take her innocence. Captain Driscoll has been very keen: to take April, rather than herself, she has to admit. Perhaps he will bid for both? He is extremely rich evidently. She has asked the Madam if he has offered for them but she snapped a non committal response which May takes to mean no.

She ponders his motives. He has convinced himself and April, that he can tell the twins apart. He is wrong and she will prove it. No one except their dear Mama could ever see the difference, not even Aunt Elizabeth was always accurate. He has had lucky guesses so far but his luck cannot continue – but no matter – he is handsome, amusing and young; compared to some of the other predators who are bidding he is a God. The question is will he bid for one of them or both? Of course he may not bid for either.

So far he has not had one of Mrs Jansen's lovelies, not even Stella has been able to tempt him. May has been amused at Stella's lack of progress in this respect but is careful not to let her see. She is a spiteful piece when roused.

May adds rouge to her cheeks and stains her lips raspberry red. She licks the tip of her forefinger, picks up the beauty spot and attaches it to her left cheek. This is the Madam's latest idea to tell them apart. She suspects May of being the more militant, and she is right. She thinks by suggesting May wear the beauty spot, when not in the public areas of course, she will be able to keep her eye on her and stop any more escape nonsense.

May has already fooled the Madam by getting April to wear it instead. April can be persuaded to agree to most of her sister's demands; she has always had a sweet, biddable nature. She has none of May's brittleness, none of her cunning.

May, being too lazy to go to Thomas for a "Lesson in Love", feigned illness so April agreed to go in her place, even though she had taken the class the day before.

'It was not arduous was it?' May asks sulkily.

'No simply degrading.' April replies tartly. 'It entails watching from behind a curtain as one of the whores pleasures some deviant specimen of a man. This voyeurism makes me squirm. I cannot imagine why anyone wants to be watched while they grunt and groan through the act.' April shudders at the memory.

'He has asked for this "peep show" you understand and of course, Mrs Jansen charges extra for the service.' April makes a face.

April had noticed his fat fingers find all the poor girl's secret places. She had closed her eyes and stuffed her fingers in her ears; she had found it all so distasteful and disgusting.

May, on the other hand, would probably have found it informative and file it away for future use

'It is part of our "education" the Madam says, May makes a rude gesture to try to make her sister laugh.

May is keen to keep up April's spirits. Her sister is always keen to please her, even though she hates this sordid life with a passion. May worries for April. Earlier she had been upset: 'You are the only friend I have in the world and I will do anything to please you. I need you to watch out for me, without your support I would die I am sure.' April had implored May to try to devise another escape plan; one last attempt before submitting to their fate.

'Perhaps Captain Driscoll will help us flee?'

May is not as naive as her sister and knows this is a reckless idea.

'He is a rich man visiting a brothel and he has entertainment on his mind, why would he help us?

May knows he holds all the power, he will do as he pleases. 'We are possibly just his latest fetish: beautiful, young, innocent girls are probably just a distraction from the day's business to him – a passing fancy to unwind after he has brokered a particularly difficult deal, a reward.'

May is of the opinion that once he is back in Glasgow he will forget them. 'Once he's back home we will both be out of sight and out of mind, he probably has a wife and children for all we know. All men are liars!'

May has not dismissed him out of hand; she is not that stupid but still thinks if they are to take flight it will be through a plan of their own devising. Of her devising that is as April is a bag of nerves and her creativity is stifled when she is worried.

There is a knock at the door. Betsy says: 'Thomas is waiting.' Good for him, May thinks. Thomas, another hired muscle and the one who services the men who like pretty boys, also provides some of the twins' "Lessons in Love".

May pats a curl, turns and checks in the mirror that her bustle is in place and centred and smoothes her wrinkled skirt. Then and only then, does she go to the faggot's room.

'You took your time. Playing hard to get?' he says smirking.

May looks at him disdainfully as he lounges back on the bed, his hands behind his head. 'I'm sure there are things you could be doing to pass the time,' she says sarcastically.

'I'm sure you are right but no man wants a whore with an opinion so the quicker you learn that lesson the better.' His soft, girly lips smile, he is wearing the same shade of lipstick as May.

He likes May, she can tell, despite her pert ways.

Although his base instinct is for men and the rougher the better, he admires May's beauty and rough tongue, he likes to spar with her she knows.

'At least you give as good as you get while smiling in a comely way, unlike your simpering, mouse of a sister. You might be able to fool old lady Jansen, but you can't fool me. To me, once you open your mouth you're as different as chalk from cheese. Wonder if it'll be the same when you open your—'

'Thankfully you will never know!'

The lesson begins. He tells her it is the last, but most important lesson she will learn. 'Is it how to preserve my dignity?' she asks wryly, 'for I cannot see how I am to save my virginity at this late stage.'

'I almost feel sorry for you,' he laughs.

Thomas might like her but she hates him; she has little experience of men and if this is a sample she is underwhelmed. He is handsome, in a feminine, sort of way but he enjoys his job far too much for her liking. He is cocky and would take liberties if she would let him. She will not let him. Stella says he swings both ways. May is unsure what this means and does not intend to find out, she thinks about hurting him to distract herself from what she is about to do.

♦

Mrs Jansen's dark eyes open wide. She is astonished. She cannot believe what Captain Driscoll has suggested; buy April, lock, stock and virginity. Is he mad? She wastes no time telling him how much she has invested in the twins. Their earning potential after the auction, which is going very nicely thank you, will be considerable. They will be a big draw for her establishment she tells him; men will come by the train load to sample the delights of her identical twins. Beautiful twins at that. Compliant, well trained, able to perform all acts requested, together or apart...

Captain Driscoll half listens and waits for the Madam to stop talking.

When the flow finally halts he says. 'Name your price Mrs Jansen.'

The Madam for once in her life is speechless. She stands and then sits down again trying not to appear agitated – but agitated she is.

'I shall have to look at the figures Captain Driscoll, I cannot conjure a number out of my head just like that. I will need time. There is the loss of earnings from May, also to consider. On her own, although a very handsome girl she cannot command so high a fee that she would if she were taken with her sister. I doubt you could afford my dear April, I should be loath to lose the sweet child.'

She underestimates his fortune clearly. In her grasping, avaricious way, she will undersell the sisters. Serves her right don't you think?

It is agreed he will come back tomorrow evening at eight.

No matter what figure Mrs Jansen comes up with Edward will pay it. Or barter her down if the price mentioned by the Madam is ludicrous, he sees her for what she is; a provincial bawdy house owner in a seaside spa town. He is a man of business and means to have what he wants at the price he decides to pay.

♣

April is waiting for May to return from her class, she is still thinking about the inescapable ordeal that awaits them. She has also thought perhaps Captain Driscoll will be the highest bidder and be the one to take her virginity. Unlike her sister it matters not who deflowers her. She will be ashamed no matter who it is. The thought makes her sick to the stomach, she shudders.

April knows, after the first assault, which will be bad enough, there will be others to follow. The prospect of the first time is uppermost in her mind, but now she has begun to see this is just the start, just the beginning of a life of vice. There will be a steady procession of the pot bellied, the bald, the hoary, the coarse and inevitably, according to Stella, the cruel, the perverted and the downright debasing. There will be no saying, 'Oh I am sorry you are too grotesque, tremble kneed and corpulent to touch me.' The men will perform any act they choose, in any way they choose without due regard to her feelings. Her young, soft body will not be her own. She will be forced to yield to any vile act; they will have paid for the pleasure to do as they like. She is to be a sex slave.

She sees her life mapped out in front of her. Not for her the tender kisses and caresses of a beloved. Not for her a loving suitor to court and flatter. She will endure shame and degradation at every turn. She will wear a mask and behind it die each time she is taken against her will. She is powerless, she has thought of killing herself more than once. She can think of no other way out of this hell hole

'If the handsome captain makes the top bid for you at

least your first time might not be such an ordeal.' May says trying to pacify her twin.

'How do you know? Behind the urbane exterior, a cruel, base nature may lurk. I have seen from behind the curtain that once the fine clothes are abandoned, so are the manners and the morals.' April curls her lip. 'In any event I should still be taken without my consent by a man who is not my husband – only a husband should do the things we witness. I shall feel the shame and the pain.' April looks ready to cry, 'Stella says it will hurt.'

'Stella is a cunning bitch – we shall have to do as the other whores say and close our eyes and wish ourselves elsewhere. Perform how the man wants us to act but imagine it is not us it is happening to.'

'If you are able to do that you are a better actress than I, for I cannot see how I am to achieve that. How can I think myself elsewhere while some sweat covered bulk huffs, paws and pants over me?' April covers her face with her pale shaking hands. 'Oh May, what can we do, I cannot go through with it, I shall be sick!'

May tries to calm and comfort her sister but knows time is running out. 'I wish we had done as you suggested and not entered the brothel in the first place, shop work and a hovel are looking appealing now.' May holds her sister's hand. 'I had been certain we would be able to escape but time is running out and we are watched constantly, I don't know how we can get away. Every plan so far has been scuppered.'

Despite what May says April knows May has lofty ideas. She has plans. Her sister is convinced when they become "working girls" their lives will change. One of them, she says, will surely secure a man of means who will become captivated and free them from this prison. Stella has filled May's head with nonsense about a mythical protector: A rich, good looking man who will pay for exclusive rights so they service him and him alone. That would be better than a succession of undesirables, May says.

April, ever the realist, remembers the slobbering, flabby vicar she saw relieve himself yesterday with a sixteen year old called Biddy. She gags. What if she ends up with someone like him as her protector – how happy would she feel then?

This route, May says, could be their way out; they could make themselves indispensable to one man so he will take them away from the brothel and set them up in their own establishment.

May is picturing a handsome sea captain. April is imaging being locked in the vicarage attic.

'Away from the brothel,' May says, 'we will find it easier to escape.' May is not fooling April with her fanciful ideas. She doubts she is fooling herself.

They have written numerous letters to Aunt Elizabeth begging her to come and get them, to save them from their plight. All have been ignored. 'Perhaps she is still abroad? Is it worth one last try?' April asks sighing. She takes up paper and ink, she has nothing to lose if she writes one last time. She is not too proud to beg.

♠

It is five minutes before eight and Edward is waiting in the Madam's office. As the clock strikes the hour, Mrs Jansen glides in all smiles and cheap perfume. She has a piece of paper in her hand on which is written the sum she has decided April is worth. After pleasantries and a regurgitation of yesterday's speech, the Madam pushes the folded paper across her desk.

'Talking about money is so coarse is it not?' she says. He is tight lipped as he opens the paper and is surprised to find an amount which is far less than he would have been prepared to pay. To Mrs Jansen the sum represents a fortune he realises, yet to him it is a drop in the ocean. He remembers this is a provincial brothel, not some London hot spot.

The price is agreed instantly, Mrs Jansen is elated. She would have come down a little in price he knows but he cannot bear to negotiate with the hateful woman.

Edward heads straight to the receiving room where he hopes April will be waiting; he is keen to tell her the good news. He has not dared mention his plan to his heart's desire of course. He did not want to raise her hopes only to have them dashed if, in the unlikely event, the Madam decided to go ahead with the auction.

♥

The twins are sitting together and are alone; no other men are present, the hour being early. May notices Captain Driscoll and nudges her sister. 'Be nice to him, he's our best chance of getting out of here.'

'But it is not...' April is silenced by her sister's warning look as he takes a seat. He raises a hand and orders champagne, May's eyebrows rise in astonishment.

'I would speak with you alone Miss April if you would allow it? April is startled as he asks the question of May;

she sees her sister is reluctant to move but can think of no reason to decline.

May smiles sweetly but April sees the steely gaze as she sidles over to the window. The warning look says: be grateful, show appreciation, we cannot afford to risk upsetting such a wealthy man. April listens as Edward tells her his news and outlines his plans.

'I have released you from this place!' he announces.

April is alarmed. 'I do not understand Captain Driscoll.'

'It is as I say; you are free of this place. I have offered for you and it has been accepted, you need not face the indignity of the auction. I will take you away to Glasgow, if you will allow it and install you in my town house.'

April's stomach heaves. She is lost for words.

'You have no need to worry about your honour, do not, I humbly ask, jump to the wrong conclusion. You shall not be my mistress, I shall move back to my brother's house for propriety's sake, initially. You will have my sister, Effie Claire for company and my staff to assist you in all things. My hope is you will allow me to pay you my attentions and then, in time, marry me. I hope that you will learn to love me as much as I love you.'

April is stunned and she does not know what to think. She looks at her sister's back and wishes she were by her side, she knows not what to say and needs May's counsel. Is this a trick she wonders, a wickedness she does not understand? Then, just as it is sinking in that she is to be free she says. 'This is some surprise – but love Captain Driscoll, you barely know me and yet you speak of love?'

Bless her heart! She is so innocent. May or Stella would

have had their bags packed and be heading for the door were they in April's shoes.

'I know my own mind, please let me do this for you my dear, you are too good to be used and abused. If you stay here I fear for you, I have seen you are not strong. You should not be here – it is a travesty you are not the type of lady to be demeaned in this vile way. I can provide you with the life you deserve, the love and security you need. Please do not be afraid as I only have your best interests at heart.'

April's mind is racing. 'Glasgow you say, I have never been anywhere but Whitby, is it not another country?'

Edward laughs and she becomes flustered. 'It is but only across the border, you need not fear – we are perfectly civilised I promise you.'

'But what of my sister Captain Driscoll? I cannot in all conscience leave May, how could I be happy knowing she would still be a slave? She does not deserve ill-treatment either; I cannot leave her alone I am all she has in the world. We have never been apart.'

♦

This is not the response the Captain has expected, Edward is thrown into turmoil. Why had he not thought of this? He chides himself: What sort of damn fool am I? Even if the same bargain can be wrought to free May what is he to do with her, he cannot marry them both. He tells April this, in a dressed up manner, so as not to offend or worry her further. He reasons with her yet sees April is immoveable. She will not leave without May.

Edward retreats, leaves the brothel and walks the

length and breadth of the harbour thinking all the while. He calls into The Angel Inn and orders whisky. It seems to wake up his brain; he can think of only one solution. He climbs back up the hill and once again asks to see Mrs Jansen.

She has been expecting him. She has seen over the past months how inseparable the twins are. She knows with a woman's instinct, one will not go without the other. Now she will extract the same price again or perhaps even more, after all the loss of earnings is now double.

Act 2

1

The day of sailing arrives "The Two Brothers" is to take her maiden voyage. April and May are aboard heading for Glasgow and a new life. Their meagre belongings are stowed below in the cramped accommodation.

'The ship was not built to carry ladies I am afraid,' Edward says jovially as he apologises for the lack of space. 'It will be a long, arduous journey for you both – let us hope the weather does not turn nasty. I hope you are good sailors.'

'We have never sailed before so it is yet to be seen,' says May brightly. Nothing can dampen her high spirits.

'We will be putting in at Aberdeen and other ports along the way. I had not expected to be carrying such delicate cargo!'

May is waving as they pull out of Whitby Harbour as if she is going on an Atlantic cruise. She knows no one on the quayside but is excited to be free. April does not feel the same excitement: she fears she is exchanging one prison for another, one cruel gaoler for a more handsome one.

'Just think April, if you can secure Captain Driscoll we will be set up for life, he has already made arrangements for us to be together at his town house. When you marry you will be mistress of a fine new establishment if we are to believe all he says. I see no reason to doubt he is as rich as Mrs Jansen says – he has paid handsomely for our release.' May sits on the bed in their cabin and looks at April's worried face.

'Yes I know but it is not you who has to marry him it is me he wants to wed.'

'I would be in your shoes if I could, I think him the most handsome and generous man I have ever met, what more can a woman ask for? Compare him to some of the gropers we would have to service at the brothel.' May shudders then laughs loudly. She will not allow April to dampen her spirits.

'But I do not love him!' April says.

May could shake her. 'You do not love him...yet. He says he will give you time to get to know each other, there is no rush. He wants to court you and win your heart and besides, we are not in danger anymore and that is the main thing surely?'

May takes April's hands in hers and looks imploringly at her twin's identical face. 'We are free my love. Free!'

May just wishes it was she who had received the offer of marriage; she is already half in love with the captain for simply rescuing them. Add to this his good looks, charm and money and she knows she will soon be head over heels. She cannot understand her sister's hesitancy.

'I have thought of a plan,' May says 'We will play him at his own game. I will pretend to be you and marry him if that makes you rest easier, I would gladly have him.'

'You forget May he can tell us apart! Do you not see we are at the mercy of this man? We know nothing about him, save what he tells us. How do we know he is not married already and going to set me up as his mistress despite what he says? He could be a white slave trader for all we know.' April wrings her hands together as if she is in a Victorian melodrama. 'Either way, even if he is telling the truth, and I agree he must be a wealthy man, am I not bought and paid for just as I would be if I were still at the brothel?'

May is beginning to lose patience. 'Let us talk of the matter again when we dock and we see how the land lies, I know you are anxious my love. When we get there and see all is as it should be we will think again if you are still unhappy. I will readily change places with you, don't forget. How hard can it be to fool him? Edward cannot know for sure which of us is which, he just *thinks* he knows. He has been lucky on the few times he has been tested.'

April is not so sure: 'Edward says he sees not one, but two differences between us, the same two differences our mother maintained helped her to tell us apart.'

If you were to look closely, their mother had said, there were violet flecks in April's eyes that were not visible in May's. There was also a mannerism which April had developed, a way of holding her head that was different to the way May held hers, a sort of tilt, not discernible unless you looked closely. Both these things convinced April he was not simply speculating.

♥

The ship eventually docks at Port Glasgow. The twins, despite the hardship of life on board, have survived the journey relatively unscathed. May had a bout of sea sickness before they even left England but soon found her sea legs.

April and May are escorted to a carriage and taken through the busy streets of Glasgow to a fine granite building; it is more than a town house. Granted it is a house in a town but in reality it is a mansion. The twins, it seems, have landed on their feet. The magnificent building, in an exclusive area of Glasgow, has huge iron gates leading to a turning circle where their carriage deposits them at the double doors.

May's eyes light up. April looks overawed. The house is in an exclusive tree lined square, secluded gardens to front, sides and back prevent ne'er do wells from looking in. A flock of servants swoop out of the house to pick up their scant belongings like birds picking up crumbs. They are taken inside.

A pair of sweeping staircases rise up from a marbled hall. They are shown into a large, well appointed drawing room papered in blue and gold. The room is restrained and elegant, not at all manly. Effie Claire is brought in and introduced to the twins. How her brother has explained their presence April does not know. April is reassured slightly as the fair haired girl appears as open and generous as Edward.

April sees her twin's face alight with joy. All is just as May has hoped for and all that she, herself, has feared; it is all too good to be true.

Perhaps April is waiting for him to twirl his moustache like a caricature of a pantomime villain? Perhaps she imagines he has a mad wife stowed away in the attic? Poor April cannot bring herself to see her good fortune just in case it is snatched away from her. Even so she still fears for her honour.

Tea is served and Edward smiles, 'I have engaged a maid especially for you April. Edith is not Scottish; I thought you would prefer to hear an English accent and besides the best lady's maids are from England. She has been here two days to prepare for your arrival.'

April can think of nothing to say but is shot a look by May so tries to look pleased. 'I have never had a maid before, you should not have gone to any trouble I—'

May interrupts, 'Captain Driscoll you are too kind, April did I not say we would be spoilt? Our every wish is to be catered for it seems.' Edward explains May is to have use of a local girl. It is the first of many distinctions that May will face, but for the moment she is far too happy to notice or to care.

The servants show each of the twins to their own suite of rooms down plush carpeted corridors. Effie also has rooms on this landing they are told. Again April hopes this is a good sign, she is clinging onto any little thing for reassurance. The rooms are imposing but comfortable and have a quiet grandeur. They are lit with gas light and there are fires in the grates.

Edward has gone away again; gone to be about the business that helps him live in such splendour. He is to return later. The servants, of which there are many, have been told to treat the sisters as house guests. With the exception of Tibbs the butler, who is far too professional to stare, the rest of the staff gawp at the twins as if they were circus attractions. Of course they have never seen identical twins before and never ones as handsome as these two.

April is shown into a bedroom of gigantic proportions which has its own dressing room and bathroom. She is in awe. Her new maid steps forward.

Edith thinks her new mistress seems ill at ease, not at all confident. She wonders why she has so few belongings perhaps? She does not even have a decent vanity set she noted when she unpacked. Edith is sure the girl has never had a lady's maid before and is suspicious something is not as it should be. She will watch and wait and hope she has not made a mistake in taking this position north of the border.

'Good day Miss, I have taken the liberty of unpacking for you. Which gown would you like me to lay out for dinner? Are you to dine in?'

'Yes we are, Captain Driscoll said so. We have travelled a long way and we are all tired I think.' The maid opens the wardrobe door and looks at the four dresses hanging there limply.

Edith has noticed the inferior silk and satin when she unpacked earlier. The dresses are not of the latest style, in fact they are over fussy and in need of attention. Repairing shabby gowns was not what Edith had expected to do when she was offered this employment. Granted the house is far above her expectations but her mistress appears unsophisticated, and is certainly not a lady of class or breeding.

'What about the grey?' she asks as she runs her fingers through the indifferent silk.

'Yes, that will do I think. I will just go and tell my sister to wear her grey too as we like to dress the same,' she explains unnecessarily.

'I will of course relay the message Miss.' April feels her face flush but then the door bursts open and May rushes in beaming.

'Well, are you happy now?' She begins to open cupboards and drawers which are of course empty, but if Edward is to be believed they will soon be full of new clothes appropriate for their new positions. 'Soon all these will be brimming with ribbons and lace! I concede perhaps my wardrobes will not be quite as full as yours if you succeed in marrying Edward, but no matter. They will be fuller than if we had stayed in Whitby.'

April shoots her twin a look behind Edith's back. 'What's the matter – do not start protesting! Is all not exactly as he said it would be?'

'Edith can you please leave us a moment.'

When they are alone April begins to cry. 'Everything is as he said but still I am the one who will have to pay for all this.' She slumps heavily on the bed. 'And tonight I may pay the first instalment.'

'Buck up my love, have faith – if need be I will sleep here with you, all will be well. I am sure Edward means to marry you first, you need not fear.' April is unconvinced but a little reassured that her sister will not desert her. 'Ring for Edith and get ready, dry your eyes and I will see you downstairs.'

When Edward left earlier he had told April to expect

him for dinner at seven thirty. He wants, among other things to discuss the arrangements for a shopping trip the next day.

April does not want to go shopping as she has things on her mind which will not be cured by buying fripperies. Edward, it seems is a good man, a generous man yet she cannot trust him to be who he says he is. She does not want him to buy her a new wardrobe as he has promised. That would make her even more beholden to him. She already owes him a debt of gratitude she can never repay, if that is, he is honest but she still fears some trickery.

April hopes to convince him to help her and her sister to find respectable work, perhaps write them a letter of reference so they might get employment as companions or governesses. He knows they have education, surely she can persuade him to let them have their freedom? She will tell him how much she admires him and that she will always be his friend for rescuing them from Mrs Jansen but she will make it clear she cannot marry him. She has not spoken of her plans to May. She fears what May will say.

Dressed in her grey silk and with her hair dressed by Edith in an elaborate style that is not to her liking, April goes down to dinner. May and Effie are already down and sitting by the fireside. Edward has returned and comes to greet April, all smiles.

'How wonderful it is to have you here, my love. Do you want for anything? Does your maid suit you?'

'Yes, thank you Captain Driscoll, I am very grateful.'

'Did I not say yesterday I do not want your gratitude, say nothing of it? It gives me more pleasure than you can imagine that you are here…free,' he whispers the last word as he kisses her hand. He does not want his sister to hear, 'And please, call me Edward, I insist.'

They eat a dinner the like of which the twins have never tasted and Edward tells the sisters a little more about Glasgow and his business. Effie is a pleasant girl and chimes in with her own thoughts; these consist mostly of where the best places to be seen are and where to purchase the best gowns and hats. Edward laughs at her chatter, not condescendingly, but as an indulgent brother.

They are all tired from their journey and so Edward prepares to leave his own fireside to go out into the gusty Glaswegian night so his house guests may retire. May, after thanking Edward, asks to be excused; she is being discreet. Effie Claire follows her lead and after kissing her brother on the cheek also retires.

April has been worrying all evening that Edward would not be true to his word. She has been fretting that once dinner is over and all have retired he will come to her room and – she cannot bear to think of it. Her mind goes back to the vicar at the brothel and she almost loses her dinner.

In her mind's eye she has pictured him stealing into her bedroom – she has noticed there are no locks on the doors. She is expecting him to claim his prize and is terrified. No matter that her sister will be there – he will evict May and have his wicked way with her and there will be nothing she can do to overpower him. She is just getting herself worked up into a state when he sends for his carriage to be brought. April is much relieved – for now.

'I will send the carriage for all three of you in the morning at ten thirty; Effie Claire will take you anywhere you wish to go. She knows all the shops and stores where I have accounts so you must avail yourself of everything you need, and May too of course.' He smiles at April as he puts on his gloves. 'Effie's dressmaker is to call in the afternoon at four so that gowns can be made for you both. You have precious little to wear from what I have seen of your baggage.'

April summons all her courage. She does not want to anger Edward but she does not mean to lead him on. He has to know she never intends to marry him. 'Please Edward, remember our conversation in Whitby? May and I will never be able to repay your kindness for what you have done for us thus far. We cannot keep on taking advantage of your kindness, we wish to stand on our own feet – you have done too much already. There is just one thing I would ask of you dearest Edward,' she adds the "dearest" hoping to make it sound sisterly, 'and that is a reference or a letter of introduction. If you could see your way to providing us with such a letter we will be able to support ourselves. If you can see your way to do this for us we would be so very grateful, it is our dearest wish.'

Edward smiles indulgently: 'Before you came down to dinner May was as excited as Effie Claire at the thought of a shopping spree! I am not sure your sister agrees with you. When we last spoke of this in Whitby I imagined you were being shy, coy perhaps? I have said I do not wish to put pressure on you, I so want you to be happy. You know my intentions, I want to marry you. I understand that after all you have endured this last six months you need a breathing space and I intend to give it to you.' He smiles and April realises she wants to believe him, but she still cannot bring herself to trust him on so little an acquaintance. 'You and May are free to stay for as long as you like, as my guests. I only seek to make your stay enjoyable.'

He takes her hands in his, April sees what she thinks is a look of longing. She remembers the faces of the punters at the brothel when they look at the girls. Her stomach turns.

Edward says: 'I want to take you about to dances, the theatre, to dinner with my friends, I want to give a ball in your honour. To do this you have to let me provide you with the accoutre so you can mix confidently in Glasgow society.'

April sees Edward has made plans and she is at a loss how to counter his ideas without appearing churlish. 'But Edward if we agree to this, how will you explain us to your family and friends? Will they not wonder where we have sprung from? What have you told your brother and Effie Claire? Not the truth surely?

Edward dismisses Morag, an aged retainer who has been hovering by the door whilst this conversation goes on. He smiles kindly. 'I had thought to be on my way now, perhaps with a chaste kiss upon my cheek in the way of thanks.' April steps back.

'I have told Alistair and Effie you are William Vaughan's nieces. I said I have invited you both to stay as you have never been north of the Border and might enjoy seeing Glasgow. Be assured my love you have nothing to fear. Alistair is never over curious if it does not concern tobacco or shipping and there are no other relatives to delude. He is unmarried and we have no aunts, uncles or cousins hereabouts, only distant relatives who live in America.'

April sees how Edward has thought of everything. She is tired and her head is beginning to throb. She decides to give in for now but resolves to only buy essentials tomorrow.

Edward interrupts her thoughts. 'Alistair is to dine with us tomorrow night so you will meet him then. He is a sound man of business and a grand chap, my big brother! You will no doubt be surprised how different we are both in looks and in temperament. We are the polar opposite of you and your sister.' Edward kisses her hand and wishes her a good night and leaves to stay at his family home with his brother at Port Glasgow.

April can hardly believe it. He has been as good as his word. He has left her alone. She breathes a deep sigh of relief. She knows he would make a splendid husband, she understands her sister's reasoning. May is right, he is a handsome man and a kind one it seems but she does not love him and does not want a husband.

She looks about the room; it is the height of good taste. The furnishings are of the best quality, there are antiques and rugs from Persia which feel deep and soft under her feet. There are paintings of the Scottish variety with stags and lochs, gilded mirrors reflect the wealth and splendour. Crystal chandeliers sparkle. April sees all this and none of this; she feels trapped. Yet even now she cannot bring herself to believe she is free to enjoy it, if only she could trust Edward. She does not want to become attached to this house, this life and most of all to this man, in case the soft, piled rug is pulled from under her feet. She sees the gilded cage is a pretty one but it is still a cage.

♣

Before breakfast, April goes to May's bedroom to talk about what is to be done. May is wearing her green day dress. As it is the first time in their lives they are in separate bedrooms, they are not dressed identically; April having chosen her blue. May is all smiles. She is clearly excited about the day's plans.

'May, we agreed now we are away from that infernal house of ill repute we shall make our own way in the world. Edward would be happy to be put upon I see, but we cannot take advantage of his good nature—'

May interrupts, irritation on her face, 'Ssh! someone might hear you!' May's maid leaves the room. 'Like men would put upon us do you mean, sister dear? We have nothing, aside from what we stand up in, so how are we to meet his friends fligged out like we were at the brothel!'

April winces. She is frightened a servant might hear and says so. They bicker on for some minutes like sisters are prone to do. April tries again. 'That is my point. If Edward provides us with a reference as I have begged him to do, then we shall need only sober, conservative clothes as would suit ladies who have to earn their own living.'

You will see from this exchange that May has no intention of working when she is being handed everything on a plate.

71

'But in the meantime as Edward's guests we need evening clothes which will not disgrace him in front of his family, friends and business associates.' May appears to capitulate but intends no such thing. 'Look around you April we have arrived at the highest echelons of society.' She is like the cat that has not just drunk the cream but has bathed in it too.

April is forced to admit this is the case and so the shopping and the dress maker are taken advantage of, but with some restraint; April's set face forces May to hold back somewhat much to her chagrin.

That evening as April descends the wide, thickly carpeted staircase, the door is being opened by a footman to a tall, dark haired man, wearing a light overcoat. When he passes his hat and coat to the footman she sees he has unruly curly hair. He spies her pausing on the stair like a child who has been caught doing something she shouldn't. He smiles up at her and his face becomes animated. If this is Alistair, he is indeed unlike his fair haired brother.

'Good evening, you must be one of two ladies I am expecting to meet this evening? Do I have the pleasure of addressing Miss April or Miss May?' He bounds up the stairs to greet her and escorts her down.

'I am April, I am very pleased to meet you sir.'

The door of the drawing room opens and Edward welcomes his older brother. April looks at them both side by side and can discern no similarity in their appearance. Where April and May are identical, the two brothers are distinctly different. Where Edward is stocky, Alistair is rangy. Where Edward is blue eyed, Alistair has dark brown eyes that are alert and sparkly. In all terms they are different, excepting in height perhaps, where they are both above average, being over six feet she guesses. They move into the drawing room where May sits by the fireside. She is making herself at home.

Alistair is introduced and at once says, 'Well, I for one will never be able to tell you apart! You are like two peas in a pod!' Alistair apparently, is more conventional than his brother. Edward shoots a sideways glance at April who misses the look.

May knows what Edward is thinking; he is remembering their first conversation at Mrs Jansen's.

Throughout dinner an amiable conversation ensues, until the two sisters' lives begin to be discussed. April is on her guard but she need not have worried as May is up to the task at hand.

May expands the lie Edward has told. She explains how they are nieces to a prominent, Whitby shipbuilder with whom they have just become acquainted since the death of their mother. May tells the fabricated story confidently and fully.

April and Edward are mostly quiet at this point, April shows no surprise as the easy lies trip from May's tongue.

Edward is taken aback until he sees she has saved him the trouble of explaining himself, and then he sees he should be grateful to her. Edward is only happy to have the lies believed.

April has the good grace to look embarrassed. Edward is filling their glasses with a good white burgundy and enjoying himself. April notices another difference in the brothers. Where Edward is gregarious and quick witted, Alistair is sober and reserved; she finds herself laughing at the stories he tells at Alistair's expense; stories from their adolescence. Alistair, it transpires is thirty five whereas Edward is ten years younger. April for the first time in months begins to enjoy herself and lets down her guard.

'Edward and I have different mothers you understand,' the older brother declares, 'when my mother passed, father remarried. Sadly Edward's mother, my step mother, also died. Then father's heart failed two years ago leaving me his heir.'

'At least like my sister and I you have each other and your sister of course.' April smiles at Alistair as the meal comes to an end.

The sisters have never been in such exalted society before but know, through their reading of novels, that at this stage of dinner the ladies are expected to leave the men to their port. They rise to leave.

'Go to the library, there will be a fire lit already and tea will be brought to you, Edward says happily. He is content now April is under his roof.

'Thank you Captain Driscoll, take all the time you need,' May says in honeyed tones as if she is lady of the manor.

♠

'I admire Edward the most but I would be just as happy I am sure, with the heir. Both are amiable, both are handsome, both are rich. In fact, Alistair is the better bet.'

April and May are sipping their tea in the library. April knows May is devising a plan; a plan no doubt that involves the two poor sisters marrying the two rich brothers. She watches closely as May stares into the fire.

May has watched Edward throughout dinner to see if she can discern any animosity between the brothers because he is the younger son, and not the heir to what must be a spectacular fortune. She has seen none.

In May's case you will notice the apple has not fallen far from the tree.

'Alistair is very personable and attractive – I had half expected a hunchback when Edward said they were very different, either that or some evil, moustache twisting, ogre from a romantic play.' April half smiles remembering her own earlier thoughts regarding Edward.

'Yes, he is quite likeable, different to Edward, but—'

'Likeable! I saw that glint in your eye! He is much more to your taste than his brother I think? I saw you, were you not attempting to flirt?'

'I was not – but yes I have always found dark haired men attractive, but as we will be moving on soon, it will do neither of us any good to form attachments.'

'What is wrong with you? Why should we even think of leaving until we are pushed?' April sees the look of exasperation. 'I see if you play your hand with Edward and I with Alistair than one of us is sure to come up trumps. Alistair is heir to a massive fortune we could be made for life. He's rich, handsome, unmarried.' She frowns suddenly.

'There has to be a catch – why has he not been caught before I wonder?' May scowls, and then remembers Aunt Elizabeth's warning that scowling produces wrinkles. She desists.

'Exactly. I think you might be setting your sights a little too high,' April says.

'But the prize is worth the effort, I would still prefer Edward despite him being the poorer but beggars cannot be choosers,' May giggles brightly.

'You make it sound so, so business like; like a deal just waiting to be struck.'

'And so it is my dear only now we are in the driving seat, not the men.' May smiles wickedly. April thinks her twin is enjoying herself.

There is no chance May is going to be working for her bread with all this luxury going begging. April will soon be made to see sense.

'At his age Alistair must surely be looking for a wife; son and heir required me thinks. A huge empire and he has no one to hand it on to! That in itself will ensure he marries, surely? He will not be looking for an heiress; he has all he needs in that respect. All he needs is a beautiful, young, fertile bride; me...or you. Who cares which way around so long as we land them?'

It is April's turn to be exasperated. 'Edward says there is a lady, but he thinks that Alistair's ardour has cooled recently, he says this is the pattern with him. He begins by being enamoured then after the chase he loses interest and distances himself. Be careful what you wish for, you may end up on the discarded pile.'

April pours more tea and nibbles a biscuit. 'Wouldn't it be something if the two sisters married the two brothers...' May looks dreamily at her twin.

'A story book ending? May, you are a dreamer, our best plan is to get Edward to agree to one of us being a companion for Effie Claire, I should be content with that. We can still live here she is a lovely girl. Sweet natured and—'

'And in three or four years she will be married with no need of a companion! We need to think ahead, think to our long term future. Marriage for one, or both of us, is the only solution, rid yourself of this romantic notion of being a genteel lady's companion. What exactly have you got against marriage? My temper is being sorely tried!'

'It still seems like slavery, just with a different master. Oh, I know Edward is no Mrs Jansen but it is all the same to my mind.'

'I am lost for words!' Edward's dog Scout, a Border Terrier, rolls on his back luxuriating in the heat from the fire, for a moment both girls watch him. 'I am trying to see things from your point of view April but I cannot.' April sees her sister's temper barely held in check.

'How can being sold to fat, repugnant, old men be the same as marriage to a rich, handsome man who adores you? It makes no sense to me. This need you have to make your own way in the world. It is not as easy as you think out there in the big, bad world. If you want melodrama go on the stage with Aunt Elizabeth! If by all this posturing you lose Edward's good will, I will never forgive you. Would you have us return to being brothel bait – I should sooner die.' May's voice has risen and her colour is high, the dog sits up and whines.

April begins to cry, tears slipping down her cheeks. She hates being bullied, she has not meant to make her sister angry. May, who has been pacing up and down, drops to her knees in front of her quietly sobbing sister.

'I am sorry.' She takes her twin's hands in hers. 'I know this is difficult for you but we have to be practical. If Edward cools because you throw his benevolence back in his face, then what will we do? Remember he has paid handsomely to free us, he naturally wants repayment for his outlay. Yet he is not forcing himself on you, he didn't have to move out, he could have stayed, he obviously cares about your reputation. He is an honourable man surely you see that?'

April dries her eyes as her twin continues. 'Let us look at it from your point of view. If we follow your path and get employment, we may not get agreeable jobs in good households; we might well end up slaves just the same. Low pay, poor conditions, picking up after some spoilt ringletted little Miss with more money than manners.' She strokes her sister's hair, something she has always done when April needs soothing. April wants to agree with her. 'Don't just do this for me dearest, do it for us both. We could be happy here, if you will just try, is it too much to ask?'

The fight has gone out of April. She agrees to try her best to keep favour with Edward. To herself she thinks she will bide her time and try to think of a different plan, one that involves marriage for May, and not her.

♦

In the dining room the two brothers are discussing the sisters.

'Well they are a fine pair of maids you have netted for yourself, do you mean to marry them both?'

'I believe that would be illegal, even here in Scotland

where the laws can be somewhat lax. I have a preference for April; she is the apple of my eye.'

'How can she be when they are identical?' He smiles wickedly and adds, 'Perhaps if you did marry them both, then when one is indisposed you could be free with the other.' He likes to tease his younger brother. 'It could be passed off as mistaken identity!' he adds and laughs loudly at his own whimsy.

'Do you really not see the difference? April has a glint in her eye, a violet hue to the iris. She also has a mannerism of tilting her head slightly that her sister does not have, it is obvious to me.' Edward pours more port into his brother's glass. 'April is softer in both manner and temperament,' he continues, May has more of an edge, a hardness which comes from being her sister's protector and provider. Just like brothers, their bond is great – greater possibly as they are twins.'

'I understand we each play a role, as older brother and younger this is to be expected. I, as the older brother, look out for you, and you as the younger look up to me with respect and admiration.' He winks at Edward who shakes his head in mock disbelief.

'What I do not understand is how, as twins, it can be the same for them; they are the same age. Why does May assume the protector and provider role?'

'Because they have different personalities of course! Just because they look alike does not mean they think alike! They have different tastes, different likes and dislikes.' Edward wonders why he has to explain such an obvious fact.

'You say you are taken with April? You have known

her how long, a couple of weeks? Is this not a little hasty? You have been in this position before only to find your enthusiasm waned as the weeks turned into months. I remember how it was with you and Charlotte Burns.'

'This is different but in any case April will not be rushed, she has made that quite clear.' He remembers the conversation of a few days ago where she asked him to help them find paid, respectable work. He does not mention this to his brother. Alistair must see them as a higher rank than mere governesses. Both girls act their new roles well, now they have the correct costumes he knows they can be passed off as ladies.

'Well at least she does not appear to be after your money, unless she is playing the long game, which is possible. Just have a care, you know nothing about this pair of pretty things. Are you not being blinded by their looks, their uniqueness?'

'I am old enough to know my own mind.' Edward is slightly irritated by his brother's point of view. 'Charlotte was years ago, do you not find May an attractive proposition? You could do worse,' he says hoping to take the heat off his own situation by changing the subject.

Alistair shakes his head. 'I am thirty five and have escaped marriage thus far, I am happy being a bachelor.'

'Does Miss Griffiths know this? The last I saw of her she was hanging onto your every word and thumbing her diary for possible dates for an engagement.' Edward watches his brother's expression intently.

'I have not seen her for weeks and don't intend to go out of my way to meet with her again; her father has begun to circle, I will not be the prey.'

'But what of a son and heir?'

Alistair looks thoughtful. 'There is that one stumbling block but there is always you to carry on the family business, you will be my heir as it were. I am sure you will marry and have sons.' He drains his glass and stands. 'Time I was taking my leave; I have an early start tomorrow.'

The two brothers join the twins in the library, just long enough to excuse themselves before leaving.

'I am pleased to have met you both but am afraid I have an early start tomorrow and so must take my leave. Perhaps you will do me the honour of dining with me next week sometime?' Alistair asks.

It is agreed and Edward also makes to leave. Once again the sisters are left alone. One of them expels the air from her lungs slowly. April is relieved she has been spared another night.

2

As the weeks pass May sees that Edward has eyes only for April. She has thought to put herself in his path to attempt to change his mind as to which twin he wants to court. She tries to show him she can be just as sweet as her sister, but it has all been to no avail. If she could win him around, April could be spared whatever it is she is scared of, and May could have the man of her dreams. But it is not to be. No matter how she tilts her head and flatters him he does not heed her.

Imagine that! The frustration she must feel.

She has to concede defeat, he can indeed tell them apart. He consistently knows which is which! May has attempted to trip him up more than once when April's back has been turned but each time she has been rumbled. But no matter so long as April keeps him sweet they will be safe; she sees Edward is just as keen, if not more so than in Whitby.

May's attention turns to Alistair. Here she has had more success. By flattering Edward, she has unwittingly drawn the attention of the older brother. While she has been so attentive to Edward, Alistair has taken a back seat. He is a man who enjoys the chase and when a woman shows him little attention, it ignites his interest.

Isn't that just like a man! Perhaps when Edward sees his brother's interest in May he might change his mind? May can only hope, men are fickle. They only ever want what they cannot have.

May notices this turn of events just in time. She continues to be polite and amusing, but still does not single Alistair out especially. Alistair grows keener. Her frustration lessens. Her hopes grow.

One evening when Edward and April are at the theatre with Effie Claire as chaperone, Alistair makes an unexpected visit to the house. May is reading by the fire when he is shown in.

'I had forgotten it was tonight you were all to go to the theatre,' he says after she explains where everyone is. 'Were you not supposed to go too? He sits opposite her by the fire and strokes Scout's ear roughly. 'Are you not a theatre lover?'

'I love the theatre but to be frank I pretended a headache, I think Edward deserves time alone with April without having me always in the background. Effie has gone too of course but will not listen to a word they say, she will have her friends to chatter to.'

'How thoughtful of you to deny yourself pleasure for your sister's sake. I hope she appreciates it.'

Earlier when he saw his brother leave the house with Effie and April he saw there was only one twin in the party. He is keen to be alone with May, so has called after he saw the carriage leave knowing she will be by herself.

Cunning.

He asks about the book she is reading and she tells him the plot failure as she sees it. May sees how he is watching her. When she has finished he says: 'I fail to see those obvious differences; those tell tale signs between you and your sister which my brother assures me are there for all to see. I have tried to see the difference but you can fool me it seems! For all I know you could be April,' he laughs.

'There are not many who can separate us, previously it has been only our mother.'

'Then I do not feel so bad! All I see is a ravishingly beautiful, young woman. Your eyes are like your sister's it is true but no matter what Edward says I cannot discern any difference in hue. You both possess beautiful eyes as far as I am concerned.'

'Thank you Alistair,' May says demurely. 'I appreciate the compliment. May notices he seems relaxed. She turns on the charm.

The next day at the office Edward and Alistair discuss the twins. 'I have been thinking about what you said the other night about producing an heir. I think May would make a good wife and mother. I imagine I could be happy with her, the getting of the heir would not be a chore at least.' Edward is surprised at the turn of events

'As a rich man I am used to women throwing themselves at me,' he laughs, 'I am old enough and wise enough to know that over the years some of them have been set on the path by their husband-hunting mothers.

Most have been after my name and fortune. Two or three I have genuinely liked. One or two even loved me for myself would you believe.'

'Yet one, and only one, you have loved above all others. You have had your heart broken but that was a long time ago now, water under the bridge surely?'

'It is true but the pain of it sometimes shocks me in the middle of the night when I least expects it.'

'I had no idea.' The brothers have neve talked so openly of affairs of the heart before.

'May, I am surprised to notice is not flinging herself at me as I might have anticipated. She has not fawned and flattered and positioned herself to show herself off to best advantage. I had thought she would be cosying up to me for a double wedding; I admit at first I cringed at the thought. But now I might he be persuaded to at least do a little pursuing to see what happens?

'Pursuing her around the bedroom?' Edward winks at his brother. 'Like her sister she is very comely.'

You will be building up a picture of Alistair no doubt. I bet you think him astute in business but behind the door where women are concerned. You might be right. Either way May seems well positioned to achieve her goal. She is turning out to be quite the scene stealer.

He tells Edward about his visit the night before. 'It was a very pleasant evening I must say. I am never one for small talk as you know but the conversation was wide ranging, intelligent and stimulating by turns and when it was time to leave I was genuinely sad to go home to my bachelor existence.'

'You sly old dog I never suspected!'

'I had gone last evening hoping I would find May alone, half to convince myself she was like all the rest; a pretty face but nothing special. I am not so sure now. I am definitely attracted to her, definitely warming to her charms.

'Both ladies are becoming sought after in our circle. Another handful of invitations came this morning.'

'I have seen the admiring glances when we dine out, especially from the men.'

'You will have to hurry and watch your step if you are to secure May, her dance card is always quick to fill up.'

3

For their part both twins know every hostess of note is keen to invite them to their dinners and dances. May is excited as she opens yet another invitation. 'The invitations flood in,' She laughs as she waves the card in front of her sister's face. 'We are mingling with Glasgow's high society and are a success; we are causing quite a stir.'

They have learnt a lot about the high life, they are becoming used to luxury for certain. They are enjoying their new positions and status. The parties, balls and theatre trips Edward promised have all materialised and been enjoyable for the inexperienced twins. They are mixing with a level of society neither of them ever imagined they would have entrée to.

April is still more reticent than May. 'We have both been admired I admit but we are a novelty – identical twins, the season's latest craze, as such we are courted but it will pass.'

'Ah but beautiful too, no one has ever met such beautiful twins before.' May laughs as she opens another card.

In truth April is enjoying herself too, too much to think about applying for positions. She has realised what May says is true; she is fortunate to be here in this beautiful house, with everything she could possibly wish for. Here there are luxuries beyond anything she could possibly imagine. Every day the post brings exciting opportunities, they are the toast of Glasgow.

Edward is kind, attentive and keen to make sure that she, in particular, has everything she needs. She has grown fond of him she has to admit. He has shown her the finer things in life and proudly escorts her about town.

After a few short weeks April has given up trying to be independent you will notice. Now she feels safe from his advances she has let down her guard, she has forgotten about having to pay for her board and lodging.

Of course Edward is careful to include May in all things, April is pleased to note but it is April who receives the gifts; the gowns, the trinkets, the fur lined cloaks and the finest kid gloves and now, the jewellery.

'Edward! You take my breath away, you are so thoughtful,' April says as she lifts the lid of the velvet box, an amethyst and diamond necklace lies nestled against the silk lining. 'It is so delicate and beautiful. How it sparkles.'

'I am glad you like it. I am the kind of man who gets as much, if not more pleasure, from giving than receiving; I am pleased to have made you happy.'

Instinctively, April wants to show her sister the necklace, then realises at the last moment, it might look insensitive. As if she is showing off. She refrains from dangling it in front of May. She knows May is happy for her but still…

There is another dinner, one more in a line of many they have enjoyed since arriving in Scotland, where April and May are introduced to the Driscoll brothers' social circle. May is often seated with young, available gentlemen at dinner. The hostesses are keen to please their male guests who often ask the day before to be placed next to the ravishing beauty so they might try their luck.

Of course April knows she has her admirers too but Edward has let it be known there is an understanding between herself and him. She suspects there is much gossip that she will soon become Mrs Edward Driscoll and so she is treated with the respect of an almost affianced lady. She is treated with kid gloves. Edward is a very important man and has many important friends and associates.

♥

Tonight May is seated next to Captain Archie Ryder, an Irishman, they have met previously at dinners and dances. Captain Ryder hails from Dublin and has the easy charm of the Irish. May thinks him inordinately good looking, not flashy but well dressed.

The old gentleman to May's left nods off between courses, he is so ancient he can barely sit upright and slumps in his seat. He has forgotten he asked to sit next to May. Other men at the table possibly resent the old fool.

He adds nothing to this story – his is but a bit part. Captain

Ryder however, will make more than a guest appearance.
Archie Ryder has not asked his hostess to seat him next to
May but he is keen to get to know her better nevertheless.

Captain Ryder has an accent that is soft and beguiling.
He has a ready wit and May knows he admires her, call
it women's intuition if you will. She likes him also as he
has a lively, engaging manner about him. He has the easy
banter of the Irish and the confidence of a self-made man.
He is interesting but not fascinating. He is not Captain
Edward Driscoll...or his brother.

After dessert, he is ready to ask May a question she
thinks he has had on his mind throughout the dinner.
'I am ashore for the next few weeks while my ship has a
major overhaul, there was an incident with a privateer
off the Normandy Coast and she suffered damage. Would
you permit me to escort you while I am in Glasgow? Name
something you would like to see at the theatre perhaps
and I will arrange it.' He looks confident she will concur.

May has been anticipating such a request for some
time and cannot understand why it has taken him so long
to get around to it. 'I would like that very much Captain
Ryder. The new play up from London looks interesting.'

Archie, she realises will make someone a good
husband. Not her she thinks, she has bigger fish to fry.
Archie has typical Celtic looks; dark hair and a fair
complexion that flushes easily when he has drunk too
much. He has heavy lidded, blue eyes which give his
countenance a sleepy look. He is ambitious, he has been
working for himself since he was sixteen years old he has
told her. He is wealthy but not extravagantly rich like
the Driscoll brothers. May sees he can be used to further

her cause with Alistair; it will not hurt her prospects if Alistair sees the good captain is casting his eye in her direction.

You will see that May can be quite a schemer, it comes easily to her. She is good at manipulating people to her own ends.

May is beautiful and like most beautiful, young women she is learning how to use her looks to get what she wants, she now sees a little jealousy will further her cause. She has been aware throughout dinner that Alistair has kept a watchful eye on her.

Sadly for him he has been seated next to two particularly "Plain Janes", of the unmarriageable variety – his hostess's daughters no doubt.

May has chosen to name a play which has had rave reviews. All of Glasgow society, such as it is, is eager to see it. Later in the evening Archie goes to the card tables with Edward. Edward is keen to promote May she knows; he sees if she can make a match with Archie she will leave his house. He thinks it would help his own cause to have April to himself. She thinks he would like to be rid of her. May feels a moment of disquiet as Alistair makes his entrance.

'You look entrancing this evening May, I thought Ryder was stuck to you for the evening.' He smiles confidently. 'Would you allow me to escort you to the play just transferred from London, I hear it is very amusing. We could take Effie Claire as escort if it would make you more comfortable?' Alistair is pleased with his suggestion she can tell.

May smiles inwardly but outwardly her face shows

disappointment, her acting skills come to the fore. 'Oh Alistair,' for they are on first name terms now, 'I have already been engaged to go to the production, how vexing.'

Alistair's face drops. 'That is a shame, I should have realised sooner that it, and indeed you, would be popular. When are you to go, perhaps if you are going with Edward and April I may be able to join the party?'

'I go on Saturday but alas,' and here she pauses for effect, 'I am to accompany Captain Ryder.' She looks up at him with sorrow in her eyes.

'I see I am behind in the queue, some other time then perhaps?' May demurs. 'It would seem so, your brother and April are to go on Friday I think,' she adds helpfully, 'Perhaps you might go with them?' She smiles a sweet smile knowing he is wrong footed and she has the upper hand.

Alistair mutters something inaudible. May knows he will not bother with the play. He sulks.

Women all over Glasgow dream about being asked to the theatre by this rich, handsome man; he isn't used to rejection.

He hides his frustration well for one who has had little practice in being bested. 'Some other time then May, let me know when you notice something you would like to see and I will take you.' He smiles, bows and moves off to speak to a beautiful redhead.

Later, the redhead will massage his injured pride and attempt to wheedle her way into his heart – and wallet.

♠

Some days later May enters her sister's bedroom and

notices it is much tidier than hers and with better furnishings. Are those new drapes she wonders and those cushions? Surely April did not have a silver vanity set last time she was here? She dismisses the thoughts and remembers why she has come.

'Is Edward to ask you tonight? I overheard something he said yesterday and guess he means to announce it at dinner.'

She has had her ear to the door.

May sees the look her sister shoots her. 'I can manage thank you Edith,' April says and waits till the maid has left the room. 'I wish you would learn to be discreet May, the other day when you had taken too much wine you were very free with your tongue about Whitby in front of one of the footmen. You need to watch out.'

May ignores this outburst, she has noticed her sister is more outspoken recently. She is not so open, not so confiding as she was a few months ago. She has begun to grow into the role which Edward has cast her in. May realises her own role is now a lesser one, a supporting part. Edward has become her sister's leading man. She is irritated.

'Well is he? She asks bluntly.

'Yes, I was just coming to tell you he wants us to marry and without delay; in three months time. He favours November 2nd.'

'Congratulations! This is wonderful news. Make sure you pick the biggest diamond you are offered,' she giggles as she hugs her sister. She is pleased their futures are to be secured but she cannot help but feel a tinge of the green-eyed monster. She wishes it were her on the receiving end of the proposal as he grows more handsome in her eyes every day. May has also noticed, to her surprise, that her sister appears to have warmed to Edward too. Still, she thinks, Alistair is showing a keen interest, so with patience I too, will secure a rich husband for myself.

Richer than her sister's even.

'I have been thinking about the wedding, should we ask Aunt Elizabeth, after all she is our only relative?' April asks.

May's blue eyes flash: 'Are you mad? After what she put us through! It is your wedding but I tell you now, if she is there I will not show my face.' May flounces out throwing a cushion from the bed onto the floor in an attempt to make herself feel better.

◆

After dinner Edward makes the announcement in front of his brother, sister and some of their close friends. Effie Claire is delighted, she imagines herself as a bridesmaid dressed up in silk and chiffon. No one has asked her yet but she knows she can persuade April if she has to. She has never been a bridesmaid and is excited at the news.

The young girl has enjoyed the company of the twins since their unexpected arrival. She had found it quite dreary at George Square with just her brother for company. Now she has female company on the evenings when they are at home. She is allowed more freedom to go about with them too. They are older and deemed more sensible.

April is kind and thoughtful and May is quite entertaining and makes witty asides, often at the expense of others; she has a wicked sense of humour that appeals to the young girl. May also likes fashion and needs no persuading to look at the latest styles. Effie likes having the sisters around.

Yesterday they had been at tea with Lady Sutherland and May had been quite disparaging about the society hostess. 'Do you suppose she shares her husband's razor or gets her maid to use scissors?' Effie had been trying hard not to stare at the lady's chin which had a covering of dark coarse hair. May had whispered back: 'Clearly not but if someone does not attack it soon she will have a beard to rival the king's. Perhaps she will send for the gardener and his shears.'

Effie had stifled a laugh and received a stern look from the lady in question.

May had openly attempted to make Effie laugh. 'I have a keen interest in gardening Lady Sutherland. Pray tell me, does your gardener favour shaving, I mean shearing your hedges in spring or autumn?'

Effie admired May the most. She had a blatant disregard for the social niceties unlike April who was seemed always keen to "fit in". May often went out unchaperoned – a thing Effie had never dared do.

Effie still cannot tell one twin from the other until they speak, and even then she is sometimes wrong. It is what they say and how they act which marks them apart for her. She has also come to see May watches what goes on more closely than her sister and is more unguarded than the sweet natured April.

Edward has agreed Effie can go to be "finished" in France next spring and she knows May has kindly put in a good word for her. She feels grown up in their company; they are like her older sisters she thinks.

Later when the guests have left Effie asks, 'Where will you honeymoon?' She sits on a footstool by Edward's feet. The fire is making her face red, May suggests she move behind the screen to protect her pale Scottish skin.

'We are to travel on the continent, France, Italy, Venice then possibly Holland on the return leg.'

Effie sees a look pass across May's face. Is she cross?

'I am so envious, when I marry I hope I get the chance to go to Europe, how long will you be gone?' Effie asks in a dreamy voice.

'You are to go to France next year, don't forget young lady. You should think yourself lucky. The trip will take us at least three months I should think.' Edward looks lovingly at his betrothed.

May looks daggers at her twin. The subtext of the look says 'Why have you not told me this?' She has not thought of a honeymoon! How will she cope without her twin? Of course they have never been apart. April has not mentioned a honeymoon and she must know of the arrangement.

'So I am to stay here with May? I do not have to go to stay at Alistair's do I? I will be forever in the carriage coming to town to see my friends.' Edward strokes the top of her head affectionately.

'Well, yes you do have to go to our brother's actually. April,' he breaks off and looks to his future wife smiling, 'would like May to be her companion on the trip, they have never been apart and she would be lonely without her. You cannot be left here, alone Effie.'

May's face lights up. She forgives her sister instantly.

'I would not be alone if you got me a companion. Then I could stay here and the house would not have to be shut up.' Effie is upset and doesn't care who knows it. 'Did you know about this May? Why would you want to go on someone else's honeymoon? That is an odd thing to do!'

Effie, with all the tact of a sixteen year old, is trying to hold onto her position. She does not want to be stuck out at the port with only her stuffy old brother for company. She will miss all the dances and the tea parties, the balls and the promenading. She flounces from the room, a sulky look on her face. 'No I did not know about this, Effie.' May says to her retreating back.

'Thank you Edward, that is very thoughtful of you.' Are the last words Effie hears as she slams the door behind her.

4

The wedding plans are at fever pitch, it is to be the society wedding of the year. Besides the wedding dress and trousseau there is Effie's bridesmaid dress, which has been redesigned three times so far, you would not be wrong in thinking Effie is being more demanding than the bride.

You will also notice only one bridesmaid dress is being made. May, one would imagine, is put out.

Edward has had a confidential word with his soon to be sister-in-law and suggested May not attend April in this capacity on the big day. 'You two being identical will detract from April if you are to follow her down the aisle. Even though you of course, would wear a different colour and style, you must see it would not do. It is April's day and she must be the one who gets all the attention.'

Must she indeed, May thinks to herself, as she is shown silks which are inferior to those shown to April and Effie Claire. Worse news is on the way for poor May as April is swept up in the fervour of planning her wedding.

The future Mrs Driscoll spends many hours with

the wedding planner, a rotund woman of fifty who is intent on bankrupting Edward. At first April is firm and overrules the odious woman but then gets caught up in the excitement and starts agreeing to all her demands. May has long since excused herself from the proceedings. She cares not whether the table linen is Irish or Indian; whether the favours are sweetmeats or sausages.

It is while she is hiding in the garden tending the rose bushes, May has discovered a growing passion for gardening, her fingers are quite green, that Edward seeks her out a month before the wedding.

'Can I have a word with you please May?' His opening gambit can hardly be refused. Which word would he like, she can do "Yes."

She still thinks him well-favoured and amusing even though he treats her as second best. Or third best, if you count Effie in the equation.

'My little sister is beginning to wear me down, she is constantly complaining about going to stay with Alistair while your sister and I are on honeymoon.' He picks up a faded rosebud which May has just ruthlessly pruned, it is a bud that never opened up its petals to the little warmth there was of the brief Scottish summer. 'It is too late to appoint a companion now and I don't want her to be miserable. Winter in Scotland can be depressing enough for a young girl like Effie. I have thought of a solution, but it requires some sacrifice from you I am afraid – if it is to succeed.' He smiles a slow, lazy smile which he usually reserves for her sister. May feels her cheeks colour – she longs for him to kiss her. His nearness sets her heart beating faster.

Instead he says, 'The only way I could agree to Effie staying at George Square is if you stayed with her. I know April will miss you, and you her, but might it not be agreeable all round if April and I honeymooned alone?' He looks on waiting for May to digest the news.

'But the arrangements have all been made have they not? The bookings made?'

'They can easily be unmade,' he says flippantly. Only the passage and the first leg of the trip are booked, it is of no consequence,' he assures her.

May is reminded that money does not matter. Edward will possibly forget to even cancel the booking. He is not a typical Scotsman; he is an exceedingly rich one. May is clever enough not to argue with Edward – it is April she needs to speak to and convince her she cannot go on honeymoon without her.

Later that evening May sends a message saying she will not dine as she is unwell. She knows her sister will come to see what ails her. May has powdered her face pale and left off any trace of rouge. She checks in the mirror and is pleased with the effect before arranging herself artfully on the bed, a lace handkerchief crumpled in her hand. The stage is set. There is a soft knock at the door and April comes in concern all over her pretty face.

'What's wrong? Do you have a headache?' April sits on her sister's bed and feels her forehead. She can detect no fever. May lets a tear roll from her eyes. 'Tell me, do you have pain?'

'Not the sort of pain a doctor can cure, more a pain here, in my heart, knowing we two will be apart for months. I cannot bear to think what it will be like. It will be like losing a limb I imagine. Oh April,' she says flinging her arms around her sisters neck dramatically, 'we have never been separated before!'

Bravo May, well played. She has worked on the speech for hours.

Separated by Edward she means, but knows better than to say. In May's defence, some of this speech she believes to be true; she will miss her sister, they are close. Also she has been looking forward to going abroad as she has never left these shores before. If she cannot be the bride she at least thought to enjoy the honeymoon. She does not intend to give up the trip without a fight.

'I wasn't aware Edward had spoken with you yet.' April looks ashamed, 'He said last night he might ask you to stay with Effie but I wanted to talk to you first.'

Alarm bells are ringing, surely she means talk to Edward in the firmest of terms saying she must come on the honeymoon, no questions asked. But no, April is talking and she is not saying the words that May wants to hear.

'We talked it over last night and I tend to agree with Edward. On this one occasion, I think you should stay with Effie Claire. We will be fearfully lost without each other my love, but we must face up to it. When I am married, and when you are married too in the fullness of time, we shall not always be together. Things will change. We will change.' May is incredulous. 'You will still live with us when we return, I could not part with you until you have a husband and a house of your own.' She smoothes May's hair, a sadness about her small face as the torrent of words splash over a disbelieving May.

'All the more reason to stay together for as long as possible,' May says attempting to regain lost ground. 'We have talked endlessly about what we will do in Paris, what we shall see in Venice, what we will eat in Florence...' She lets another tear drop down her cheek streaking a path down the white powder.

May cannot believe April has such a hard heart – she never used to have. 'I think you are being a little selfish, my love. Edward has never asked you to do anything for him before. Now he asks you to stay and be with his sister. Can you not find it in you to do this for him? Last night when Edward and I talked of this he made a suggestion, an idea I am sure you will like.' April takes May's hands in hers. 'Edward is so thoughtful and generous, he said as a consolation you might like to accompany Effie to France in the spring when she goes to be finished. He thought the two of you could perhaps see a little of France and perhaps take a trip to Rome or Venice before your return.' April smiles at May as if she has just presented her with a glorious gift.

Indeed you might be thinking, it is a wonderful gesture he offers. After all what red blooded man wants his wife's sister tagging along on the honeymoon? Two's company...

May is derailed. She sees she is fighting a losing battle. Go to France as an unpaid companion to chaperone his sister! May is incensed. April has grown a backbone and May is not happy about it. She needs to keep her influence over her sister; she needs to secure her place in this house. The next thing Edward will be suggesting is she takes a separate house after the honeymoon. May shivers. She will have to think of something to maintain her hold on April.

♣

It is decided. May is to nursemaid Effie Clare. May tries to put a positive slant on it and tells herself she will spend the time working on Alistair. She had thought while she was away, absence would make his heart grow fonder but now she will have to decide on a different plan of attack. She must not lose sight of the goal; both of them should make good marriages. She does not mean to live her life the poorer relation.

Since moving here she has gained ambition. She wants what her sister has – she wants to be centre stage too. She will achieve this at any cost she tells her reflection in the mirror

5

The wedding, all tartan kilts and Highland flings is a 'splendid do' as they say in these parts; no expense has been spared. The bride looks radiant – for one who has been so reluctant for so long. The bride's sister, while not exactly dowdy, has been sidelined once again.

However, Alistair has made himself indispensable to May, so she is not too despondent, he is at her side throughout the service, when not performing his duties as Best Man.

At the wedding breakfast he says, 'Will you try a few steps May? I know you have been having dancing lessons with my sister and April?' He looks well in tartan. His sturdy legs suit a kilt. They dance a reel and May gets giddy when he spins her round expertly. She is enjoying being flung around in his strong arms.

'I did not know you danced so well,' she says truthfully.

'All boys are taught Scottish country dancing at school. Girls too, of course; it is our heritage. I learnt how to dance on crossed swords from the age of ten. I felt very manly I can tell you,' he says laughing at himself.

More than one guest notices the looks between them and wonders if there will soon be another reason to celebrate.

April has gone to change for her honeymoon and as her bridesmaid Effie has been chosen to help her. Again May feels demoted. No doubt this too, was another of Edward's suggestions.

He is becoming fond of making suggestions. Usually they are of the kind that separate the twins from one another. He possibly finds having a replica of his betrothed about constantly, quite trying to say the least.

It would have been May's last chance to be alone with her sister for three months and she has been denied even that small favour. A resentment is beginning to form in the pit of her stomach. First there had been the inferior clothes; next she was still putting up with the local girl acting as her maid: May could hardly understand her Glaswegian accent – it was impenetrable. Then there was the taking away of the honeymoon trip and now this. As the guests wait for the happy couple to emerge from the reception May arranges her features into the semblance of a smile. The newlyweds are to sail that evening and the carriage is waiting to take them to Port Glasgow.

April, on the arm of the man May loves, despite his interfering, trips lightly down the steps and catches sight of her sister. She lets go of her new husband and flings her arms about May's neck. 'I will miss you, my love,' April whispers in her twin's ear.

'I will miss you too, enjoy yourself. Do not forget to write,' here she pushes her sister away from her so she can see her face and holds both her hands in hers, 'Remember what old lady Jansen taught you. Edward will at least be a happy man on his wedding night with all the "lessons in love" you had,' she says witheringly. April's face shows confusion.

May, resentful of her sister's happiness adds bitterly: 'Tonight he will see what a good return on his investment he has.' May watches April's face as she tries to hide the shock and hurt she feels at May's acerbity.

For her part, May had wanted to sting her sister but had not meant to stab so deep.

'I love you dearest,' she adds wishing she could take back the barbed words, she hates this jealousy that builds up inside her, yet she cannot help herself. The feeling of resentment has taken hold and is beginning to build despite herself. May wants the one thing she cannot have.

The guests close in around them and Edward regains his bride but not before he leaves May with a speech of his own.

'Goodbye May, take care of Effie for me and do not take any nonsense from my little sister. Don't forget if you need anything Alistair will be there to guide you.'

Edward is a happy man now he has secured April. Effie muscles in and plants a last kiss on his cheek – at the same time he leans in to kiss his new sister-in-law and is jostled by the over enthusiastic Effie. The kiss he has meant for May's cheek lands full on her lips; May colours slightly. She feels the softness of his longed for lips, smells his musky cologne, her insides turn a somersault. Her jealousy knows no bounds.

Every event seems designed to rub salt in her wounds. Tonight, she thinks, her sister is to have what she does

not really care for, the love of Captain Edward Driscoll
and May, alone and unloved will lay in an empty bed
wishing with all her heart she could swap places with her
ungrateful sister.

♠

Effie Claire is more pleased than May of course at the
change of plan; now she gets to stay in town and meet
with all her friends. The young girl is also in the throes
of first love with the young Laird she met at the wedding.
He has departed to his remote castle in The Highlands.
This adds to the romance for Effie and she has discussed
the situation with May endlessly. The young lovers are
corresponding and Effie has shared the letters with May.
May has pronounced them to be very good letters and
this thrills the inexperienced young woman. Despite
May's own heartache she has listened patiently to Effie's
prattling with good humour. The young Laird has asked
if he can see Effie on his next visit to Glasgow in two
weeks time and Effie is excited at the prospect.

'You will have to speak to Alistair, I cannot give my
permission,' May says after the letter has been read out
to her.

'I know, but will you put in a good word for me, you
know how stuffy my brother can be? He is to call this
evening after dinner. Please May,' she wheedles.

'I will of course but whether he will do as I bid, who
can say? He need not take notice of me.'

May is grateful for the information that Alistair will
visit this evening, now she knows she will borrow one

of her sister's more superior gowns. She has quite taken a fancy to some of them and has worn one or two when Alistair has taken her and Effie out and about. May has also availed herself of some of the jewellery April has left behind thinking them too precious to risk losing abroad. May would have no such qualms.

'Oh but I am sure he will, he holds you in high regard I know. When he called last and you were out with Captain Ryder he was very sorry to have missed you. In fact I believe he had called to see you, rather than me, I think he is jealous of Archie'

'When did he call? You did not say.'

Effie can see May is paying more attention now, she is a clever little minx.

After an initial sulk over being left behind, May has been amusing herself while her sister has been away by going about, chaperoned of course, with the good captain. He has taken her about Glasgow, showing her the sights, such as they are, and taking her to galleries, exhibitions and the theatre. He has naturally been at sea for some of the time April has been honeymooning, but no matter, for then she has had Alistair to fall back on, she is enjoying playing one off against the other.

That evening Alistair calls, as expected, and May is looking especially lovely. She is wearing lilac shot silk with an amethyst and diamond necklace she has "borrowed" from April's jewel box. It brings out the colour in her eyes.

'Do you know you have a violet hint to your eyes? I have never noticed before,' Alistair says as he kisses her hand. May files this away for future use as this information might be useful. She is sure it is the colour of the dress and gems that enhance her eyes.

Effie is happy when Alistair has no objections to her meeting her young Laird when next he comes to town. 'That is if May will be kind enough to act as chaperone if I am unavailable,' he says smiling at her. Effie disappears after planting a kiss on her brother's cheek. She is excited at the prospect of meeting her beau again. She will write to him at once and agree to meet him.

'Effie will have to be watched carefully in France,' Alistair says after the girl leaves the room. 'I can see she will get into all sorts of bother otherwise.'

'You make me sound like a maiden aunt charged with watching her every move! Try to remember I am but two and a half years older than your sister,' May says.

'I am sure you were not so silly at her age.'

'She is in thrall to the young Laird, I doubt she will be prone to wildness in France.' Alistair laughs at the comment.

'Then you have more faith in her than I! She is a determined flirt.' He suddenly becomes more thoughtful. 'It will be strange, your sister will return and you will leave. I will miss you – or will I?' he half jokes, I will of course, have your doppelganger to hand.'

'As for your missing me, I swear you will not even notice I am gone I'm sure.' May is on a fishing trip. She waits for a compliment that does not materialise. Alistair changes the subject.

'Have you missed April very much?'

'I have. In the last letter I received she said they would be back by January twenty first at the latest. Edward wants to be back for some business reason I believe.'

'Yes we are about to take over another company, I need him for the merger.' For a minute or two Alistair thinks of the business deal. He remembers his manners and his reason for calling.

'Allow me to pass the time more quickly for you by planning some more diversions, let me take you to dinner at the Blythswood soon.' He names one of the most elegant and renowned hotels in Glasgow. Its restaurant boasts a French chef, one of only a handful in the whole of Scotland.

'It is very kind of you to think of me I should like to go very much. In the meantime I am looking forward to our next visit to the Theatre Royal.'

♥

On Saturday evening Alistair escorts his sister-in-law to the theatre on Hope Street. It is a play he has chosen particularly. May is beautifully turned out in aquamarine silk taffeta, with delicate, white lace trimmings. The neck line is quite daring for a single lady to wear but then it was not designed for a single lady; it is her sister's gown. She has had an enjoyable afternoon trying on the contents of her sister's wardrobe.

April of course, has had a whole new wardrobe made for her honeymoon. May is of the opinion the gowns left behind will be out of fashion by the time April comes home so they need an outing. She will not care if May has borrowed one or two, she tells herself. Alistair looked very appreciative when he called for them.

It is the interval of the play and they are discussing

the first half.

'Well I think it the dreariest play I have ever had the misfortune to see,' Effie Claire announces putting May and Alistair in no doubt what she thinks of the production. 'Do we have to stay for the second half it is so boring.'

Before they can answer, a lady dressed in crimson taffeta suddenly appears from May's left, she has not seen her approach.

'Good evening May what a pleasant surprise to find you here in Glasgow.' May is stunned. Standing before her is Aunt Elizabeth. She pulls herself together quickly.

'How lovely to see you – it has been so long.'

'Indeed it has, so long you will not have heard I am now Lady Vennor.' She smiles triumphantly. 'But where is dear April?' Elizabeth looks with interest at Alistair. 'Are you to introduce me to your handsome escort May?'

Elizabeth knows exactly who the man is. What she doesn't know is how May comes to be here in Glasgow with one of the wealthiest men in Scotland.

'Yes of course, I am sorry, where are my manners. Lady Vennor, this is Mr Alistair Driscoll my brother-in-law.' They exchange greetings.

'April married! How splendid, when did this occur?'

The interval bell sounds. The second half of the performance is about to commence. Saved by the bell May thinks.

'Oh dear, what a bore,' Elizabeth says, 'May dearest, call on me tomorrow I am staying at The Blythswood Square. We need to catch up, please say you will call and bring dear April as well of course.' May just has time to say that April is on her honeymoon, as her Aunt sweeps back into the auditorium.

Effie says, 'Who was that? I never saw anyone so old look so beautiful!'

'Effie!' Alistair admonishes his sister. 'You are too outspoken it is offensive – please apologise at once to Miss May.' He is half smiling, for no doubt he was just thinking the same thing himself. Not that he thinks Elizabeth old, but she is stunning in a mature, older woman sort of way.

May is trying to gather her thoughts. She mutters that no apology is needed. She notices them both looking at her expectantly.

'Mrs, er, I mean Lady Vennor was a friend of my mother's, she lived in London but used to come to Whitby to take the spa waters. You are right Effie; she is still a beautiful woman.'

'Oh not a relative then?' says Effie Claire blithely, 'But you two look so alike she could be your mother. She knew you were May and not April – how is that I wonder for I still mistake you when you are together.' Again Effie is chastised by her brother for being forthright. May mutters something about it being a lucky guess.

'I can see what Effie means,' Alistair says, 'It is the shape of the eyes and the fullness of the lips; not many women have such winning features in one package.'

May blushes prettily and tries to change the subject. She is still recovering from the shock of seeing her Aunt. She has no wish to see her again after all she has made her suffer but thinks she will have to if a disaster is to be avoided. She has seen the look on her aunt's face and is worried she will become meddlesome.

It is one thing Edward knowing their past but she does not want Alistair to know of their heritage. Can you blame her?

Not that she thinks her aunt would spill the beans; she is much too careful for that yet May does not want Alistair to know she is related to an actress; an actress who sold their souls to the devil woman who is Mrs Jansen. She is keen for his good opinion, she has a growing regard for him. Would he marry the niece of an actress? May thinks not. He is much more conservative than his brother.

'I take it we are not seeing the second half of the play,' May says lightly. 'I tend to agree with Effie, it is a little tedious, but if you want to see it Alistair then we had better make a move.' May would be happy to sit in the darkness of the box and think about the dilemma of whether to call on Aunt Elizabeth or not.

'No, I bow to your superior wisdom, I am happy to give it a miss. It is not as appealing as I expected it to be.'

'It is too early to go home yet,' Effie adds hopefully, 'can we go to The Scotia, the Music Hall will be much more fun than this.'

'You are far too young for such places. Dear God, I need to think whether to lock you up until you are twenty one or married, which ever comes the soonest,' Alistair laughs, only half joking.

'I hope I am married before I am twenty one! I shall be an old maid by then.'

♦

The next morning May dresses demurely, needless to say, in one of April's most elegant day dresses – she wants to bolster her confidence and to gain the upper hand. She doesn't know what she is going to say to her aunt yet but she has lost any regard she ever had for the woman.

As she dresses she thinks about Alistair and Effie saying Aunt Elizabeth could be her mother. Now that May is older she sees the likeness. Indeed she thinks both of us look more like our aunt than our dear mother. Their mother, poor woman, had been a beauty in her younger days but working for her living had affected her looks – she was old before her time.

She wishes April were here to talk to. Her head begins to throb. She would like to tell her aunt exactly what she thinks of her but knows this would not be sensible. The best she can hope to achieve is to keep her at arm's length and hope she is not in Glasgow for long. If needs be, and if Elizabeth is to be around, May thinks she will be "indisposed" until her aunt leaves. She hopes she is gone before April returns.

May takes the short journey to Blythswood Street in the carriage and is shown into a suite of rooms at the hotel. It is a far cry from The Angel Inn she thinks.

'I am so glad you could come May, I have been simply dying to know how you come to be here in Glasgow and being escorted by one of the richest men in Scotland.' They sit opposite each other and tea is ordered. Aunt Elizabeth, resplendent in ivory satin sits upright and fans herself indolently.

'I told you, Mr Driscoll is my brother-in-law, April is just recently married to Captain Edward Driscoll. They are honeymooning on the continent.'

'I am sorry to have missed her. How fortunate April is

but by the look on Mr Alistair Driscoll's face last night my dear May you will not be a spinster sister for much longer. I dare say you too will be enjoying your own honeymoon soon enough.'

May is furious with her aunt as she has just named the very thing she wants most in the world. May has been thinking of late if she can procure Alistair she will have a higher station than her sister. After all Alistair has his inheritance which makes him a far better catch than Edward.

To her aunt she says, 'You seem to be doing well for yourself Aunt Elizabeth, is your husband with you in Glasgow?'

'Sadly not, he passed away while we were abroad. I am not really out of mourning yet.' May remembers the blood red taffeta her aunt wore the previous night. 'He was much older than me of course. Sad but as you can see, he left me well provided for.'

'How fortunate.' May spits out.

She composes herself while a maid brings in the tea. This woman has no idea May thinks, what she has put us through. It is clear to May her aunt has not given them a minute's thought until last night. She wishes her aunt's late husband had left her penniless then she would know how it feels to be compromised.

May has every right to feel aggrieved don't you think? Elizabeth, remember is their birth mother. She had it within her power to spare the girls in the first place; even when she became rich she still did nothing for them. She acts true to type.

'I am glad you are well situated aunt for I would not

want April to return and find you wanting handouts.'

Elizabeth raises a perfectly shaped eyebrow. 'May dearest, why the bitterness? Have I not always shown you both the greatest care and attention?'

'Yes aunt, I am sorry. I had forgotten the apprenticeships you found for us in Whitby. What fortunate positions they were!' May is furious and tries to swallows down the bile in her throat.

'Do not furrow your brow so you will get wrinkles before your time.' Elizabeth smiles benignly at her daughter. 'You have to understand I did the best I could for you at the time, back then I did not have the resources at my disposal to help you more. Your dear Mama left you very poorly off. I was only trying to take care of you both.'

'By placing us in a brothel! When you found yourself in a better situation you obviously went straight to Mrs Jansen and asked her to release us into your care did you not?' May's voice has taken on a menacing, sarcastic, quality. 'Of course you didn't! For you only care for one person in this world and that is yourself! Do you know what kind of life we had in that place? Do you even care? It was hell; my sister was close to the edge every day we were forced to stay there. Had it not been for a lucky encounter with Captain Driscoll we would still be in that pit now being used and abused by all manner of wretched, old men.'

May had not meant to say any of this but now she has started she finds it hard to stop.

'Those girls, some of them even younger than us, were forced to perform lewd, indecent acts. They were ill-treated and knocked about by Mrs Jansen's "gentlemen".

All she asked is that the men did not use their fists on the girls' faces because that would have spoilt them for other punters and lost her precious coin. Soon it would have been our turn to be used in any way the men saw fit.' She paused to get her temper under control.

'Your own flesh and blood yet you cared nothing for us, just so long as we were not a burden to you. We were out of sight and out of mind.' May has warmed to her theme. 'Our mother would be ashamed of you for treating us so badly, she would have expected you to do more for us than cast us adrift in a den of vice. Captain Driscoll could see what you could not – that we did not deserve to be in such a place.'

Quite unperturbed but a little shocked by May's unladylike outburst Elizabeth pours the tea. 'My dear had I only known.' May is about to continue her tirade when her aunt continues, 'It has intrigued me I must admit how you came to find yourselves here with the gentry, and ridiculously rich gentry at that? Did the good Captain meet you both at Mrs Jansen's? Was April taken from there to be his mistress? Men rarely marry their mistress,' she says forgetting old Lord Vennor did just that.

May looks venomously at her aunt. 'We cannot all be bought and paid for so easily. What do you care anyway? You showed not the slightest interest in us from the day you sold us to that woman, Captain Driscoll rescued us in the nick of time.'

'I bet he did.' Elizabeth sips her tea. May ignores the slight and fights the urge to throw something hot and sweet at her. She stands to leave. Elizabeth continues, 'In that case you should be grateful to me my dear, not reprimanding me so harshly.'

'Grateful! For selling us off like cattle in a market!'

'Think about it May dearest. Would April have met her rich husband had it not been for me putting her in the Captain's way? Would the handsome brother be casting his eye at you now if it were not for me? Seeing you both in such a place allowed Edward Driscoll to act the gallant. Men love to rescue maidens in distress I always find.' Elizabeth simpers. 'April would never have met the likes of him in The Angel I can assure you of that.' She nibbles shortbread and smiles. 'Now you are both set up for life. As I say, you should be grateful to me.'

May has reached the door and is about to leave. 'Please May, do not take on so, let us not part on this sour note. Come, take tea with me for tomorrow I leave for England and who knows when we will meet again.'

'In that case aunt I will bid you farewell and pray we never see each other again. As far as we are concerned and I know I can speak with confidence on April's behalf, you are dead to us. Good day to you Lady Vennor.'

♣

That was quite a scene. She certainly deserves a round of applause after that. But, I wonder have you been wondering about April? Are you curious to know how the honeymoon progresses? Let me fill you in. It is two months and three weeks since April said 'I do' and became Mrs Edward Driscoll. Since then she has endured her wedding night and seen the sights of France; she loved Paris, especially the galleries. The food she could take or leave. Next she travelled extensively in Italy, she loves the food here, it is like tasting sunshine, she thinks in one of her more poetic moments. The weather is still cool, it is only February but it is dry unlike England, or Scotland for that matter. They have finally arrived in Venice and April has fallen in love. With Edward you ask? Both Venice and her husband it has to be said have stolen her heart.

Edward, throughout the honeymoon, has been kind and solicitous, courteous and loving. He has behaved as any new husband would when the woman of his dreams is on his arm and in his bed. April is shy in the latter but he is not complaining – she is compliant enough. He loves April more and more each day. They make an attractive couple.

He saw how his wife was unsure at the start of their journey but now she too has begun to relax and warm up in his company. He is gratified she is showing much more interest in him, especially when they are alone. She laughs more readily, is carefree and interested in finding out more about her new husband's likes and dislikes. She sees that they have a lot in common. They like the same artists, share the same dislike of snails, appreciate the Italian architecture and they both adore Venice.

They have just returned from a romantic ride on a gondola, it is the third such trip they have enjoyed. April likes to watch the world go by from such a vantage point. She loves to sit by her husband's side as they go under the many bridges, as he whispers romantic poetry in her ear. Things could not be better for the young couple.

You know it cannot last. The honeymoon is almost over and real life is about to rear its ugly head. Poor April is about to have her honeymoon ruined.

♠

They are walking through one of their favourite piazzas, Santa Lucia, and admiring for the last time the towering campanile when April feels a pain in her back. It is a sharp stabbing pain which takes her breath away.

'What is it my love? Edward asks as she stops abruptly.

'It is nothing, just a twinge – it has gone now. I must have been sitting awkwardly in the gondola, it is very low down and perhaps the air is damp on the lagoons.' They continue to walk but April feels the pain spreading across her lower back and leans heavily on her husband's arm. They decide to return to their hotel earlier than planned.

'Perhaps you should rest a while, my love. We have done such a lot of walking of late, take a siesta. I will leave you with Edith and be in the bar downstairs if you should need me.'

April is feeling sick now but she does not want to worry Edward. They ate a pasta dish with a rich lobster sauce earlier and she thinks it has disagreed with her.

She is wrong.

Sadly for her, she is soon to find out the honeymoon baby she had not known existed is about to be lost. April clutches Edith's hand as the pain starts to grow stronger. April lies on the bed and the maid sees her mistress is bleeding. Edith begins to panic.

'We are in a strange country with doctors who do not speak English and doubtless have different methods,' Edith is worried. 'What shall I do?

'Get help, find my husband.' April is doubled over in pain. Edith rushes from the room to find the master who is reading a newspaper in the bar. Edward always a quick thinker, calls at the hotel reception and demands a doctor be sent immediately to their room.

The hotel of course, being the premier establishment in Venice, has its own doctor who speaks perfect English so Edith need not have worried.

The doctor quickly assesses the situation but by the time he arrives it is more or less over. The baby, such as it was, is gone. Husband and wife are left alone to come to terms with the news they were about to become parents and now they are not. It is a shock to them both.

Their journey home is delayed. When April feels better she writes to May saying they are enjoying Venice so much they plan to stay for two more weeks. She does not want to worry her twin and so makes no mention of the miscarriage. The doctor has advised her not to travel until she feels strong enough. She already feels well again but Edward is erring on the side of caution, he is taking good care of his wife.

When May gets the letter she is vexed as it comes on the back of other bad news – the very worst news. She has lost the man she thought she had snared. She has spent the last two days in a foul mood veering between anger, sadness and frustration. Now this!

What can have happened I hear you ask? When last we saw Alistair and May together things were going splendidly. They were on the verge of declarations surely?

One evening shortly after May's meeting with her Aunt, Alistair calls on one of his frequent visits. On the evenings when he is not showing her around Glasgow, and when she is not making him jealous by going about with Captain Ryder, he has taken to dropping in on his way to or from his club, on the pretence of checking on his sister.

On this particular evening he has not been to his club but has come from the house of a lady. An old friend you understand, an old lover is nearer the mark.

He sits opposite May, as his is wont, stares pensively into the fire and sips brandy. May is not perturbed for when she saw him two nights ago he was keen to assure her of his affections. Things were at last beginning to move and he had taken her hand and kissed it with more feeling than ever before. She had been sure if Effie, the minx, had not burst in upon them he would have declared himself then and there.

At last he turns to look at May. She tells herself he is rehearsing the words that will make them inseparable, the words that will join them together.

She is wrong.

'It is strange is it not how fate plays her hand in our lives? A chance encounter, a different turn in the road and our lives can be altered drastically.' She smiles waiting for him to go on. 'Today I have learned of something I know will change the course of my life, something I could never have imagined, I feel I had to come and speak of it with you straight away my dear May.'

'Some business matter do you mean Alistair?' she asks still not alert to any danger. He often talks over issues concerning the business now Edward is away. She has been flattered he trusts her judgement, although she knows nothing about imports and exports, he says he has found it helpful to use her as a sounding board. She was taught by the Madam to listen, men like to talk she had said. If you are a good listener you might hear something to your advantage. It has been the only piece of useful information she received from the vile woman.

'No, a personal matter. A matter I thought was over many years ago.' Now her eyes dart to his face. Now she is watchful.

'When I was younger,' he pauses and looks from the dying embers of the fire to May's expectant face, 'twelve years younger, I met a lady named Beatrice and well, we fell in love.' May is on high alert now. Panic is beginning to rise in her breast. Her mouth is dry.

'She was an aristocrat and an heiress. She had an overbearing father who did not want his only daughter to marry "trade" as he saw fit to call me. No matter about my wealth I was not titled, I was "new money" in his eyes. When he saw my intentions, Bea was kept away from me and quickly became betrothed, against her will, to an English Lord old enough to be her grandfather. She was distraught as you can imagine, as was I. The marriage took place with undue haste as her father was sure we would try to elope. There was no opportunity for such a thing as she was watched day and night. As the wedding drew closer there was nothing I could do, I could not even get a message to her.'

He stops his speech suddenly and says. 'I am sorry to pour my heart out to you in this way but I feel I owe you an explanation.' May cannot frame a sentence and he carries on. 'I heard on the grapevine she bore him two sons; an heir and a spare! As I say, this was twelve years ago and her husband's estate being in Yorkshire I never saw her again – until yesterday.'

May can feel her world unravelling but clings to a slender thread. 'Has she returned to see her family?'

'Her father has been dead these last seven years and she has no other relatives in Glasgow. The reason for her return is because her husband has died, he was so much older than her as I said. Yesterday she sought me out to tell me she has returned home. She is still a very beautiful woman, despite all the years of loneliness and heartache she has suffered married to an old, unfeeling man. It was only ever a marriage of convenience, her father's convenience that is.

May's face is set, her teeth clenched. She can hardly breathe. She knows what is coming and cannot bear to hear it. She sits frozen to the spot. 'Does she plan to reside here in Glasgow?' May asks not caring where the damn woman lives so long as it is not within two hundred miles of here.

'Hopefully, all I know is we have to be together – we have been given a second chance. There is nothing and no one to stop us marrying now. All these years no other woman has come close to her for me, every woman I ever met had to measure up to her and they all fell short. That is, until I met you of course May,' he adds hastily. 'I think I could have been happy with you and possibly, you with me? I am sorry, I do not know whether you knew I had feelings for you, but now all is changed. I hope this does not come as too much of a blow. I will always be fond of you, my dear.' He sits by her and takes her hands in his. 'But I cannot waste any more of my life apart from the one woman I have always truly loved. Tonight I asked her to marry me and she accepted. His face has a bright, happy smile of joy and contentment upon it.

Every word he is uttering is like a fresh stab wound to her heart. The blows keep raining down. It is not that she loves him passionately, she admires him and might have learned to love him; she certainly desires him – and his money. She has imagined he would be a thoughtful lover. It is the life she could have had with him, the life which is being cruelly snatched away that is killing her. The loss of rank, status and wealth is what she will miss.

Before May can gather her thoughts he adds. 'Please do not hate me May, try to be happy for me. I am sorry if you had expectations.'

May struggles to compose herself. Later she can barely remember what she says to him in reply. She is in shock. She had hoped on her sister's return she would be giving her some news of her own, news that would see her elevated even higher than her sister. News of moving to her own household with her own staff to command, where she would wear finer silks and finer furs to ward off the cold, Scottish winters. She would have had status and wealth beyond her wildest dreams. She has worked tirelessly to that end. She deserved a new life. Now Alistair will be the one with the news of a wedding and it will not involve her.

She takes to her bed. Her hopes and dreams are smashed. What is there for her now? Captain Archibald Ryder is no substitute for what Alistair could provide, any alliance with him would be a backward step. There would be no mansion house, no fine jewels, no position in Glasgow society, no life at all.

Effie, concerned for May, comes to see what the matter is every morning but May will not see her. For two days she makes excuses and stays in her bed. She cries, she rants, she throws things, but most of all she feels sorry for herself and the life she has lost. A piece of her heart freezes solid. She will have revenge.

Act 3

1

At another dinner on another evening April, home from her honeymoon, watches May toy with her food. She is concerned for her sister who is clearly unhappy. They have of course, talked of Alistair's marriage which took place with all due ceremony last week. As it is six months since Bea's aged husband made her the happiest of women by dying, Alistair has wasted little time in securing her as his bride.

The wedding, which May bore with fortitude, was attended by all of Glasgow society. Now they are on honeymoon at Bea's late husband's estate in Yorkshire. Alistair is making up for lost time with the woman he never thought to possess.

'Are you still feeling under the weather dearest?' April asks as they retire and leave Edward to his port, or rather his single malt.

'You hardly ate anything again this evening.'

'It is a bilious attack I think I shall have an early night

if you don't mind.'

'Of course I don't mind but wait a while and have some tea with me. I am sure tea will settle you.' May knows why she is being detained; she knows what is to come. She has seen the looks between husband and wife. She has noticed a change in April's waistline and sure enough when the tea drinking is underway April tells May her news.

'I hope you did not mind me holding you back from your bed but I wanted to share some news with you. I wonder if you can guess. I am to have a baby!' April blurts out before May has a chance to speak.

'How wonderful my love.' May says and she means it, she would mean it more fervently if jealousy was not eating her up. May has been so dejected over the past few months. Firstly there was Alistair's news, followed by the ordeal of meeting the "other woman" Beatrice. Then there were the wedding preparations and the "putting on of a brave front" all of the time. It has been exhausting. Thank God she is not an actress, she thinks. It is harder work than she imagined playing the role of happy, poor relation.

Finally the wedding is over and Alistair is gone from her life and now this; the final insult. April is to have Edward's child. Her beloved Edward is to be a father. If only she could have been his wife and given him his longed for son.

'It should have been me!' She screams to herself back in her own bedroom. Now April is back she has returned to her old, smaller, inferior suite of rooms and resents that too.

Did I mention May had moved into April's suite when her sister was abroad? Well wouldn't you have taken advantage of the palatial suite, with all its amenities while you had the chance? She misses the water closet. Her own apartment is hardly a mouse hole but May has lost all perspective. She is a woman whose glass is always half empty. She sees her sister has everything she wants and with Alistair lost to her, she has no way of obtaining the same.

April has told her sister about the miscarriage in Venice and how sad they had been to find the baby lost. She has said she is delighted to be with child again and the doctor has told her he does not expect any problems this time around.

He is wrong.

Three weeks after May learnt of the pregnancy she is woken in the early hours of the morning by the news that April has miscarried again. May does all that she can to help her sister over the ordeal. She sits with her, talks with her, orders her favourite foods to try to help her to recover her strength. They are inseparable once more. It is as it used to be before April's marriage.

May, though not intentionally at first, realises her sister has come to rely on her for most things. She still loves her husband but he has his business to distract him from the heartache of losing another baby.

'He is a man', she tells May, 'and he does not feel the loss as I do.'

The twins spend much time together. They are as one. May begins to see a way ahead.

After her own loss, of Alistair that is, May has given Captain Ryder his marching orders. She has no time for him while she comforts her twin. He has served his purpose and now he is surplus to requirements; better to stay in splendid spinsterhood in luxury than to move down the social ladder and marry him. She plans to take a lover, and has even had a braver idea.

May has noticed that far from Edward not caring about the loss of another child, he has taken it quite badly. During this sad time he has confided in May.

'I cannot tell April how I feel.' he says, 'for fear of upsetting her further, she is so sad and thinks she has let me down.'

May has also noticed that Edward has begun, slowly at first, to drink more. He has always been fond of a particular brand of single malt but May has seen how the bottle is emptying quicker during the weeks following the miscarriage. He has started to sit alone with the whisky bottle after dinner.

When April takes an early night, he sits and talks with May and pours himself a large slug of the amber liquor. May is a sympathetic listener. She talks of other chances he and April will have to conceive. She says April is young and strong and is sure to carry the next child to term. She is full of platitudes. She hopes this will be the case for he has often spoken of a son and heir and without one May worries for both their futures.

Gradually May makes herself indispensable to her brother-in-law too, as she tops up his whisky glass and listens with rapt attention. She acts the part of wife and confidante and talks over business deals as she used to with Alistair. She admires his handsome face and the broadness of his chest. She looks at him lovingly and wonders what it would be like to love him fully.

One evening he is feeling quite garrulous, the whisky and port are doing their job when he says. 'You know May I admire you, although there was a time when I was quite jealous of your hold over April. I thought you sought to influence her against me but now I see you have nothing but our welfare at heart. You have been a devoted sister to my wife, especially lately when her spirits have been so low. You are a kind and loving sister-in-law to me. He takes her hand and kisses it for longer than a brother-in-law should.

May, who is sitting close by him, leans in and looks up at him through long lashes. She has yearned for this moment for so long and now it is here she wants to hold onto it forever.

'Edward you know I would do anything for you,' she murmurs. Shall she risk taking it further she wonders?

You can almost feel for her. He is constantly before her, yet she can do nothing without being disloyal to her sister. It is a predicament, a daily battle she fights within herself. The temptation is great.

'You must know that I love you – as a brother,' she adds quietly. She places her head on his shoulder and closes her eyes. The weight is barely discernible. She hardly dares breathe. She expects him to pull away but he does not. In fact he keeps hold of her hand and again raises it to his lips, May turns into him and their lips meet. She places her hand on his shoulder and they begin to kiss gently. His touch becomes more ardent and May can feel herself yielding. At that moment the door is flung open and Effie, you might have guessed, bursts into the room. She is just returned from a night out with her friend, Lady Amy.

'Look at you two love birds,' she says giggling. She still cannot tell one sister from the other and imagines it is his own wife he is making love to. 'We have had such a good time, I am quite fagged' Edward straightens up and is about to remonstrate with his tipsy sister when she announces. 'I'm off to bed and I think you two should follow suit!'

The saucy little thing!

She flounces out again slamming the door behind her. The spell is broken

2

Christmas comes and goes; the household is not in the mood for celebrating. Effie Claire spends more time at Lady Amy's where the mood is altogether jollier. Her love affair with the Laird has fizzled out, absence has not made her heart grow fonder and she is enjoying playing the field once again. With May as chaperone, she has had more freedom of late, as Edward is managing the business single handed whilst Alistair is in Yorkshire.

By early spring it has been decided Effie will not go to be finished this year after all; May cannot be spared to go with her. April is with child again. It is late May and April is almost six months into the pregnancy. All seems to be progressing well. Effie Claire is enjoying herself so she is not too despondent.

April, against doctor's orders had been desperate to conceive again. Perhaps May has been whispering in her ear.

Since the night when Edward first kissed May there has been no repetition of the intimacy between them although they have continued to spend time together. April often retires early. Both husband and sister have encouraged April to take care of herself and Edward has confided that now his wife is past the critical time when she has lost the two previous babies, he is allowing himself to feel optimistic.

It is short lived.

Once again poor April miscarries the baby she has longed for. This time however, the pregnancy being that much further advanced the blow is so much harder to take.

'This time the ordeal has meant not only have I lost my child, I almost lost my wife.' Poor April is near death for days before finally rallying. 'She has wanted to die, prayed to die, so heartbroken is she. This time she had been sure she would have a child to show for all the inactivity she has suffered over the months; she has been so careful.' Edward is distraught. May too is distressed.

The doctor takes Edward to one side concern written on his face.

'In my medical opinion I deem it unwise for Mrs Driscoll to risk another gestation. She has steadily got weaker with each loss. I fear her constitution is not strong enough to withstand another pregnancy. Should you try, I would not give her favourable odds of surviving.'

It is a bitter pill to take and Edward is devastated. 'How will I break the news to the love of my life?' he asks May who is downcast.

'I wanted this child so much.' He is plunged into despair. Again he is consoled by May and the whisky bottle.

Once a sober man, he begins to depend on alcohol to sleep through the night. May has been "a rock" he says to Effie, who with all the callousness of youth just wants everyone to cheer up.

May has been grieved over her sister's loss too; she would have been a hard hearted sister had she not been affected. May has done all she can to support April. She had feared for her sister's life but when her sister cannot bring herself to get out of bed and is often sedated for her own good, May spends time with Edward, time trying to cheer him and raise his spirits. She remembers the lessons at Mrs Jansen's where they were taught how to raise men's vital principles. She has been patient and thinks she should now start to reap the rewards that are her due. The once happy house has become dull and moribund; Effie spends even more time at Lady Amy's.

'I have tried to bolster Edward and help him through this difficult time.' Alistair tells May one day as he is about to leave. 'When I see my brother during the course of the working day I see his distress; now I am back in the saddle I have tried to take over the reins but he will lock himself away with his head buried in work!'

'You are good to try to help him but I too am worried for his well being. He is as you say trying to divert himself with the business.' And the bottle she thinks to herself.

Sometimes Alistair and Bea come to dine to try to lift Edward's spirits. Last time, Alistair took May aside. She thought he was going to confide his marriage was not working out as he expected. She had noticed there seemed little love lost between the newly married couple.

She was wrong.

I have tried in vain, to get Edward to dine at our house to take him out of himself but Edward has refused to leave April, he says she cannot be prevailed upon to leave the house.'

She can hardly be prevailed upon to leave her bed some days, poor woman, let alone her house. She is despondent. She knows she cannot supply the heir her husband wants and is at a loss to know what to do.

The next time Alistair dined he tried again. 'Can I persuade you to join us for dinner, will you have a word with April? May will take good care of April – or perhaps you both might enjoy the carriage ride over? What say you? Shall you ask her Edward?'

'I will ask, but I fear April is still too weak and too sad. I do not know what I would have done without May; she has been tireless in her support.'

'Well then why not leave Effie Claire with April for a few hours, she will be sleeping anyway. Let May have some respite from the sick room and bring her to dine, it will do you both some good.' Alistair will not take no for an answer this time as he can see his brother is brought low.

It is arranged that Edward, along with May, will dine from home for the first time in weeks. May is excited and makes good use of Edith's superior hairdressing skills, while her mistress sleeps deeply.

'Pile it higher,' she says as her hair is hoisted in soft curls that cascade over her soft, peachy shoulders. May looks at herself in the mirror and is pleased with the results. There is a glint in her eye and a smile about her lips as she surveys her reflection. She is eager for company.

When Alistair was paying court to her before "Blasted Bea" made her unwelcome appearance, he once brought over a bolt of the finest silk she had ever touched. 'Look,' he had said unrolling the fabric, 'what colour would you call this? I would say it is orange but you will possibly put me right, ladies always know about these things.' The silk had arrived that day on one of his ships just come from China. 'I have noticed that although you are not kept short of anything, you do not always get what you deserve,' he had said. May had been warmed by the observation. 'Is it not a glorious shade? When I saw it I knew it would suit your colouring.' He held it up in front of her and she had looked at her reflection in the over mantel.

'You are right! It is a beautiful colour, but you are wrong in thinking I would know what shade it is as I have never seen the like before. I would think the best description would be a burnt orange for it is not gaudy and bright like the fruit. It is much more subtle than that. When it catches the light it has a depth to it the like of which I have never seen. There is a sheen yet no shine. As you say it is not garish, in fact it is very sophisticated.'

She had ordered the dress maker to make her a glorious gown with the silk. It was a gown of the latest design and cut revealingly low. At the time she had thought to be wearing Alistair's engagement ring and knew she would be able to carry it off escorted by her future husband. Of course that never happened. In fact the dress had never seen the light of day; until now.

Edward is waiting for her to go to Alistair's for dinner. No doubt he wishes it were April who is to accompany him to his brother's house. As she comes down the staircase she watches his face.

'May you look stunning. You have made such an effort, is that for me?' he jokes almost like his old self. He has already taken whisky she thinks while he waited for her.

'Of course, she quips back, 'Who else?'

She is looking forward to the evening, play acting the role of wife will lift her spirits she hopes.

In the carriage he says: 'I hope April will sleep, she has taken a draught.' May wants to be cheerful for a change, she seeks to reassure him. 'Then I am sure she will not even miss us. We both need respite do we not?'

'It is not that I do not enjoy your company May, you know I do but I just want my wife well and happy and by my side as it used to be. I miss her, miss her laugh, her smile, her affections.' May frowns and sighs in the half light of the carriage.

They are greeted by Alistair and when he sees what she is wearing as he helps her off with her cloak, he is very appreciative. 'I said that shade would suit you and I was right. You look good enough to eat May.' Bea is out of ear shot talking to Edward. May feels her spirits rise. 'Thank you sir,' she says flirtatiously while Alistair's wife's back is turned. She has had little to smile about of late and intends to make the most of tonight. She seldom gets to take the lead role.

He hands her through to the drawing room. May is at first disappointed to find there are other guests. She had hoped she would be the star in this production; an intimate group of just the four of them. She has imagined herself playing the role of Mrs Edward Driscoll to perfection, then she rallies and sees a star needs an appreciative audience and she has one she hopes.

May is introduced to a dour looking old gentleman whose name is Smythe, he reminds her of the clientele at Mrs Jansen's. She shudders at the thought. Next she meets another new face, a more interesting face than the ruddy, pock marked face of Mr Smythe, who even now is leering at her breasts.

The newcomer's name is Captain Christopher Charterhouse. He is also in shipping. He is the grandson of a shipping magnate who made a fortune a century ago by sending coal from Newcastle to all parts of the country and abroad. He is English which also pleases May; she has spent many dinners since coming to Scotland trying to understand indecipherable Scottish accents. Tonight will make a pleasant change.

The captain has a very handsome face which is made even more handsome when he smiles. His hair is thick, dark and curly. He has strong white teeth and hazel eyes. May is immediately interested. She is gratified when he is seated next to her at dinner.

Besides herself the only other woman present at dinner is Bea – this pleases May. She knows by comparison the woman is a poor second, even though she is fair enough. When May had first met Bea she was surprised, almost shocked. She had been expecting the heiress to be beautiful, tall and vivacious; Alistair had described such a woman. He had loved Bea from afar for all those years and doubtless his judgement must be clouded by love.

Bea was not a troll but neither was she a beauty. She was now in her mid thirties and any freshness had long perished, her pale hair had touches of grey – May would have banished them without hesitation. She was at best attractive, with regular features and pale skin but she was no oil painting. She was tall but after two children any slenderness had been replaced with sturdiness, especially around those child bearing hips. May sits taller when she is by Bea's side. She knows comparisons will be drawn and she knows who will come out best.

Meow.

May is happy to be the only other single woman this night, all eyes will be on her. She will enchant, smile and flirt and, at last, enjoy herself. May is entertained by Captain Charterhouse. 'Call me Kit. I insist, all my friends do and I feel we are going to get along.' At four and twenty he is as yet unmarried. She is even more flirtatious when this nugget of information is let slip by Bea. 'I come to Glasgow from Northumberland regularly on business,' he tells her. She flatters more. May is savouring the evening; she is exceedingly pleased with everything and everybody.

Well not the Smythe character, he holds no interest for May.

After the sadness and the nursing of her sister these last weeks May is opening up like a bloom in the rays of the summer sun.

But wait, you might be getting the wrong end of the stick. May is not thinking the captain husband material. She is far too canny for that.

She does, however, think he would make a more than passable lover. He could keep her entertained she thinks between bouts by the sick bed. May is still too besotted with Edward to ever think of leaving his house and besides, there are few men in the country who can match up to Edward's wealth.

She has decided, quite ruthlessly you might think, that if she cannot have Edward she will not lower her standard of living by taking a husband. That would be folly.

Even the charismatic Kit she thinks, is no match for Edward and anyway if her plan comes to fruition she will have everything she needs in the fullness of time.

Kit is a man of the world. He is as much interested in May as she is with him. 'I have travelled the world and enjoy the company of beautiful women,' he tells her confidently 'but you are by far the most beautiful woman I have ever seen.' May remembers to look coy. He continues to tease and flatter so both are oblivious to anyone else at table, except that is not quite the case at all.

May sees exactly what effect her behaviour is having on Edward. She knows he watches her closely; she makes sure to tilt her head at a slight angle whenever she notices him looking her way. She tips him a tantalising smile from time to time opening her limpid, blue eyes wide.

After dinner and after Bea has chatted over tea with May, the gentlemen join them. May has noticed Edward has made free with the wine throughout the meal and he looks as if he has been liberal with the port bottle also. He is now cradling a glass of his favourite single malt.

May smiles and encourages him to join her but Mr Smythe, though old and gouty, is fleet of foot it seems. He picks himself the seat next to May and sits far too close; when he talks he speaks to her bosom. Edward looks furious and the captain disappointed. May looks gratified. She does not, of course, want an old clod like Smythe for company but he is serving a purpose.

'Do you hunt Miss May?'

'No sir I do not. I am afraid I do not know one end of a horse from the other.'

'Don't hunt! Don't ride!' I never heard such a thing. What does a young filly like you do for entertainment?' He is gross May thinks. His innuendo has not gone unnoticed.

'May is it not time to take our leave?' Edward says. 'April has been left long enough I think.' He turns to Alistair stiffly and thanks his brother for the evening and they make to leave. A footman brings May's cloak. This time Kit is quick off the mark.

'Allow me to help you,' he says taking the cloak and placing it about May's shoulders. He whispers in her ear. 'May I see you again?' May offers her hand, looking up at the handsome face through thick lashes, before nodding and taking her leave.

In the carriage Edward's face is fixed. She is trying to discern his thoughts when he suddenly says: 'It is somewhat perplexing seeing the image of one's wife being made love to all through dinner.' A silence falls between them. May holds her breath wondering what turn the evening will take. She does not have to wait long.

'It is confusing to the senses as in front of me I see the woman I love but my sensible self tells me she is at home, hopefully resting and recovering after her ordeal.' He turns from the carriage window and looks intensely at the woman beside him. 'Then I look at you and my mind is tricked and I want to lean across the table and swipe the look off Charterhouse's handsome face.' He takes May's gloved hand in his. I feel a jealous, possessive rage at his forwardness as he is talking to my wife as a potential lover. Then I see it is you, my sister-in-law and I reprimand myself.' His penetrating gaze assesses May and again she tilts her head just enough to spark a recognition. 'You look so beautiful tonight, I cannot blame the captain for admiring you.' He sighs deeply. 'I have been so lonely recently.'

Again a silence falls, only the night sounds of Glasgow in the background. He leans in, hesitates, and then begins to kiss May, softly at first but then he takes hold of her shoulders roughly and kisses her harder with a passion May has never experienced before. She responds and kisses him back, all the desire she has ever felt for him rising to the surface. His hands roam about her body. His cologne mingles with the whisky on his breath, she is intoxicated. She presses her body closer to his and pulls at her cloak's ribbons to loosen them. He pulls the cloak from her shoulders and reaches for her breasts. The carriage draws to a halt. They are home.

3

May goes down to breakfast, knowing Edward will have left earlier for the office, but is surprised to see her sister at table.

'Good morning May,' she says a bright smile on her pale face.

'Good morning to you too, how nice to see you up and about. You are feeling better?'

'I am. I feel like I am finally turning a corner, I slept well again last night. Finally the nightmares are receding.' A cloud passes through her eyes momentarily. 'I thought I might enjoy a trip out in the carriage later, if you will join me?'

'Where do you wish to go? Of course I will come with you, it will be my pleasure.'

'I have a fancy to go to The Botanical Gardens, I thought we could see the Kibble Palace again. It seems an age since we were there. It will be warm in the glass houses and you might get more ideas for your garden.'

'My garden, yours don't you mean my love?' May is slightly nettled but does not want to spoil her sister's mood. 'What a good idea! Perhaps I will see a new rose to tempt me. Robins is knowledgeable, of course, but I think a fresh approach is needed in some of the beds for the summer. I wonder if peonies would tolerate the harsh winters here. I shall be ready as soon as I have eaten.'

A footman brings a card on a silver tray and hands it to May.

'Please ask the gentleman to wait in the morning room and tell him I will be with him presently.'

'Gentleman? What is this – an assignation? What have you been up to while I have been indisposed!' April teases. May is pleased at her sister's cheerfulness.

'Hardly an assignation but interesting nevertheless. It is Captain Charterhouse; I met him last night at Alistair's. You remember we dined there last night.' May tells April all about him.

'He is obviously very keen calling at this unseemly hour,' she says when May has filled her in on all the details.

'He is possibly leaving Glasgow today I expect.' May is gratified he is so keen. 'April, I have had an amusing idea; do you remember how we used to trick people into thinking you were me and the other way about? We haven't done that for years – it used to be such fun when we were girls. Shall we see if we can trick the captain? Would that not be diverting? You could go to him and pretend to be me – while I go and change ready for our trip.

'I wonder will he be one of those "You are like two peas in a pod, I swear I cannot tell one from the other".' April and May mimic the familiar refrain laughing. May thinks it is a relief to see her sister light hearted again.

April thinks for a moment and then giggling agrees to the subterfuge. She goes to the morning room and greets May's guest.

'Good morning I am sorry to arrive so early but I was keen not to miss you. I imagined if I came later you may have gone out.'

'And so you should have for I have just planned to go to the Botanic Gardens with my sister, she has just gone to make ready.'

'That is such a shame for today is my last day in Glasgow I am away on the morning tide tomorrow. I had hoped—'

'Then why not join us sir? I am sure my sister would not mind.'

It is all agreed before May joins them. April and Kit chat easily as they wait for May to make an appearance. When May enters the room the sisters wait for him to comment on their likeness.

'I knew you were twins of course, you told me so last night,' he says looking from one to the other. 'Pardon my staring I know you will be used to it as everyone will want to see how alike you are but—' The twins wait for the familiar words to trip from his lips. 'Give me a minute or two and I will see a difference, there is always something.' The two sisters look askance. This response is at least novel. May smiles with pleasure – she decides she will have him as her lover.

'Captain Charterhouse is to join us at the Botanical Gardens this morning, he has never seen them before. I was just telling him about the Kibble Palace, April says grinning.'

Kit is still staring. 'Shall we set off then? I am sure the carriage will be ready,' the real May says. The twins move towards the door and the footman opens it for them to pass through.

'I think there is some mischief here.' Kit smiles a twinkle in his hazel eyes. He has not moved and the twins turn matching eyebrows raised. He looks directly at May. 'I do believe you are the lady I met last night – no please do not try to contradict me.' He raises his hand laughing to stop May from denying it. 'I will explain how I know you have plotted to deceive me if you will permit me.' The twins laugh knowing they have been caught out but are still keen to keep up the charade.

'You see, even though you are identical there is always some tiny thing that, if the onlooker pays particular attention, is discernible. You, Miss May, have a habit of lowering your eyes to the left and you Mrs Driscoll,' he says correctly identifying April tilt your head very slightly away from the viewer.' He stands upright and proud. The twins laugh and admit for the deception.

'I had thought it would be easy to tell you apart as you Mrs Driscoll, being a married lady, would wear a wedding band but I see I am wrong in the assumption.' May quickly explains her sister has been ill and her fingers have swollen so that she cannot wear her rings. She continues:

'We had taken a bet you would say what everyone says when they first encounter us and that is—'

'I know what they say, "You are like two peas in a pod" – am I correct?' Kit finishes May's sentence and the twins laugh.

He says amiably, 'What you both don't know is what makes me such an expert on twins.' He stands arms outstretched theatrically. 'I too am an identical twin! I have a brother who is my spitting image.'

April and May are surprised. 'I should love to meet your brother, what fun we could have confusing people!' May says.

'My brother and I have spent our whole lives hearing the same phrases as you two I bet. So ladies, you see how I come to know what you were up to, for William and myself have played the self same trick to amuse ourselves on many an occasion. I should like to see if you think we are "like two peas in a pod"! Our parents were the only ones to tell us apart.' May thinks she likes the captain even more as they leave for the West End.

They walk about the gardens and April is purposefully a poor chaperone as she loses herself in the shrubbery pretending interest in reading the plant labels. She is thoughtfully giving the couple some time to get to know one another. She sits on a bench feeling tired and just a little sad.

She would be able to add 'shocked' to the list if she heard her sister's conversation.

Kit has been very gallant and has talked to May in such a candid way that she believes he is interested in beginning a courtship with her. May has other ideas. She asks Kit if she can be frank with him and he says she can. She tells him she is prepared to be his lover, but nothing more.

At first he is shocked into silence. Then he recovers

himself.

'Well May you are very forthright I must say! I will not ask you why you spurn my advances although I am intrigued, I am sure you have a very good reason.'

'I do and I thank you for not prying – let me just say that although I have no wish to have a formal attachment with you, I am happy to have, shall we say, a less conventional liaison if you are agreeable.

He is agreeable. He is a man. He cannot believe his good fortune. Cake and eat it!

He says he will make arrangements for this very evening and send for her as soon as he has planned where they can meet. He is thinking quickly and in no time has formulated a plan.

Men can shift themselves when the need arises, and his need, has indeed, arisen. Sorry gentlemen but you know it is the truth. Had he been asked to organise a dinner date without strings attached, I'll wager he would have dallied a while longer.

He will have to firm up the plan he says a smile upon his lips. By the time he has left April and May back at George Square, May is confident tonight she will spend an enjoyable night in the arms of her new, handsome lover.

♥

When Edward returns home in the evening he is happy to see his wife in the drawing room looking radiant and cheerful. She tells him about her day and about their visitor. She is so beautiful he thinks, as he listens to her tell how they tried to dupe Kit Charterhouse. He sees she is recovering her sense of fun.

'That is marvellous news that you have been out my love. You like the Botanical Gardens I know. I should have suggested we go there, what a fool I am not to think of it myself.'

When he had left her last night to go out with her sister, he had never thought she would be so much better so soon. He feels a little guilt. 'I never expected to see you up when I came home this evening. Do not overtire yourself, my dear. Have an early night if you need to but I am glad we will be dining together.' Out of habit he pours himself a whisky.

'May and Effie have already dined. They are expected at the Chesters later so we shall be able to dine alone. I have been looking forward to it all day my love. I feel so much better.'

'The Chesters? I thought Charterhouse wanted to court May you said. Is he not keen to see her before he leaves Glasgow?'

'He is but she has this previous engagement and he had a business meeting he could not cancel and so she will see him next time he is in town. I am so happy for her. He seems a very amiable man, and handsome too. May deserves some fun. I do not know what I would have done without her recently.'

Edward knows it is the truth but cannot help but feel jealousy. Then he tries to think about what he feels about the captain. Is there not perhaps a little jealousy there too? The man has been quick off the mark he thinks. Edward allows himself to feel peeved. His mind flits to last night's carriage ride. What if May marries this fellow?

150

Should he look into his background? He thinks he will ask Alistair about him, it cannot do any harm. The man only met May last night and he is proposing a courtship on so slim an acquaintance. He swills the whisky around his glass.

Then he remembers how he felt when he first met April. It was love at first sight – for him at least. He tries to think what he feels about his sister-in-law. He wonders if like April, she is slow to warm to a man's touch? He thinks about April. About Kit Charterhouse. About his childless marriage.

He is doing a lot of thinking! He reaches no conclusion.

He refills his glass as a footman announces dinner is served. Husband and wife dine alone for the first time in weeks and enjoy the experience. It is like old times Edward thinks, except he detects sadness in his wife's beautiful eyes, a sadness he doubts will ever leave now it appears she will never give him a child.

May returns from a tedious night at the Chesters. It was an engagement that was made to please Effie because there was to be dancing and Effie loves to dance. She makes some excuse to go to her room when she sees Edward is talking by the fire with her sister. A slight tinge of green seeps into her eyes as she remembers Edward kissing her, embracing her – was it only last night?

However, she has plans of her own now. An arrangement has been made for her to be with her lover this very night. She has had a note from him suggesting how they can meet. She feels the excitement in the pit of her stomach. She is no shrinking violet yet she has a little apprehension. She has watched, from behind Mrs

Jansen's curtains, what happens when a man and woman lie together; it will be different when it is she who is the one performing.

Once in her room she dismisses her maid and re-dresses in a different gown, a more revealing one she has 'borrowed' without asking from her sister. She tidies her hair and sits down to wait until everyone is abed. Why are some minutes longer than others she wonders as she checks the clock for the umpteenth time?

At last she deems it safe to venture out. The house is quiet. She puts on her cloak pulling the hood carefully over her head. Out on the street it is ghostly quiet. The carriage Kit said would be waiting is across the Square. She approaches and an outrider jumps down and without a word hands her inside the plush interior. They arrive at Blythswood Square Hotel. It is one thirty a.m.

There are still one or two people milling about, some returning from the theatre, others from dinner engagements. She feels a thrill of excitement mixed with anxiety.

This is to be her first time laying with a man remember. She is the one choosing who takes her virginity – Mrs Jansen would be livid to hear she is giving it away for free. Or is she...

May pulls the hood lower over her head and makes her way to room sixteen on the first floor. She knocks lightly. Kit opens the door almost at once a glass of champagne in his hand. He lowers the hood from her head and pulls the ribbons at her throat and releases her cloak. He throws it over a chair. He sweeps a lingering look from her head to her toes. He smiles lazily and appreciatively. He has removed his jacket and is wearing a startlingly white, silk shirt which shows off his tanned face.

It is a suite of rooms, not unlike the one where she met her aunt. They are in the sitting room. He pours champagne and proposes a toast. 'To us and to an interesting night and many more of them,' he says grinning, He is handsome, a dark curl falls over his brow. May's heart beats faster when he leads her to the bedroom.

4

Back at George Square May trips lightly down the stairs and into the breakfast room. She feels light and happy. She is surprised to see Edward at table then remembers it is Sunday. April has finished eating and pours her sister's coffee. They chat while Edward continues to read his newspaper. 'I need to get on I have things to do,' says April vaguely.

'What things?' Edward asks folding his newspaper.

Anyone would think he is afraid to be alone with May.

'Oh just things,' she answers vaguely leaving the room after she plants a kiss on the top of his head.

Edward looks at May for the first time that morning. Her face flushes slightly. It is, she thinks, as if he can tell I have been up to no good. She tries to shrug telling herself not to be ridiculous. She gives him her brightest smile. She wishes she had given herself to him last night – not that she didn't enjoy the experience with Kit but still...

Or should that be experiences. Plural.

'Did you sleep well?' Suddenly she is on high alert. Is this a trick question? Again she chides herself. It is an innocent enough question. She errs on the safe side.

'Eventually I did. I had trouble dropping off.' This is no lie she thinks. In fact the only sleep she has had was an hour or two since she returned from Blythswood Square.

Edward stands and comes around the table to sit close beside her.

'I came to your room last night,' he whispers and looks disappointed. 'When there was no answer to my knock I let myself in thinking you must be sleeping but your bed was empty.'

May swallows hard and puts down the knife she has been buttering bread with. 'I could not sleep so I went to make chocolate. That usually helps me drop off.' She nibbles the bread. 'I am sorry I missed you.' She thinks quickly hoping the lie is believed.

'Why did you not bring it back to bed? I waited in your room for some time.' His voice has a slight whine to it, like a petulant child who has been told he cannot have another sweetie.

'I decided to read, so I went to the library to fetch a book. By then I was wide awake and drank my chocolate and read some poetry. How long did you wait?' She smiles and squeezes his hand in compensation. 'If I had known—'

Fate is a strange thing she thinks. Of all the nights since she came to this house the man she adores chooses the one night she is elsewhere!

Edward stands up quickly. 'Of all the nights to choose,' he grumbles echoing her sentiments exactly. He returns to his seat. He sits heavily and looks irritable.

Fate is indeed playing cruel tricks. Had she known what

was on Edward's mind she would sooner have lost her virginity to him she is certain.

Edward glowers, mutters something about orders to the stables and leaves the room scowling.

May stares at the crumbs on her plate and thinks of what might have been. It has taken the shine off her happiness. After some time she goes in search of her sister and finds her in the garden. 'Here you are. I wondered where you had disappeared to,' May says looping her arm through her sister's. 'Are you feeling well? You look brighter.'

'I just needed some air.' They saunter down the path, the gravel crunching under their slippers until they reach a seat and April confides in her sister:

'Last week when Caroline Cressy called to see me, she told me something very interesting. She too has suffered miscarriages, five of them, poor woman.' May mutters a consolation. 'She has a doctor – a man who she says is a miracle worker. You are aware she now has two sons? Well, it is all down to this doctor apparently. His name is Sinclair and he specialises in women's problems. Caroline says he helped her to keep her babies. Like me, she could conceive but not carry to full term.'

'Really! And are you thinking of consulting with him?' May asks trying not to sound concerned.

'He has some very modern ideas and I am interested in his methods. I have already contacted him, he is sure he can help.'

'April, I thought you were to give up trying? Your doctor says it is too risky to try again. He knows your history this Doctor Sinclair does not! You cannot put your life at risk, is it not foolhardy to say the least. What does Edward think?'

'I haven't told him. I want to see what Dr Sinclair says first. I do not want to get Edward's hopes up in case... he is still distressed over the last time. We both are naturally.'

May tries in vain to dissuade her sister from seeing the doctor, but April is adamant. 'If you only knew how desperate Edward is to have a child, especially a son,' April says a pained look on her face.

May does know. Has he not opened up to her frequently when April was recovering and he had drunk too much? Although May has reservations when she sees her sister is determined to see the specialist she agrees to accompany her. If, as she suspects, the doctor turns out to be a quack, she will tell Edward and he can put a stop to it. She cannot let her sister put her life at risk by trying some fakery at some back street practice. She will not stand by and watch April endanger her life. And besides it does not fit with May's plans for her sister to want to try again for a baby.

May has another scheme in mind. Since the last miscarriage she has seen a way to secure both their futures.

♦

April and May arrive to see Dr Sinclair at his office. It is in the West End of Glasgow. It is a well appointed house with a brass plaque bearing his name and qualifications. Not a back street fraudster at least, May thinks. April does not want him at George Square in case Edward should be at home and puts a stop to her seeing him.

The twins are shown into his consulting room. He

is young looking, perhaps thirty five, and has thinning red hair and a flushed complexion. After asking many questions of a very intimate nature, he sits back in his chair and steeples his fingers under his double chin. He has examined April behind a screen. She has returned flushed.

'I see many ladies in your predicament Mrs Driscoll and I have helped a great many of them. Not all, it has to be said, but a fair few. Over seventy percent I should say. As far as I can ascertain there is no reason why you cannot carry a child to full term. You are young, healthy and have no medical problem that I can see which might account for your losses.' He smiles kindly at April. 'I will give you a paper to read outlining my methods. It has been compiled after years of research and has been widely acclaimed. I would suggest, when you have read it, you come to see me again to discuss any issues you do not understand or have concerns about. I am sure you will find it helpful. Speak with your husband and see what he thinks. I cannot promise, but I am sure all will be resolved most favourably. A positive outlook, on your part Mrs Driscoll, is also necessary.'

He outlines the treatment. Summing up he says 'My method means that your womb is cultivated made ready as it were, to take your husband's seed, made more receptive, stronger. Once the seed is sown in a fertile womb it will grow and mature safely. It is imperative you take the tinctures I prescribe for at least six months, and practice abstinence in the marital bed at the same time. Your husband will comply do you think?'

'I hope so,' April says her face the colour of beetroot.

'He makes it sound like gardening.' May giggles when they are on their way home. 'Perhaps you should have consulted with Robins, he also makes up his own concoctions. He was showing me some putrid, foul smelling stuff he has stewing from comfrey leaves to make fertiliser. I am sure it will be just as good as the doctor's stuff and no doubt cheaper,' she teases. 'I think you should throw the paper in the bin my love. It all sounds strange to my ears.'

April reads the pamphlet thoroughly. When she has read it she hands it to May who takes it to her room to read. May is interested to read what it has to say if only to dissuade her sister from getting her hope up. Yet May sees it is a revelation.

It is a general paper about women's health and fertility. It is something Sinclair has written after extensive research he says. Not only does it outline how to get babies and keep them to term, it outlines ways of stopping them. This is the part May reads with particular interest. Now she has a lover it is as well to know all the latest ways of stopping anything unwanted occurring. It talks of charts and temperatures and fertile times of a cycle. Mrs Jansen would be most interested in the good doctor's findings; much more scientific than a milk-softened cundum.

'Have you read it?' April asks when they are alone after dinner.

'I have. It is just as he explained. You are to refrain from marital relations for six months and during that time you are to take a combination of herbal tinctures, medicines and potions to make your lady garden stronger and more pliable.' May giggles. 'You are to rest and avoid extreme exercise. What exercise does he think women like us take one wonders?'

'Riding, one presumes,' April returns boldly and they both laugh. I shall not mind taking the supplements, though Caroline says they are vile tasting, but it is the abstinence for six months that will be hard to bear for poor Edward. Caroline did not mention that!'

May has been thinking about this and as usual has a plan to hand.

Since reading Dr Sinclair's pamphlet she has seen an opportunity, a chance to build upon her original plan. She watches her sister's face closely.

'I know what I am about to suggest will be abhorrent to you but hear me out before you condemn the idea out of hand.' May smiles at her sister kindly.

What she is about to propose is shocking but if April can be convinced then May sees both their futures will be guaranteed. April looks anxious; she cannot imagine what her sister has in mind.

'It is Edward's greatest wish to have a son is it not?' She pauses and April nods a look of regret on her beautiful face. She feels after all he has done for her, for them both, that she has let him down.

May continues. 'If you follow Dr Sinclair's instructions this may in time, be possible but Edward would have to keep away from your bed for a lengthy period of time. Most husbands would not like the idea. Will Edward do as you ask do you think? Will he be able to show restraint?'

'I think so. He does have certain appetites like most men. Caroline did not mention this part of the treatment as I said. I had not thought to inconvenience him.' May rolls her eyes at her sister's last remark but holds her tongue.

'I do not think he will be convinced of the efficacy of Dr Sinclair's research,' April continues, 'he thinks it is nature's way of saying we cannot have a family. Yet I would give it a try. I want to try for his sake as well as my own. But if it is to work, you heard what the doctor said; I have to follow the instructions to the letter.' April looks crestfallen. May interjects, 'Yes you must otherwise it will be a waste of time.'

'I can keep the fact I am taking medication from Edward but how am I to explain he is not welcome to share our bed without telling him why? If I tell him I am undergoing treatment I am not sure how he will react, he worries so about my health.'

May nods. 'Of course you must follow the Doctor's plan if it is to stand any chance but there is no point in paying good money and not following the advice exactly. Are you adamant that you will not tell Edward?'

'He would stop me I think. He says we cannot risk my life. He is prepared he says, to use other methods so that I do not fall pregnant – you know what I mean. We both learnt about these things at—'

'That is all well and good but the potions might not be as efficacious if you are being...interfered with shall we say.'

April looks discomfited now the conversation has taken a more intimate nature.

April is much more inhibited than her sister you will see. It is a good job Edward took her away from Mrs Jansen's; she would possibly have died of embarrassment.

May sits quietly waiting to launch her idea. She knows she will have to tread carefully if April is to be convinced. 'You know I would do anything to help you my dear,' May says, a look of pity on her face, 'It seems so cruel that some women only have to look at a man to become pregnant. They produce a child a year without effort.' May pauses to let this statement sink in. 'I have thought of a way to help. Will you hear me out? You will think the plan is outlandish, perhaps ridiculous, but think before you condemn it out of hand.' April looks alarmed but agrees to listen.

'What if during those six months I see to Edward's needs.' May waits for the words to penetrate.

'Are you mad! April cries getting to her feet. 'Firstly how do you think you would get Edward to agree, dear God May, this is your idea of helping? You have always wanted him. Is this your way of getting what could never be yours?'

May is shocked at the personal attack. 'No dearest! I think only of you.' She follows her sister to the window. April has her back to her looking out at the dark, wet night.

'Consider it April. If you are unavailable to him for six months, what do you think he will do?' Again she pauses to let the picture develop. 'Like any red blooded man he will look elsewhere.' May looks imploringly at her sister's horrified face as April turns to her. May pushes on. 'He is not the type to take a mistress I don't think – but where did we meet him?' May is pressing home her point. Again she waits to let this point linger in the air between them. She continues, 'He will go to whores. Should you want that? If he does, who knows what diseases he will bring to your bed in the future? He will hide his indiscretions from you, to spare your feelings, but he will go nonetheless. Most men would, it does not mean he loves you less, dearest,' she adds sympathetically. 'If he is not getting his needs met at home he will look elsewhere.' May takes her sister's hands in hers.

'If you cannot fulfil his needs then why not let me? Better me, who is unsullied than some disease ridden strumpet.'

April pulls away from May's grasp. Her palms are wet with sweat.

'I shall not go through with the full treatment then. I will not keep him from my bed. I will just have to resign myself to not giving him a child. Or I can tell him I am still too ill or something to accommodate him. He will understand.' Tears fall from her eyes and May sits down and waits, biding her time.

May knows she will have to be patient. She knows her sister is not going to hand Edward over without a struggle. She presses on. 'Six months is a long recovery my dear, I am not sure you can keep him at arm's length for half a year!' She lets the statement sink in. 'If you are to keep Edward, do you think he will be happy without a son and heir? You say he wants to keep you safe and is prepared to take precautions but he wants a son, my love! Men are like that, fruit of their loins, to show the world how virile they are!'

April slumps in a chair. 'What if he comes to resent you for not producing a child? Do you think there is a chance he would? If he were to take a mistress and she gave him a son what then? Do you think he would not replace you?' April is horrified at the way May is defaming her husband.'

'He is not the cold and calculating man you are making him out to be! He is loyal and soft hearted. It grieves me sorely that I am unable to give him the one thing he cannot have but he is steadfast I know it. He will not desert me!'

'You only ever think of the present, April. I know Edward loves you now but what about in ten years time when he is still childless? You must see things can change, then where will we – you be,' she corrects herself. I too cannot risk losing you my angel. I could not live without you. Just think about my idea do not be hasty, think of the future. 'April has dried her tears but is still pained.

May says, 'If I pretended to be you, you know he would be safe. You would be safe.' April is moving listlessly about the room. She is agitated and confused. Part of her can see it is a plan which could help but she loves Edward and does not want to share him, or lose him either, for that matter.

April bursts out angrily. 'Even if this plan were possible, it could never work. He knows us apart; he always has been able to tell one from the other.' Her face is flushed and beads of perspiration form on her top lip. She looks triumphant

May of course, has an answer for all April's questions and anxieties and explains the ways around the obstacles.

'There is a saying "All women are the same when the candle is blown out." First of all you tell him about the treatment but you do not tell him about the abstinence part. You only tell him what he needs to know. Next we change rooms. When he comes to share your bed, by invitation, I will be in it. The lights will be low. I shall speak in a loving sort of whisper, for our voices are a slightly different timbre I concede. Surely he will not notice when he has taken whisky and is in the throes of passion.' May says encouragingly.

A tear escapes and rolls down April's cheek. May has to leave off her speech to calm her sister. 'Why would he imagine anyone other than his wife would be in his bed?' May murmurs persuasively.

'My unclothed body is different to yours now especially since the last pregnancy. He would notice.' April smoothes the silk of her gown over her belly where it is more rounded than it used to be. 'You have forgotten about my belly and stretch marks! His hands, if not his eyes will notice the difference.'

This is the one thing May has not thought of. Under her stays May has imagined April's figure to be the same as hers. 'Well, you will just have to say that your body has changed back or something. Or rather I will have to think of something to say if I am pretending to be you.'

April looks directly at May. She is breathing lighter now. 'I see the folly now of even listening to this spectacular scheme! All Edward has ever wanted, besides me, is a son,' she states the fact quietly swallowing a sob, 'although I know it to be his dearest wish I cannot go through with this outrageous plan. I cannot lie to him. I would feel great disloyalty. I know you say you are doing this to save my marriage, but I know Edward. He would never throw me out if he does not get a child. He is kind and good he is not the monster you say he is. We can be happy without a baby.'

May speaks soothingly to her sister trying to ease her mind.

Do you think May is about to give up her scheme? I see you have the measure of her. She will bide her time, be patient and wait for April to see sense. She knows she will get what she wants if she can put doubt in her sister's fragile mind. She has planted seeds of her own and she expects them to germinate.

5

Kit Charterhouse has become a frequent and welcome visitor to Glasgow. At least once a month he finds himself on urgent business that takes at least two days and usually, three nights. The plan he devised in the beginning of their affair works like clockwork, both he and May are more than happy with the arrangement.

'May you are proving to be a treasure. You are alluring, willing and, it has to be said, experimental in ways I can scarce believe.' They are lying in bed at The Blythswood Hotel.

'You certainly know how to please a man. Better even than some of the best whores in Paris and I should know. I cannot think how you know such things.' He strokes her belly and is aroused again.

'I cannot tell you all my secrets my love. A woman must remain mysterious but you know I was a virgin when we met.'

'That is the surprising part. I cannot account for it.' He rolls on top of her.

They have been meeting now for months but what

Kit does not know is that May has another lover, one who it has to be said, is much nearer to home. May is a happy woman. Perhaps she will give these assignations up; after all she knows which lover she prefers.

♣

After putting her proposal to April about swapping roles, May has waited patiently hoping small insecurities will grow and fester in April's mind.

April has started on the course of treatment as suggested by the good doctor but as yet has not banished her husband from her bed. Or at least that is what she leads May to believe. May has found out that since the last miscarriage Edward has not returned to the marital bed because he has not wanted to injure his wife's health.

If you want to know what is happening in a household ask a servant. No wonder he has been cosying up to May.

A few nights after May and April's "talk", Edward again comes to May's room. This time she is ready and waiting. Kit is not due back in Glasgow for two more days so Edward's nocturnal visit is more than welcome to the amorous sister. May knows Edward has taken a good amount of whisky during the evening. His consumption is still on the increase. May has been at pains to drop hints to Edward about April's poor health; she insinuates her sister is not as well as she pretends to be. She is good at sowing seeds of doubt.

There is a light knock at her door when all are abed. She is not surprised when she sees Edward standing there. She lets him in quickly, lest the nosey servants are poking about where they shouldn't be.

'I am sorry May but I need to speak to you,' he says. Odd, May thinks, that is what he has been doing all evening since April retired with a headache. 'But I just—' He takes May in his arms and kisses her thoroughly before pushing her back on the bed and leaving her in no doubt about what it is he wishes to debate.

♠

Of course by breakfast next morning, Edward is sober and full of remorse. He can hardly look at May, or his wife. He hides behind his newspaper, fidgeting. April again excuses herself and leaves the pair alone.

She is such an innocent. If she only knew how disloyal her husband is and how two faced her twin is being!

'I am so sorry about last night May. I swear I will never bother you again. Can you ever forgive me?' Edward says the minute they are alone. May has not expected this. She knows he is a good husband to April but she also knows he has the same weakness that all men have. May is put out. She does not want to be a "guilty secret". Last night had been the greatest night of her life. He had been everything she had ever hoped for. Now he is apologising!

'Edward think nothing of it.' She bats away the apology. 'If it were not me then it would be some common prostitute and then I would fear for my sister. We both have April's best interests at heart, and if during this trying time you need to avail yourself then I feel it my duty to help. After all you have done for me it is the least I can do.'

She is spitting feathers. It is her turn to feel bought and paid for.

169

'It is so easy to be with you as you are so like April. I can almost convince myself I am laying with my wife.' He scrapes his knife across his plate in agitation. The sound grates on May's nerves. 'I need to restrain myself and take greater care of you and your sister. You are right. She is not as strong as she says. I intend to be patient with her.' He looks convinced.

May is livid. She is still, even after last night, playing second fiddle. How dare he she thinks, treat me like a slut. Outwardly calm May says, 'You too, have been suffering. I see that Edward. I know it is your dearest wish to have a son and with this new treatment who knows what the outcome might be. It may well work?'

'But I cannot risk the love of my life. I have told her this but she will not listen. I never knew her to be so strong willed. She means to do her very utmost to conceive again. I told her I did not want her to undergo treatment. The stuff she is taking is no doubt expensive sugar water. The man is a charlatan I would wager.'

You will notice, despite May's protestations, April has told Edward about Dr Sinclair and his modern methods. Well some of them.

'You must bow to her will. She is a grown woman and knows her own mind. After the treatment you can review the situation. Yet I fear you are right Edward, it will all come to naught.'

Men like it when you concur with them. May knows this; it makes them feel important. 'I agree with you Edward, what happened last night can never be repeated. I too feel the betrayal. She is my sister and I love her dearly, I only mean to take care of her and show you my gratitude—'

'Yes. I must not put you in this situation again. It is wrong of me to make you feel beholden to me. I am ashamed of my lack of will power and beg your forgiveness.'

May sees Edward for what he is; a weak man. A weak man who when he has taken spirits gives in to the temptations of the flesh. Yet his touch is still fresh in her mind and on her body and she knows she would still have him if only he would come to her again. She loves him despite herself. He is her one weakness. Of all the men who pour blandishments in her ear, she cannot have the one she is desperate to possess.

She is still lauded at dinners and balls – sometimes she has to fend them off with a stick. Not only is she beautiful there are those who would be keen to be related to the Driscolls. There is possibly a decent dowry to be had too, who knows?

'Besides you have your own burgeoning relationship to consider, he says brusquely, 'I have ruined you for him – I feel the guilt of that too,' he adds looking shame faced. He is jealous of Kit Charterhouse.

He is in a pickle. He's a lapsed catholic did I mention? The guilt, the lust, the frustration. What is a man to do? It is a heady mix.

'Has Charterhouse made you an offer? 'He asks as an afterthought.

May thinks, he most certainly has but not the sort that you mean. She needs to put Edward off the scent so smiles enigmatically and is evasive.

'If you decide to marry I will provide you with a handsome dowry, have no fear. It is the least I can do for my wife's sister,' he says magnanimously.

There it is! That is what he can do to salve his conscience. Salve it by providing the one thing he has much of – money. You can buy your way out of so many of life's difficulties with money.

May is reminded of a time when her sister said she was exchanging one gaol for another. May once again feels bought and paid for. It affords her no pleasure.

May, a steely look in her eye says, 'I have told him I need time to consider. I have said I am prepared to meet with him when he is in town next but there is no formal understanding.'

May is pushing down the pain she feels. She sees Edward has no more feelings for her than some back alley tuppeny whore. She wants to go to her room but he goes on. 'You like him though?' Is there a little envy in the question? She is clutching at straws.

'He is a good match for me I think, but in all things I think of April and I would be loathe to leave her, especially now, when she has need of me. We have never lived apart. She would not want me to leave her and nor could I, until she is stronger at any rate. Any union with him would mean my removing back to England of course.' She searches his face hoping to see hurt at the thought of her leaving. She sees none.

Edward smiles and stands to leave the table. His thoughts are elsewhere, he is thinking of his next meeting. He reminds himself to look into the man's background, Alistair might know something about the captain. To May he says, 'You are a good sister to put April's needs before your own. Thank you May. She feels dismissed.

6

After much soul searching and persuading April has agreed to May's plan. She is to share her husband during the treatment in the hope of stopping him straying. 'Although the jealousy will upset you my love, May tells her, 'it is better than him visiting some cunning piece like Stella.' April is full of trepidation. She has concluded, regretfully that it is "better the devil you know."

April is fearful Edward, once in an intimate situation with her sister, will see the difference, feel the difference. She cannot think what will happen if they are discovered to be deceiving him. How he would react she can only speculate. She puts it to the back of her mind in a drawer labelled "unthinkable". She knows her husband well enough to know he has needs, needs that have to have an outlet regularly if he is to be content. 'I want more than anything for Edward to be happy, after all he saved me from a fate worse than death when he rescued me from Mrs Jansen's. I will be forever grateful.' May assures her she is doing the right thing.

Despite her misgivings when she first came to Glasgow,

she has learnt to love him deeply. He is devoted to her. He is a caring man and has given her far more than she could ever wish for. He has showered her with love and affection, gifts and even provided for her sister; he need not have done the latter. He has made her happy: she is mistress of an imposing mansion, she has a social standing in Glasgow as the wife of one of the richest men in Scotland. She feels safe and secure. She is risking it all she realises and shudders. She is in hell.

There is only one thing spoiling their perfect life together. It is the one thing she is afraid will drive a wedge between them. If she cannot give him a son she fears she will lose him and his love, and along with it, her security. Loathe as she is she has to try this monstrous, wicked scheme. She has to trust May will be able to keep her husband from straying. She only hopes her sister will not prove to be too tempting a proposition.

♥

It is arranged. May is to spend the night in the master suite and April is to remove to May's set of rooms. The interconnecting doors make it easy for the practicalities and to avoid the all seeing eyes of the servants – not that they can tell them apart.

April says, 'I have intimated that I would welcome a visit to the marital bed this evening. I assured him I feel well enough.' May tries not to smile.

April feels sick with dread, anxiety and most of all, jealousy. She clutches her stomach as it churns and heaves. She tells herself she is doing this to save her marriage, to keep him at home and away from the whores he might otherwise be tempted by. She tries not to judge him for this perceived failing.

'He is a man and men behave differently to women it is simple biology. You have witnessed this at first hand at the brothel May reminds her.

The stage is now set. The players await their cues. May, taking the role she has always dreamed of is ready to perform the role of her life and take centre stage. She lies in the marital bed to await the man she has loved from the moment she first saw him.

They have lain together before of course, but this is different, that seemed like a dress rehearsal.

A shiver of anticipation passes through her. The gas light is turned off and candles are lit. Edward enters the darkened chamber from his dressing room.

'Candlelight my love? How romantic,' he says smiling and climbing into bed beside her. He sighs deeply as he leans towards May and kisses her softly. He strokes her hair and face. His eyes are closed. 'This is nice, is it not?' he says softly as he nibbles her ear. May responds without words. His kisses become more urgent, more searching, more amorous. He lifts May's nightgown gently.

'I think you have lost a little weight my love. Are you sure the potions the doctor prescribed are suiting you?'

'Yes, I feel well,' she whispers. She kisses him back, only partly to stop the conversation. He strokes her face, her arms, her belly, he moves slowly caressing and probing, he is a caring and gentle lover.

Afterwards he has drifted off to sleep. May lays awake. This is the life her sister has, she realises covetously. She wants this life, this man. She wants to please him, love him and have him return that love. She watches him as he sleeps and her eyes fill with tears. What cruel twist of fate made him choose April? May leans in closer and smells the light cologne he always wears. She closes her eyes and breathes it in, wishing time would stop and she could stay in this moment forever.

May has expected him to leave to sleep in his own room, April had said he did sometimes if he had an early start and did not want to disturb her. May knows she cannot risk being seen in the cold light of day. After some time, she reluctantly and quietly slips from the bed picking up her night gown as she leaves. She creeps to the door, looking one last time at his handsome face. He is sleeping contentedly.

The adjoining room is May's own but her bed has not been slept in by April. May goes through to her dressing room where her twin is sitting, cold and trembling.

May raises her eyebrows questioningly. 'I could not sleep in there knowing what was happening on the other side of the wall,' she says as a single tear rolls down her cheek. She is pale and her eyes are red and swollen. She has clearly been crying all night. May feels guilty even as the warmth from Edward's body is still on her. She feels for her twin but she does not feel shame.

'I know – I am so sorry,' she says using the opportunity to score a point, 'Imagine how bad it would feel if he had spent the night with – you know what I mean. Try to remember why we are doing this.'

'At least if he went to a whore I would not know, it would not be happening under my roof with my own sister.'

"Our" roof May thinks blanching. April paces the room much as she has done all night. May thinks to pacify her sister. 'Why not go to him now, he is still sleeping I think.'

April looks horrified. 'I could not! He would see betrayal written all over my face!'May tries to calm the troubled waters. 'No he will not. When he wakes he will see the face of the woman he loves lying next to him after a happy reunion.' May talks in a soothing voice and takes hold of her sister's hands. 'Come, wash your face and go to him, we have to keep up the pretence.'

♦

April does as she is bid. She opens her bedroom door quietly. Hesitating, she climbs into the bed, still warm from her sister's body. Edward is disturbed by the movement, wakes and yawns.

'Good morning my love,' he turns to look at his wife. He is alarmed when he sees her red-eyes. 'You look tired dearest, oh I should not have come to you last night! Do you feel unwell? Tears again threaten to fall from April's eyes. She tries to reassure him.

'I am fine. I did not sleep so well that is all, you did not bother me,' she says noting the irony of the statement, 'I am so happy to have you here beside me. I have missed you in our bed.' She is telling the truth and so does not feel all the disloyalty of earlier. He strokes her hair affectionately and then thinks to check the time. Knowing he should have left by now for a meeting he rises from the bed and plants a kiss on April's cheek. 'You stay abed and rest. Can I get you anything? Shall you break your fast in bed?'

'Later,' she says, 'I will see if I can get some sleep now.' He smiles down at her and whispers in her ear as he leaves. 'Last night was like our first time all over again. Only now I love you more than ever my love.' April holds back a sob. She is left alone with her guilt and her heart which she feels certain is shattering into a thousand shards.

Has this act turned to tragedy?

7

May has been enjoying the favours of Kit Charterhouse for some time now. The excitement of the stolen meetings has begun to fade a little for her although she thinks he is happy with the trysts. Since having Edward in her life and in her bed, Kit is beginning to feel like second best. She has had an idea to spice up the liaisons.

'I thought to try something different for your last day tomorrow', she says while he helps her to put on her stays. It's a two man job negotiating the whale bone and the fiddly hooks without a maid.

'You do 'different' rather well, my dear. What have you in mind or is it to be a secret?'

'It cannot be a secret for what I have in mind. I thought we could still meet here, but in the afternoon...'

'I see – how risqué. Will that not be a little hazardous though? What of your reputation?'

'It will be both risqué and risky. That is precisely why I suggest it.' She laughs beguilingly at her lover.

'Then let us make it more interesting by taking tea first in the dining room,' he says grinning. He is wondering if she will rise to the challenge.

'But what of my reputation, as you say? Unchaperoned?' She tidies her hair in the mirror as he puts her cloak about her shoulders.

'Leave it with me, I will think of something,' she says as she leaves the warmth of the bedroom to go out into the chilly, dawn air.

♦

'I thought you were not seeing Mr Charterhouse anymore? Why are we taking tea with him and here of all places?'April asks a touch of irritation in her voice. May and April are at tea at the Blythswood. Kit is late and April is nettled. She hates to be kept waiting. She is saved further explanation as at last he arrives, all apologies.

'I am so sorry to keep you waiting, ladies. My meeting overran and I could not easily get away.' He sits opposite May and smiles winningly at April.

'It is so nice to see you again Mrs Driscoll and looking so well.'

'Thank you Mr Charterhouse. I am sorry you have had to be dragged away.' She is won over immediately by his smile. She remembers how good looking he is and cannot think why May dithers and says she is to give him up 'I was glad of the excuse. The man I had business with is an infernal bore. Our business was concluded an hour ago but he would drone on about technicalities. Shall I order a fresh pot?'

They enjoy tea and the time passes well enough. April watches the interchanges between her sister and Captain Charterhouse and hopes May is trying to rekindle the courtship. May has told her she is not interested in him. April knows from past experience you can never be sure where her sister is concerned.

April would like to see her sister married although she would not like her to leave Glasgow. She knows one day they will have to live apart. If May married Kit she would naturally live with him in England. April watches as the two talk flirtatiously and thinks Kit means to have her sister. She thinks he would jump at the chance to marry her. She sees what a good match it would be for May and as April wants her sister to make a happy marriage Kit could be the answer. He lives in Northumberland but he comes often to Glasgow. The two sisters need not be estranged by the distance. There are trains she thinks.

She lies to herself of course as the very thought of her sister living in England makes her heart sink. Even though it would be just a short train journey to see each other April knows in her heart she could not live so distant from May. She will put her mind to finding a suitor who is nearer to home she decides.

Tea is over and the twins are about to take their leave. Kit is looking quizzically at May waiting for her to give him some sort of sign of what is to happen next. They leave the dining room and stand in the lobby waiting for their coach to arrive. Kit hands April in and turns expectantly to May. Is she teasing him and means to go home with her sister? He never can tell what May is thinking. It is partly the reason he admires her, yet it is a trait he would not wish in a wife; he knows he could never trust her.

'April, you go on ahead I have forgotten I need to call at Bryant's for some ribbon to go with my Jet drop. I can walk back afterwards – it is not far.'

'Alone? We can call on the way home. I will wait for you in the carriage.'

'I should rather walk as it is but a little distance.'

'It is no prob—' May steps back from the carriage and the outrider closes the door after a nod from her. 'I will see you at home,' May says smiling as the coach lurches off. April is left with her mouth open. May turns and looks at her lover. 'You had better go up first and I will follow in the fullness of time. I do hope you have the champagne on ice,' she is smiling. Kit smiles back as he bows and re-enters the lobby. May's interest in Kit is reignited that afternoon.

♠

Effie Claire and Edward are laughing at something Effie has said and May, only half listening turns to speak to her sister. They are at dinner. May, having just returned from her afternoon assignation has had little time to change before the gong sounded.

'Did Mr Charterhouse escort you to Bryant's?' April asks, still piqued. Edward's ears prick up.

'I told him I did not need an escort.'

'You should not be seen out and about alone, it is not seemly. You will get a reputation.'

If only you knew my love, May thinks. Edward interrupts her thoughts. 'You saw Charterhouse today?'

'Yes,' April answers, 'we took tea at The Blythswood with him.'

'Why was I not invited? Effie bursts in. 'I think him a fine-looking fellow, I should take your leavings May.' Effie's eyes light up with mischief.

'Effie! You are inappropriate.' Edward chides. 'You are too young for such thoughts and besides, he is spoken for.' He meets his sister-in-law's look.

'He was late! He kept us waiting a good half hour,' April says. She is still disgruntled by his bad manners May suspects.

'I saw him earlier,' Edward says looking first to his wife, then at May. 'He was with his fiancée.' May keeps her countenance impassive; she will not show him his arrow has hit home.

'He was handing her into a carriage at the port. He had possibly been showing her around. I believe she is here with her brother on a visit. I heard she too is Northumbrian. She is taking an interest in his affairs now they are to be married I expect.'

'A business acquaintance told me Charterhouse is quite wealthy. His family made their money from coal and whaling. My acquaintance told me his family are keen to increase their wealth still further so he has recently become engaged to an heiress.' May is tight lipped as her sister glances at her to see if she knows Kit is engaged to be married.

May remembers the easy lies that fell from her lover's lips earlier about what had made him late. She wishes the dinner over so she can go to her room to decide what to think.

Edward continues. 'I thought you would catch him May but when you said he was not for you, I expect he got this lady on the rebound.' Edward watches her face closely but the mask she is wearing tells him nothing.

'She is a plain little thing from what I saw today, not that one should judge, she is possibly a very nice young lady. Though I should not think more than seventeen; he must be ten years older.'

She is aware he is waiting for a reaction and so says lightly. 'See Effie, your brother is wrong – if Kit's lady is seventeen then you are not too young, in fact you have missed your chance. You will be an old maid like me if you don't watch out.' She smiles around the table acting as if nothing is amiss.

She is her mother's daughter through and through.

'You are not old May! You are scarce older than me.' Effie laughs. Did I tell you Lady Amy is to be engaged to Lord Darnley's eldest son? Edward weren't you at school with him about a hundred years ago?'

Effie chatters on and May is allowed to retreat into herself until the dinner ends. She is grateful for the girl's lack of sense. May knows April will be curious to know how she feels about this new situation, so she excuses herself from sharing tea with her sister and Effie Claire feigning a headache.

In her room she thinks about what she has learned. She quickly comes to the conclusion it is of no concern to her that he is engaged. She admires him and he is a good lover but she has never loved him. She has never longed for him as she longs for Edward. There has only ever been one man for her and he is downstairs drinking whisky with his wife – her sister.

She is more concerned with Edward's motivation in

announcing Kit's engagement; was he trying to hurt her? Perhaps he is curious to see whether she still has feelings for the man? He clearly had not shared the information with his wife. April would have told her, of that there is no doubt. She wishes his motive were jealousy but cannot be certain.

Either way May thinks she will let Kit Charterhouse know she is aware of his position. She will ask him if he means to end their affair after his marriage. She will leave him in no doubt she understands perfectly if he does. She begins to unpin her hair as she does not want her maid chatting on so does not ring for help. It will be very inconvenient if he does end the affair she thinks. Then she remembers she has another more attractive lover to occupy her for the next few months at least. Kit Charterhouse can go to hell for all she cares.

8

May is late down to breakfast the next morning; she has been catching up on her sleep. She has felt a little faint and thinks she has not been getting enough sleep while Kit has been in town. She is aware of a buzz of excitement as she selects toast and eggs.

'May, we are to go on a trip,' Effie Claire bursts out hardly able to contain herself. 'To Whitby to take the waters, Edward says it will do April good to take the cure and he is to rent a house there for the season!'

Edward shakes his head and smiles at his sister. 'It is Whitby not the South of France!' There is no need for such excitement so early in the day. Good Lord, calm yourself! I wish I had waited until this evening to tell you. No matter, you can chatter on as much as you like now – I am away to the port. I only wish it were the South of France my dear,' he says kissing the top of April's fair head, 'But I cannot spare more than a week at this time of year, you know how busy I am.' He excuses himself and leaves the breakfast room. Effie follows him saying she has to decide what she is to take to Whitby.

'What is all this?' May asks her twin.

April explains. 'Last night we had a talk, Edward and I. He thinks I am looking indisposed.' She wrinkles her nose. 'This is based mainly on what I looked like the other morning I think. He feels guilty for "over exerting" me in the marital bed.' May cannot decide if her sister is angry with her or just hurt.

'It is his suggestion I go to Whitby. He says it will do me good and be a change of scene. He thinks I will enjoy seeing my old home town again, and so I will, partly.' She folds her napkin and lays it by her plate. 'He is to come for the first week and then leave us to enjoy ourselves for the rest of the month. I am not sure I want to go but Edward is determined to improve my health one way or another. He is so kind hearted.'

This last comment is quite pointed and is possibly to demonstrate he is not the bad man her sister makes him out to be.

'When you say "us" who do you mean?'

'All of us, Effie Claire and you, of course.'

'Oh. I had not thought to be included.' May's brain is working fast. She smiles as she sees a way forward. 'Would it not be more fitting for Effie and I to stay at home initially? You and Edward could have some time alone. Would that not be more appropriate, more romantic? Effie and I could come down when Edward returns and travel back with you at the end of your holiday.'

May is plotting again. You know she has an ulterior motive but April, being naive, does not.

'Are you sure? That would be perfect. Thank you for thinking of us, it is good of you to give up part of the holiday.' April is all smiles. 'Oh but I am not sure Effie will be as pleased when she learns her holiday is delayed.'

'Leave her to me,' May says. 'I will promise her a secret trip or two to the music hall so that should help take away the sting.'

A week later April and Edward leave to stay at a house he has let on the Mulgrave Estate at Sandsend, two miles from Whitby. He has chosen it because it is distant enough from Mrs Jansen's establishment – he does not want to rekindle bad memories for April – but close enough to the spa by carriage. The house is newly built, bright and airy with sea views from its cliff top position.

Edward is relieved to see by the end of the first week how April has colour in her cheeks and is looking relaxed. She has taken the waters every day and insisted that Edward does too. 'You are in as much need of recuperation as I,' she tells him, 'you work far too hard.'

They have promenaded along the harbour, visited one or two of April's old haunts and kept well away from Madam Jansen's establishment. Edward has also kept well away from April's bed saying he does not want to undo all the good work the spa and the sea air is doing for her.

The more cynical of you may be wondering if he remembers the charms of a certain whore named Stella. She was his type after all remember and it is but a short walk to West Cliff. Perhaps, just for 'old times' sake' he has made a visit? April has been indisposed a lot over their marriage and as we have already established like most men he has needs.

'It has been like a second honeymoon,' he says as they

sit in the conservatory over looking Sandsend Nab. It is pleasantly warm behind the glass, out of the westerly wind.

'You work far too hard my love. It has been an age since we holidayed together. I am so glad you suggested this trip, even though at first I was a little unsure. Having this time alone has been wonderful and thanks to May's suggestion we have been able to rekindle our love. I feel quite restored already.'

'Rekindle? I had not thought we needed to elicit romance in our lives. Perhaps I neglect you more than I imagine. The business does take up a lot of my time. I will try to appreciate you more in future.' He takes her hand and kisses her fingers. 'I would have suggested we come alone myself if I hadn't thought you would have wanted May with you but I too am grateful to her. You look happy and refreshed.' They sit in companionable silence watching the waves roll in and out, creaming the edges of the sand. The sea sparkles in the morning sun as they watch a schooner leave Whitby Harbour. A maid enters the room with the mail on a tray.

Edward takes the solitary letter. 'It is for you my love,' he says as he hands her the envelope.

'It is from May. I recognise the beautiful handwriting.' She opens it and begins to read. Edward watches as the schooner tacks north billowing sails dazzling white in the bright sun.

'How vexing! May has a chill! She is to put off her trip for a day or two until she feels better. She says it is nothing to worry about but does not feel up to travelling. With two or three days' bed rest she will be well enough again she hopes. Effie is spitting feathers at the delay apparently.'

'That is a shame. Poor May and poor Effie! I hope my sister has calmed down by the time I get home, you know how impatient she can be. Will you be content on your own for a few days? I can stay one extra night but then I need to get back.'

'Of course. I have Edith and there are the other servants in the house, I shall not feel alone. Do not put off your journey on my account now your bags are packed.'

Edward says he will catch the later train so they go for one last walk across the cliff tops. Arm in arm they stroll enjoying each other's company. April has wanted to say something to Edward for the last few days but she has not wanted to break the spell of their happy time together. She knows if she does not speak now then he will be gone and she will have lost the chance.

'These last couple of years have been very trying for us both, with the miscarriages I mean,' she states simply.

'Yes, for you especially my love.'

'You have suffered too I know, even though you have tried to hide it from me.'

'You have had enough to worry about – I did not want you worrying about me too.'

'How can I not when the events have disrupted our lives in so many ways. I need to tell you something, something that you will not like.' Edward raises his eyebrows. 'The second part of Dr Sinclair's regime stipulates you do not lie with me for the duration of the treatment in case it hinders my recovery.'

'Oh. Well then I will not if that is what you want.'

'It is not what I want but it is what needs to happen if I am to carry a child—' She breaks off anguish in her voice. 'If our marriage is to come through this, this phase, this sadness,' April is close to tears,

'I have a suggestion to help us through as six months of abstinence is a long time for you my love. '

'Name it April! You know I would do anything to make you happy. If you want to stay on here for longer you can. If you think it will help you to take the waters for longer, I can extend the lease on the house?'

'No it is not that. It is something altogether more personal – to you that is.'

He does not understand her meaning. 'Very well, I will just come out and say it.' April flushes. 'I know men have needs, it was Mrs Jansen's daily refrain I seem to remember. I know you have needs and while you feel you cannot satisfy them with me, then I want you to visit a... go with—' April cannot find the right words and stares at the grey, North Sea. 'What I am trying to say is—'

'That I should feel free to avail myself of whores!' Edward laughs, incredulous.

April looks embarrassed. 'Well I shall not want to know about it but if you are discreet and it makes you happy then—'

Edward takes her in his arms. 'My love, do not think of such things, you will upset yourself. I do love you and I thank you for your concern but until I can lie with you again I promise you I will not be visiting the harbour brothels, I can assure you of that.' He kisses her gently and she is relieved. He has passed the test she has set for him. She knew he would not roam. She cannot wait to tell May.

Or has he? Poor April is relieved now she has his promise. You however, realist that you are, will have noticed perhaps his meaning can be taken in different ways. It could mean what he says, plain and simple. He will not go with one of the disease ridden, tuppenny whores that frequent the harbour taverns and bawdy houses. He never promised not to visit the higher class brothel not a stone's throw away on West Cliff though did he? You and I know there is also another option available to him. An option which means he does not even have to leave the comfort of his own home.

He catches the two thirty train to Glasgow assured he will receive a warm welcome on his return.

♥

May is not ill. Not in the conventional sense at any rate. She has told the white lie for two reasons; firstly she wants to be here when Edward returns. She knows she can tempt him to her bed – with April out of the picture she knows Edward will relax his morals. Secondly, although she has not had a chill, she has been feeling a little under the weather. A little light headed, she almost fainted yesterday at the smell of fish. She unaccountably feels queasy and she cannot bring herself to eat eggs at any price. This coupled with the fact she has now missed three courses can mean only one thing.

At first when she realises she is with child she feels panic rise within her; she is alarmed to say the least. However after she has calmed herself she begins to see possibilities. Ideas have begun to form in her head. The one main issue, and it is an area of concern she has to admit, is the parentage of the child. She hopes it is Edward's but it could just as well be Kit's. It is, she thinks, more likely to be Kit's. She has lain with him more often. There is nothing she can do about it so she will just have to wait and see.

While her sister and brother-in-law have been away she has veered between getting rid of the baby and keeping it. She has thought of a few ways to achieve her aims. Thanks to Dr Sinclair's pamphlet she knows there are ways and means of getting rid of the unwanted child. Ways that are relatively safe if his research results are to be believed. Then she decides that perhaps this catastrophe could be the answer to a prayer – her sister's prayer as well as her own.

While May has the freedom, afforded by her sister's absence, she has taken the opportunity of making an appointment in her sister's name of course, to consult with Dr Sinclair. May, in the guise of April, has told him what she suspects.

'I think I am three months pregnant. I am sorry we did not follow your instructions to the letter but my husband could not be prevailed upon to leave me alone.'

Doctor Sinclair smiles to himself and can understand why.

May explains. 'However, I want to conceal the pregnancy from my husband to save him from building up his hopes as he has had them dashed three times already.'

Dr Sinclair is very understanding. He assures her she can continue to see him without her husband's knowledge at his consulting rooms.

'I understand your worries and know in my professional capacity how important it is for a woman with your history, to remain as worry free as possible,' he says. 'I will do my utmost to make sure you carry your child to full term this time.' He prescribes another tonic.

May is not sure how she is to conceal this pregnancy but she is sure she need not hide it from her sister. She has to tell April about her plans. She has to have April on her side. Without her sister's collaboration she will be cast out and she cannot have that.

♦

Edward is relaxed and content after his sojourn in Whitby and has been back in Glasgow for three days...and nights. He has been happy, talkative and attentive with May. He has not however visited her bed.

For her part May has flattered, flirted and taken care to wear her most revealing gowns. Gowns made more revealing she notices now her breasts are changing due to her condition. It seems that on this, the fourth evening Edward has finally noticed too. Effie, at May's suggestion, has gone to stay at Lady Amy's over night. They have the house to themselves. May intends to pulls out all the stops.

'You men,' she says throwing her head back and laughing at a funny story Edward has just told. He once said, a long time ago he thought she had an infectious laugh. She remembers every compliment he has ever given her. They are sitting side by side on a sofa. He has been reading to her from a sartorial paper. She has moved closer to look over his shoulder. She can feel his breath on her cheek – she sees he's noticed how revealing the gown is.

He puts the paper to one side and takes her in his arms. He kisses her with some urgency and not a little passion.

No doubt he remembers the words his loving wife said before he left Whitby. Perhaps he feels he has his wife's blessing to stray if he has needs. Edward does have needs. He tells himself this is surely better more considerate to his wife to have his needs met by May. May is not a whore so there will be no risk of disease being passed to April.

He suggests they go upstairs.

The next morning May writes to April saying she is still too unwell to travel but Effie is to join her in her stead. Effie has been keen to go and is delighted her brother has agreed for her to leave immediately. He sees the advantage of having Effie out of the house.

Left to their own devices May and Edward act as husband and wife. May is enjoying the role immensely. They are mindful of the servants of course but for the next week they are together every night... and sometimes in the forenoon and the afternoon. May has never been happier. The only cloud on the horizon is she knows she cannot put off the inevitable for much longer. She has run out of excuses. She has told April she is well again but that two social engagements had to be fulfilled. She knows April will become suspicious if she does not leave for Whitby soon.

Prior to her departure May has another check up with Dr Sinclair. He tells her everything is progressing well. She is still not showing signs of being with child. 'This is of no consequence, some ladies grow enormous while others barely show until near the later stages,' the doctor tells her. May hopes she is of the latter category.

She tells him 'I am to visit the spa at Whitby as Captain Driscoll thinks it will do me good.'

'I agree, the sea air and spa waters will be a twin tonic.' He smiles at his little jest.

'I will not see you for the foreseeable future you understand.' He gives her more of the potions and tinctures. She will pass them on to April. As luck has had it her sister has asked her to see the doctor with a view to filling her prescription so May has not even had to lie to Edward as to her whereabouts when he comes home early and finds her not at home.

'April seems to think they are doing her good so I am glad you have thought to get them for her,' Edward says when she tells him where she has been. It is to be their last night together as May is on the early train tomorrow. They make especial care to have dinner early and give the staff the night off.

9

May is met by her sister at the station and when the baggage is loaded onto the carriage they head out along West Cliff to Sandsend. Of necessity they pass Mrs Jansen's establishment.

'It feels like a different life now to what we had then,' May muses looking from the carriage window at the building that was once their gaol.

'We both have only one man to thank for it. What would have become of us if we had been forced to stay there?' April shudders.

'Fate certainly dealt us a good hand the day Captain Edward Driscoll came a-calling,' May says in a brighter tone.

'That is the difference between us. I believe you would have grown a hard shell about you, a sort of armour to protect yourself. You would have played your part well, even though you would have detested the role.' April sighs. 'You would have shielded me too I know. I do not have your resilience so I believe I would have turned inward and become a sad, self pitying creature. A woman who endured the life and resented every filthy man who touched me.' May sees her sister shiver.

'No you would not! You have proved you are strong, look what you have had to endure of late. You do not pity yourself over the miscarriages. You are more resilient than you think.' May squeezes her sister's hand. 'You are right about me though. I would have become hard, brittle and resentful. My daily cry would have been "Why Me?" I think I would have begun to inflict harm on any one around me fighting against my gaolers. I should never have stopped trying to get us out of there whether through an unguarded door or on some man's arm.'

The two sisters look seaward out of the other carriage window, turning their backs on their pasts for the rest of the short journey.

When they are settled in the conservatory at the house, April asks after her husband.

'How was Edward when you left – busy I expect?'

'Yes I think so. He is very driven in his work I have hardly seen him. We had dinner last night, however. He sends you his love and there is a letter in my luggage for you.'

'How thoughtful he is,' April says watching May closely. 'He has not said anything to make you think he knows about the deception?'

'Of course not.' May says getting up and looking at the view from the window. May is pondering when to break the news of the pregnancy to her sister.

Is April steeling herself to ask her sister if she has slept with her husband again?

May has used the train journey to think over her

options. She has realised there is more than one way to accomplish her plan. She decides to wait a few days before telling April anything. That will give her time to sort out the fine detail and make sure every lie is accounted for. She is keen to tell as few as possible knowing this will be the safest option.

For once May does not get her own way. They have seen Effie off on the train to Glasgow; Effie Claire has tired of Whitby's charms now and has her mind on a ball she is to attend. May has gone to the spa with her sister to take the waters. An attendant pours them glasses of the effervescent water. April says, 'It is gassy is it not?' She holds the glass up for May to look at the bubbles. 'I think it has a strange taste too. A little sulphurous I think? It takes a little getting used to but I am sure it is doing me good.'

May takes a sip and then another. Before May can answer her sister she loses her breakfast over the attendant's feet. 'Oh, perhaps it might take you longer to acquire the taste,' says April as she helps her sister to a seat.

Back at Sandsend, April is scrutinising May's appearance, worried she might be sick again. 'The water is strange tasting and can cause gas but your tummy, which is always so flat, looks bloated? Do you feel nauseous again?' April says concern on her face.

May is thrown off course but decides she may as well confess now and get it over with. Her thickening waist and rounded tummy have been noticed and to concede now will mean telling fewer lies.

It is April who feels sick when she is told May is with child.

'How are you pregnant? You only lay with Edward once, or that is what you told me!' April shouts at her sister all concern for her well being gone. 'Have you lain with him again? Her suspicions are roused.

May denies it strenuously and is at pains to convince April her husband's seed must be potent but April is not fooled or flattered. May tries again. 'After all have you not been with child three times in as many years?' May reminds her sister.

April paces up and down. She likes to pace when she is anxious and she is very anxious now. She even wrings her hands melodramatically.

'I knew this plan would not work,' she almost screams at May. 'Why ever did I allow you to sleep with my husband. It is sinful. We are being punished and if he finds out he will be rid of us both.'

'Why should he find out unless you tell him and to do that would be foolhardy. It is as you say, he will throw us both out onto the street if he finds he has been gulled.'

April storms out of the room leaving May to mull over the next step. But she is not left alone for long. April rushes back into the room and thrusts a book in front of May. She sees it is a Bible. May stops herself from rolling her eyes.

'Put your hand on the book and swear to me you only lay with Edward once.' April's face is contorted with rage. Pain, jealousy and confusion fight for supremacy.

May puts her hand on the good book and swears the oath. She waits to be struck down but God is obviously busy with bigger problems for bolts of lightning there are none.

April it has to be said, has the biggest tantrum May

has ever witnessed from her usually mild-mannered, timid sister. She is surprised at the outpouring of venom. 'You are manipulative, jealous and I hate you!' She rants 'I should never have listened to you; this outrageous idea was doomed from the start. How could you use me like this – go against me with my own husband who has only ever shown you kindness.' She feels the need to hurt her sister and make her feel miserable too.

April hurls one last cutting remark. 'Early in my marriage I had to plead with Edward to let you live with us. He was all for sending you back to Whitby.' She paces, hands on hips, chin jutting. 'You do not know how hard I had to beg to keep you with me!' She rants and rages meaning to hurt.

May is shocked both at the vitriol and the fact Edward has tried to be rid of her like some bothersome child! She glares at her twin. Her fury begins to build. Her first instinct is to throw the acid back in April's face and tell her the truth, well as near the truth as she dare. She is just about to hurl some vitriol of her own, when she sees the folly of it. To go down that road would surely lead to her ruin. She calms herself – reflects and self preservation kicks in.

May decides on a more conciliatory approach. She decides to faint. She slides elegantly to the floor almost hitting her head on a small table she has failed to notice. She lies decorously on the floor. She needs time to think and she knows April will feel regret at the awful things she has just said.

April rushes out of the room shouting for Edith and a maid of all work to come and help. The cook, asleep by the stove is of no use at all. Between the three of them they get May up off the floor and onto a chair. May pretends to faint once more as the servants are dismissed, playing for time. Smelling salts are thrust under her nose and she almost vomits again.

Later May lies on her bed thinking. She needs to revise her plan she realises.

♣

Things are not going to plan you will have noticed. It is three days later and there has been so much water under the bridge that the river is about to burst its banks. May has submitted her plan for approval and April, with a sense of the inevitable, begins to come around to her sister's way of thinking.

She has ranted and raved and made herself ill. Now she is allowing herself to be convinced May's plan could be the answer to her prayers. Throughout her marriage April has always felt sorry for May. She has always known that May loves Edward and felt, at first at least, sorry he did not pick her twin to love. After all, she did not care for him as a husband when they first moved to Glasgow but she did care about her sister.

In the beginning, when she had not wanted Edward, she would gladly have given the position of wife to her sister. Yet he had been determined there was only one woman for him. Later, when she had started to fall in love with Edward, April had tried to hide it from May. She knew it would cause her pain. When May suggested she sleep with him to help her, she wondered whether the gesture was altogether an unselfish one. She thought not but April, having a kind nature, tried to walk in her sister's shoes. On balance she could see the reasoning behind the scheme. Her head could see the reasoning, her heart could not, for unexpectedly she loves Edward deeply.

'Edward has been devoted to me since the moment we met. Patient when I was against marrying him, attentive when I was dismissive. I love him now more than I ever thought possible and it is this love, this all consuming love which makes me consider this unorthodox plan.' April looks at her sister's face and sees pain. She knows this confession will hurt May. 'If I gave my husband a child, perhaps even a son, I would repay him in one fell swoop for all he had done for me and for you'.

After all it would be his child she tells herself; his and May's. Her heart is breaking whichever path she chooses.

'Unlike you though, I know if I cannot give him a baby he will never abandon me, I have more faith in him than you, I know him to be honourable.'

April thinks she knows him intimately yet May has planted a seed of uncertainty. April has seen how the miscarriages have affected him, especially the last time; they had been sure this one would hang on. They had both been convinced that when she reached the six months stage all would be well. Yet again their hopes had been dashed.

April is close to tears. 'His drinking to excess is a worrying development. I know he is using whisky as a crutch, a support.'

May agrees. 'Yes, before he seldom drank more than was socially acceptable, now sometimes he sits alone after dinner and drinks until he falls asleep.'

April wonders if she has let him down. She begins to think in her pain and sadness, she is not enough for him. She begins to consider May's scheme.

♠

They are sitting in the conservatory sewing a piece of fine linen. May has told April she will need a baby bump; 'The fabric will be sewn into a sort of pillow and stuffed with goose down. A part of one side will be left open so that during the remaining months more feathers can be added to make the bump grow. It will fasten with ties around her your waist.' April has tried it on and is feeling quite broody.

'Since Edward never touches me when I am with child – since losing the first baby that is, I am not much worried about wearing this,' she says feeling the weight of the deception. 'What does worry me is Edith. She helps me dress and undress, she will see I am not with child.'

May is calm. 'Edith has been with you three years now. She is devoted to you, is she not?'

'She is but—'

'She will keep her mouth shut I am sure if you pay her enough. Why would she risk losing her position? There is no reason she should tell Edward or anyone else for that matter. That is the beauty of money – it can buy almost anything.'

'I suppose so. She is loyal, I trust her, she knows how desperate I am for a baby.' She chews her lip. April is the type of person that when she has solved one problem she looks for the next. She is a born worrier. 'What about the actual birth? I can see how we can act the rest,' April says, 'but the birth?' She is standing sideways on looking at her reflection in the mirror. She places her hand on the "bump" and is reminded of her losses.

'Somehow we must convince Edward – you must convince Edward to keep this house on. I pretend some illness over the summer and stay here to take the waters and recuperate and when it is my time I will send for you. That way he will not see me growing bigger. You then do your part by pretending the baby has come prematurely while you are here visiting me.'

May as usual has a well thought out scheme.

'What about someone to take care of you? You will need a midwife, a wet nurse and a doctor if there are complications?'

'I have thought of that. At the spa there are always advertisements for nurses and the like so I intend to make enquires. If I engage a nurse, and explain I am unmarried and in a predicament the nurse being local will know who I must approach regarding doctors and a wet nurse. I shall need money of course as I expect palms will have to be greased. Also did I mention that before I left Glasgow Edward finally agreed I should have a more able lady's maid and Effie is to go to be finished in France.'

'Effie is going to France to be finished? When was this decided?'

'Lady Amy asked Effie to go with her and so Edward agreed she could go. He knew I would be disappointed as I was supposed to chaperone her. It was my consolation prize remember for not going on your honeymoon.'

A shadow passes over May's face. 'I caught him in a

weak moment and managed to persuade him I should have a more experienced maid – at last!'

The lies flow from May's tongue. While it is true that Effie is to go abroad, it was in a different way that May persuaded him she could not "make do" with the girl she had a moment longer.

'I intend to get an English maid like you. The Scottish accent is harsh to my ears.' May sees the looks her sister throws her. Sometimes she thinks April sees her for what she is; devious. Now is one of those times. May has not finished and adds. 'If Edward keeps the house on for the summer you two can come and visit me as I shall be lonely on my own.'

'What! How can we? You will be showing – we cannot take such a risk. I can come alone I'll choose a time when Edward is busy with work and would find it hard to get away. It is madness to risk him seeing you.'

'I will be in recovery remember, I think I shall contract Scarlatina. It takes some getting over I think. Largely I will keep to my room, but you can sit with me. It will stop the boredom. When I come downstairs I will be swaddled in blankets, like an invalid. It will be easy to cover up.' May is unable to imagine being without Edward for months, she will miss him. She is prepared to take the risk.

May is as confident as always, so certain that all will go as she intends. Her twin just hopes she is not over confident.

10

It is easy to convince Edward to keep the house on as he sees Whitby is doing April good and he wants to please her. April says she intends to visit Whitby all summer to get fresh sea air as well as the spa waters. He also sees the benefit for himself.

May can go there too – alone. Perhaps he needs temptation out of his way?

In early April when May has been in Whitby for a few weeks she writes to her twin to say she has scarlet fever. April looks suitably horrified at the lie when she reads the letter aloud to her husband over breakfast. April says 'I must go to May at once.'

'April that is out of the question you cannot risk your life! You must promise me you will not to go to Whitby until May is out of danger, Scarlatina is a highly contagious disease.' Edward looks imploringly at his wife.

April pleads, 'I must go to her – what if, god forbid, she does not recover then how should I feel? I have to go to her.'

'Very well but I insist on accompanying you, though I

am not happy about it. I understand the close twin bond – if it were Alistair lying ill, I would want to be there. If you are to go then we shall both risk infection. I cannot let you take the risk alone,' he tells her gallantly.'

There is no risk of course. When they arrive at Sandsend, May has taken to her bed. She has hired a plain young maid to train up. Flossie is being paid above the usual rate to ensure her loyalty she tells April.

'Miss May's fever has broken and the rash subsided, she is still weak and will need several weeks of recuperation the doctor says but she is not infectious now.'

Flossie has learnt her lines well.

After several hours April joins her husband for dinner. 'I am sorry she did not want to see you my love. She is very tired – she has been so ill; the doctor thought she might not survive the night on Monday Flossie says.' The lies May has made her rehearse are sticking in her throat. She does not lie easily and cannot look her husband in the eye.

Unlike some we could mention. With little else to do May has been learning her own lines and April's as well.

'Dear me, that bad! Well put your sister's mind at rest and tell her I shall keep the house on for as long as needs be. Until the autumn if she would want it. Does she need a nurse, one could be got?'

'Thank you my love you are so generous. I would like to look after her myself. A nurse would be so impersonal and I should feel better knowing I was doing my best for her.'

'Of course, I know you will only worry if you cannot see her but you won't leave me for weeks on end over the summer will you? I would miss you too much, my love.'

'Of course not, I will come home as soon as she is better.' She holds his hand and sits beside him. 'I have another reason for wanting to be in Whitby – a reason which will shortly become apparent I hope. They say the waters are good for pregnant ladies.'

'You are with child? But...'

'It must have happened the last time...you remember.' She names the time when he was deceived.

'But the risk! I knew I should not have lain with you. I thought I had been careful! My love I am so very sorry to put you in danger again.' April assures him there is no risk to herself. As she knows this to be the truth this time, she is very convincing. She tells him Dr Sinclair will be consulted when she comes home and all will be well.

Edward is overjoyed of course but anxious nonetheless. He returns to Glasgow the next day leaving April to help in her sister's "recovery".

♥

It is late April and Edward writes asking his wife to come home. April is eager to return to her husband – after all May is not ill and never has been. She tells May she is to return to Glasgow but before she leaves May adds more goose feathers to the "bump";

'Edward needs to see the pregnancy is progressing, since he saw you last you need to have grown bigger.'

April no longer feels guilty at the lie; she is far too excited. She is almost beginning to believe the lie herself – thinking she may soon have a baby handed to her is making her giddy.

One evening when she has been home a few weeks, April and Edward have Alistair and Bea to dinner. They have been discussing how gravely ill May has been with the scarlet fever.

'She is lucky to be alive you say,' says Bea, 'and I can well believe it. One of our servants has lost four of his children and his wife to it. Scarlatina is a vile disease and highly infectious, I am surprised Edward would allow you to visit her.'

'We only went after the fever and rash had gone and there was no chance of catching it,' April says.

'She looked well in my opinion when I left,' Edward says, 'she must have a strong constitution.'

'I think the spa waters helped in her recovery although at first she found the taste disagreeable. They are an acquired taste I think.' April adds.

'I should like to try them as I have had a persistent sore throat this summer.'

'Then why not go and stay with May,' Edward says all generosity.

'May would welcome the company and it would help April too. It would save her another journey to satisfy herself that her beloved sister is doing as well as she says she is. The house is very comfortable, isn't it my love?'

April has gone white. The last thing they need is "Blasted Bea" poking her nose in. 'Yes it is,' April stutters, 'but I am not sure Bea would like it in Whitby. It is a little provincial and gets very crowded in summer.'

'Nonsense,' says Bea. 'I am not such a sophisticate as all that.' Her tinkling laugh grates on April's nerves. 'I lived in Yorkshire for many years and have a fondness for the county although I never went to Whitby. I was once in Scarborough and enjoyed the sea air. Are you sure you wouldn't mind Edward? I could go next week when you are away Alistair.'

It is all arranged and there is nothing April can do save write and warn her sister she is to expect a visitor. April loses sleep over this. She thinks it could spell disaster.

♣

It is a glorious June and the summer and May's pregnancy are progressing beautifully. May is feeling languid and happy, she is blooming. She has often wondered how much can be achieved when one has money. As she suspected one of the spa staff has connections and has found her a midwife and assures her when the need arises she will be able to secure the services of a wet nurse. She has supplied her with the name of a doctor. She is unconcerned about her health.

She is made of stronger stuff than her sister.

May has travelled twice to Glasgow to see Dr Sinclair. She has not of course told her sister. The doctor is happy with her pregnancy and attributes her well being to his potions and ministrations. She attributes her good health to her happiness. For the first time she sees with the birth of this child, Edward's child, her position is secure.

She has no particular maternal feelings for this creature which inhabits her body. It is a means to an end because the child will make her indispensable to her sister. Edward will see how happy April is and will be content himself. He might even continue their liaison.

The one cloud on the horizon for May is she worries she might not have such a tiny waist after the birth. Still, she can lace her stays tighter if she has to she supposes.

Vanity, vanity all is vanity! May it seems takes after her dear mother in most ways. She clearly does not have maternal feelings unlike her sister. Surprising perhaps when you recall how protective of April she always is. Another way she resembles Elizabeth is her ability to practice to deceive. And lastly of course, there are her acting skills. Soon she is going to need recourse to these.

May receives the letter from her sister telling her about the proposed visitor. May's heart sinks. 'Dear Lord, May exclaims to Flossie, "Blasted Bea" my sister-in-law is to make an appearance! I am supposed to be on the road to recovery, I cannot be bedridden all day or swaddled in sheets as I was when Edward visited, Bea will not be as easy to fool as Edward. Men see only what they want see.'

'Your belly is big, not so big as to be unsightly, of course, but too big to pass off as weight gain,' the maid says unhelpfully. 'You are still slender everywhere else,' she adds tactfully.

May looks in the mirror and sees that from the back she looks the same size and shape as before, it is only the bump which she carries high, that gives the game away.

'Either way, May says, I cannot hide under blankets in this heat. I would faint away. Another plan has to be thought of.'

May is whip quick to see the obvious; April, without feather bump, will take up residence at Sandsend. You will notice once again how May directs her twin. Actress, director, producer – there is no end to May's skills.

213

May will go away for a few days, they will swap places. She writes to April outlining what she must do.

♠

When April receives her instructions she is none too happy. She is tired of the plotting and lying – she is forever on her guard. She is not so accomplished a liar as her twin. She just longs for the baby and for a quiet life.

May suggests Edward is told she will spend a few days at Dr Sinclair's clinic as a rest cure prior to the forthcoming birth. This facility is outlined in the pamphlet; it is thrust under his unsuspecting nose. May gives thanks daily for this paper. Edward's attention is drawn to the paragraph by his wife.

'Of course you must go. You should have gone earlier my love, why did you not tell me of this? It will do you good I think to be under the doctors supervision. He smiles and pats her bump lightly making April want to shrink away. 'Nothing is too good for you my love.'

Keep up in the cheap seats! Of course it is not her that will go to the clinic, but May.

So it is on a late summer's day, that April travels south of the border to Sandsend with bump removed, to await the arrival of her tiresome sister-in-law. May on the other hand has travelled north and is enduring bed rest – again, at Dr Sinclair's special 'laying in' clinic near Helensborough.

It is all smoke and mirrors. April however, is not such a consummate actress as her sister and is worried sick she will "slip up." Poor girl.

'Bea fortunately for us has never been able to tell us

apart.' May laughs.'

'I am not such a skilful liar as you sister dear, I have had to have my wits about me for the whole of the visit.'

The visit has passed off without incident. April is relieved that Bea has left and May has returned.

'I have such a headache,' April moans. They are to spend one night together before April goes home to Glasgow. 'I kept forgetting who I was supposed to be and what state I am supposed to be in! I could not relax for one moment these last three days. I am no good at subterfuge. First I pretend to be with child then I am not. My head spins!'

'Just remember it will all be worth it in the end my love. Just think in two months' time you will be a proud mother.' May knows just the right thing to say to soothe her sister's ragged nerves. April softens and says. 'The next time we meet the baby will be born. Do you think it will be a boy?' she asks excitedly.

'Or a girl,' May jests. April giggles and the two sisters discuss babies, clothes, layettes, the colours for the nursery and of course names.

'We have been thinking about names, Edward and I.' April says a serious look on her face, 'You are doing so much for us May so I should like you to choose. I can easily persuade Edward to whatever name you would like.'

She looks at May's belly and wishes things were different. Throughout the pregnancy April has worried May would lose the child; she thought perhaps they might both have the same defect but it seems not to be the case.

April cares deeply for her sister. 'I would be grieved if you were to suffer as I have done. Naturally I wish I was the one to provide my husband with a child but it seems it is not to be.' She sighs. 'This is the next best solution I hope. He will be so proud whether it is a boy or a girl.'

They have talked of names and of course, he would like to call the baby Edward, Ted he thinks would be a good diminutive. If it is a girl he likes Fay after his mother.

'Are you sure? I thought we would have talked of it before now but I know you are superstitious about such things.' May is genuinely grateful. 'I expect Edward would want a boy named after him and I think it only proper that if it is a boy his son should bear his father's name. As for a girl's name I have always liked June. Do you remember we used to talk about it when we were children? Then she would follow us: April, May and June! I also like Fay.'

Tosh and piddle! There has been pillow talk I'll warrant! No doubt about it. Poor April is duped again.

Either way April, bless her heart, is elated. 'May that is wonderful! We think alike for I said to Edward that I liked June and he chose Fay!' The matter is amicably settled to everyone's satisfaction.

♥

May is left alone as April returns to her husband again. April has shed a tear or two before leaving; 'I should like to stay for the birth both to be a support for you and to see the baby as soon as possible. Dr Sinclair's paper talks a lot about mother and baby bonding, he even advocates the mother breast feeding her own child!'

216

May screws her face up in horror.

The month of September is hot and surprisingly humid. May sits staring out to sea from the conservatory. 'I am bored.' She sighs, 'I do not want to go out until after the birth, I feel so large and ungainly.'

'You could look at the magazine you ordered?' Flossie offers.

'I have looked at it, I do not want to stay at home with nothing to do but read and no one but you for company.' She is irritatable.

Despite her frustration the young maid is shaping up well May thinks. She is a quick learner and with the right incentives she is sure she can be discreet when they return to Glasgow. May has started "training" Flossie. She has told her new maid a little of what she is to expect when they return to Glasgow.

'Mr Driscoll is extremely wealthy and revered; he is an important man as is his brother. The house is well appointed, large and elegant and George Square is a sought after address. There is a large staff and you will be well looked after and treated respectfully if you toe the line that is. If you can be tactful Flossie and learn to turn a blind eye from time to time you will be handsomely rewarded.'

May shoots a look at Flossie and adds: 'I just hope when we return home you will not be able to tell my sister and I apart and if you can you keep your own counsel – do we understand each other?'

Flossie knows which side her bread is buttered.

Flossie has brought a bowl of cool water for May to soak her feet. Her ankles are swollen from the heat; the conservatory is like a hot house. May lowers her feet in the soothing coolness, sits back in her chair and closes her eyes. Flossie passes her mistress a fan. Twenty minutes pass and May is dozing when she suddenly is aware of something not quite right. She realises the dampness she feels is not just her feet. She takes a deep breath, opens her eyes wide and grabs hold of her belly with both hands. Her labours have begun earlier than she expected. The show is about to begin.

◆

This time there is no ticking clock, no baby born either side of midnight with the help of a prattling midwife but there is a long, arduous labour. Flossie is almost despatched to fetch the doctor at two in the morning but at the last minute May finds inner strength, some willpower she had not known she possessed and delivers the boy in the early hours of the morning with just Flossie in attendance.

The maid it turns out has eight siblings and as the second oldest child has helped her mother in the delivery bed on several occasions.

She has been a treasure May thinks. As she recovers her strength the heat of the last few days dissipates and rain pours from leaden skies. May is cradling the child as the rain lashes at the windows.

'Look what you have done,' she says soothingly to the sleeping infant, 'You have made it rain! Are you always to be so troublesome I wonder? I had hoped you were going to be the harbinger of peace and harmony but alas—' Thunder booms out reverberating from the cliffs.

The sea beneath the cliffs is turbulent and whelming on the rocks. Flossie smiles as she takes Teddy and lays him in his cot. May sinks back on the silky pillows and falls into a deep, satisfied sleep.

♣

When the labour began a telegram was despatched to April; May had planned everything down to the last detail. They had decided to send a coded message just in case Edward, as was his right, intercepted his wife's correspondence and read it.

The telegram read: AM WELL ENOUGH TO COME HOME STOP COME AND FETCH ME STOP.

When April receives May's cipher she can hardly stop herself from ordering the carriage to take her to the station straight away but she knows this is not part of the plan so restrains herself. The baby must have come early she thinks – she hopes all is well but she cannot help but worry. Edward is opposite her at the breakfast table when the missive arrives.

'Dear God! Could she not send a letter via the usual post! Why the need for a telegram? Should we put the flags out for her return!' Edward has been enjoying living with his wife without her sister forever in attendance. The strain on his nerves trying to avoid temptation has been eased no doubt.

April smiles sweetly at her husband. 'I know she is extravagant but it will be lovely to have her home.'

'Extravagant with my money,' he says smiling back at his wife seeing her pleasure. 'Why must you go? I am surprised she needs a chaperone.' he says with a raised eyebrow. In your condition it should be her waiting upon you not the other way about! Tell her I cannot spare you.' April stands behind her husband, puts her arms about his shoulders and kisses his ear. She knows this is a sensitive spot and a sensitive situation. In a cajoling voice she says, 'Don't be churlish, it doesn't suit you! You know it will please me to fetch her. I will go down tomorrow or the next day.' She nibbles his ear and he smiles.

'When I was there last we talked about my helping close the house up. We will do so then return together. I should like to see Whitby one last time, it has been lovely having the house for the summer.'

'Is that not what servants are for; to close the house up?'

'Of course, but you know what staff are like if they are not supervised.'

'Well let May do it. She has had all the benefit after all! You should not be gallivanting all over the country, you will tire yourself. Are you not supposed to be resting? Have a care my love.' He usually capitulates easier than this but no doubt he is anxious about his wife's health. The last thing he wants is for April to miscarry again.

'Edward! My sister almost died remember!' she says pulling out her trump card. 'Besides I want to go, Dr Sinclair says I am well – there is nothing to worry about. I feel completely different this time. His ministrations have worked, I know they have. I shall only be gone two or three days at the most.'

♠

May is in her bedroom feeding the baby when her twin

arrives. April's eyes open wide when she sees this intimate connection. She wonders where the wet nurse is. She moves closer to May and sees the baby feeding hungrily, he has dark hair and his eyes are closed in concentration as he suckles. May is radiant as she looks up at her sister. April's stomach contracts.

'Come and meet your son,' May says quietly. April's heart misses a beat. 'He is falling asleep now he is sated, he is such a greedy boy.'

'A son, Edward will be thrilled! So am I. Oh May he looks so small!'

'You would not think that if you had laboured to give birth to him,' she says with all the insensitivity of a sledge hammer. 'He was over six pounds at birth, large for a premature baby. He will be gaining even more weight if he carries on guzzling this way.' May turns the baby deftly and starts to wind him.

'Why are you feeding him – is there no wet nurse available?'

'I remember reading in Dr Sinclair's pamphlet that if a mother can feed her own infant it is beneficial to both the mother and the baby. It is one of his new ideas. I do not feed him in the night of course. I need my beauty sleep and this gluttonous little tyke is feeding every two hours. The wet nurse takes over while I rest.' May looks lovingly at her son. The light in her blue eyes has never been brighter.

April looks shaken. Then reminds herself she is his mother now.

'Might I hold him?' Her sister passes the baby, who is now sound asleep. April, emotion threatening to overwhelm her, looks at the tiny bundle. She searches his face for recognition. She sees her own button nose but no other trace of a likeness.

'Where does he get the dark hair from I wonder? We are blonde and Edward is fair, yet look at the dark hair. He has such a lot of hair!'

'Yes he does. It does not signify. We could have dark hair in previous generations. It is a throw back – perhaps it will change as he grows older. Alistair is dark haired'

May has had two days to think of what to say about this anomaly but has been so deliriously happy she has not given it much thought at all. He could clearly be Kit's son from this one trait but she cares not. She has safely delivered what her sister could not. She wants him to be Edward's son. She needs him to be Edward's heir. He is a healthy, happy baby boy so what does it matter what colour hair he has?

For the next two days the sisters dote on the boy, both vying for his attention. Both are experiencing emotions they had never imagined existed. One small bundle has wrought much change; so many feelings are brought to the surface.

The sisters have kept each other afloat through the years but now they are uncertain what lies beneath their usually calm surface. One sister has to begin to let go and the other to accept something that is not of her body to become part of her. The bond which hitherto has been a strength may now break them apart.

From the moment April sees Ted she is in love. She already thinks of him as belonging to her. 'I cannot stop myself from adoring him and cannot wait for Edward to meet him.' As she cradles him in her arms she begins to make plans for his life. 'You are a very lucky boy if only you knew it. You will have a life which will be privileged and full of love and attention. We will protect you and care for you little man, you will want for nothing. You are the most wanted baby ever born.'

♥

Soon the sisters realise they have to turn their attention to the father. The next part of May's plan is ready to swing into action.

As you would expect Edward, poor man, is to be told yet more lies. If he could only guess at the fabrication that is being presented to him he would surely shrink from both women.

You will notice April is so bound up in this tissue of falsehoods she is as guilty as her sister of duplicity. Yet Edward is blissfully unaware. All he knows is what he is told. Lies!

He is sent a telegram telling him his wife went into labour in Whitby and has been delivered of a healthy boy. He is a proud father at last. He has his longed for son and a wife who did not die in the childbed. He gives thanks his prayers have been answered. He sets off immediately for Sandsend to meet his son and heir.

The telegram is sent in fact three days after April's arrival at Sandsend on account of May saying they need time to adjust without the father fussing. It is an emotional reunion for everyone when he arrives to meet his "newborn" son.

It is April who shows Edward his heir. 'I am so proud – more so as a son has been longed for and lost before.' He looks at his beautiful wife cradling his beautiful boy. 'I am a happy man! You look radiant my love. I never thought to see the day.'

He does not question the blackness of the hair. He does not see the proprietary look upon May's face as she stands aside, watching.

♥

May is forced into the realisation that her son, her beautiful boy, who she loves to distraction can no longer be hers and hers alone. She has brought him into the world but cannot own him. He has to be given up, not entirely, but partly. She is shocked at the turmoil that is raging inside her. She is drawn to him like the moon pulls the waves upon the shore. He is her star, her leading man. Yet she will not be his leading lady. The spotlight will shift and she will be forced to accept a lower billing, a lesser role in his life.

Before the birth she had thought she would be glad to pass on the responsibility, to get her figure and her life back but now she is not so sure. The bond between mother and baby is strong, more powerful than May ever realised it would be; it is as though the umbilical cord was never severed.

She is consoled by reminding herself he will be with her always. When they return to Glasgow she will still be part of his life yet she knows she will be pushed into the background, sidelined and called "aunt". The wet nurse will take over, the baby will be presented to his "mother" for inspection while his real mother is forced to stand aside and watch from the wings. Life is to change for everyone. A new male principal has made his entrance.

A star is born.

April on the other hand, with all the status that money can buy, does not simply hold a baby she holds the power. Her married status and her husband's fortune ensure the baby will grow up in their likeness. The twin bond, the connection which binds the twins together for the first time in their lives is exposed and weakened.

'Oh East is East and West is West, and never the twain shall meet.'

Act 4

Chapter 1

It is six months since their return to Glasgow and the days have begun to form a routine. Both sisters have relaxed their guard slightly as Edward has never for a second suspected any subterfuge.

The proud parents see Ted clean, fed and usually sleeping when his new nursemaid, Lizzie, brings the son and heir for his parents' praise and attention. This is most evenings when they are at home. May is always present and fawns over him nearly as much as his mother and father.

'May dotes on the boy,' Edward says one evening.

'It is not remarkable,' says April quickly, 'Most spinster aunts show an interest in their sister's offspring, he is her nephew – of course she spoils him.' In between times the sisters visit the nursery, either together or singly as the desire takes them.

The wet nurse and Lizzie cannot tell whether it is the aunt or the mother who visit; they are of the "peas in a pod" brigade. Flossie impressed with her new surroundings has learnt to see only what concerns her; it is no business of hers what rich folk get up to behind closed doors just so long as they keep paying for her loyalty.

Often when April and Edward are at the theatre or dining out May goes to the nursery to spend precious time with her son. As she holds him, he has grown plump over the months and is a weight to lift, she whispers to him and he laughs and gurgles. She sings to him and he chortles and wriggles. He has a sweet disposition. Often she goes to him just before retiring when her hair is loose and he grabs a handful and tugs. She smiles at his strong grip. May cherishes these times when she is alone with her son. She can be his true mother, no acting is required. She knows April adores him but a mother's love is stronger she thinks. April can never have the bond she shares with him.

On the surface, the arrangement is working yet as you might imagine there are undercurrents in the form of jealousies. Each twin is jealous of the other as they jockey for position. It is placing a strain on their relationship – a strain which has never been there before. You do not need a crystal ball to see trouble ahead.

As May gets ready to retire one night she shares her feelings with Flossie. 'I have noticed the way Teddy favours being held by me, rather than April. If she picks him up he often cries; he only ever smiles when I, his real mother, hold him close. It is as if he recognises his birth mother. April it seems is an understudy. I am convinced he can already tell us apart. It is possibly a sense a baby has for his birth mother – a bond that cannot be broken.'

'He is much loved by both of you,' Flossie says neutrally. 'he is a lucky boy.'

As the weeks pass, jealousies begin to rise to the surface.

'You will turn him into a brat,' May says sharply as April swoops to lift him from his cradle the second he begins to cry. She had just been about to go to him herself and this time has not been quick enough. She is peeved.

'Don't lay him on his front he does not care for it,' April snaps on another occasion as May puts him down. Each "knows best" as mothers invariably do. Both are tight lipped in front of Edward not wanting to show the division or arouse suspicion.

'Suspicion! Of what?' May laughs when April suggests Edward might one day become mistrustful. 'With all the self-awareness a man can muster, Edward sees nothing but a wife, a son and a spinster sister-in-law doting on his son and heir. He is a happy man. He has all he could ever want. Money, power, a loving wife and adorable son. He needs nothing else!' Not once in six months has he thought to question his son's, thick, dark hair.

Are you curious to whether his affaire with May is still ongoing? As I said he has all he could ever want. Draw your own conclusions.

One evening when her sister has retired early with a headache and Edward is out, May makes a last visit to the nursery before turning in. She is in the habit of sending the wet nurse and Lizzie away so she can be alone with her precious son. The two are glad of the excuse to go and eat cake and drink tea in the warm kitchen with Flossie; the March nights are still long and cold.

May lifts Teddy out of his crib and holds him close. He is awake and looks up at his mother with almond shaped, blue eyes that are identical to her own. She murmurs to him and sits in the nursing chair by the fire. Ted, still a hungry boy, pushes his tongue in and out searching for milk. May's body cries out to reward him. She has been in this predicament before and has squashed down the urge to put him to her breast. She knows the girls will not return until she rings for them but she also knows she must not take the risk.

The house is quiet, the only sound is the snuffle of the child in her arms. Teddy looks hopefully at his mother. May never expected to feel maternal, so bonded to her boy. The urge is hard to resist. She struggles with herself before at last Teddy begins to winge then cry. The urge is too strong. She pulls at her nightgown's ribbons and lets Ted feed. He quietens and latches on enthusiastically. Every fibre of her body yields to him as she smiles down at her son, relief flooding through her at the familiar feeling; a feeling which she has denied herself for months. She watches as his chubby fists knead the air rhythmically. She has never felt so fulfilled, so happy.

May is so lost in her contentment she does not hear the nursery door open slowly. Edward on soundless feet stands at a distance and watches his wife feed his precious son.

Or who he perceives is his wife I should say.

'I did not know you fed him yourself sometimes?' he whispers smiling. He too often comes to say goodnight to his handsome boy.

May's head shoots up. The gas light is turned low but

she senses danger. She tries to swallow down the panic rising in her throat. Her heart is pounding as Teddy feeds on unaware of any risk. She cannot speak. She cannot move.

Edward, curious when he receives no reply, moves closer. At first he is not suspicious, why would he be? He sees his wife feeding their son. Unusual but nothing to be alarmed about. Then he sees what he is not supposed to see. He sees the terrified look on May's face. Her mask has fallen and given the game away.

He looks closely at the woman holding his son and sweeping a look down to her ring-less left hand, knows fear. He looks at the eyes that are not his wife's. Recognition hits him like a thunder bolt.

'What are you doing?' he asks still not certain he can believe his own eyes. 'How is this possible?' He looks over his shoulder as he hears footsteps behind him and April comes upon the scene. Time stands still as they each try to make sense of the situation. A bond is irrevocably broken.

◆

It is later and May has fled the room after April has taken charge of the situation.

Yes April! May has gone to pieces – she has dried, forgotten her lines. Had she been prompted she might not have frozen. If only she had not given in to the impulse to feed her own flesh and blood! She is infuriated with herself for her weakness, for her recklessness. How could she have risked everything she had worked for?

April had taken Teddy from his mother's arms and

yelled 'Get out of my sight.' It is a cry of self preservation as she thinks quickly what she should say and do next. Her future depends on the next few minutes. Edward standing by his wife's side protectively says, 'I don't understand?' Bemused he looks to April for answers that will right his world which is spinning on its axis.

'How can May feed our son?' April swallows hard as she lays Ted in his crib, playing for time. She rings for the absent servants. Ted begins to bawl. April takes Edward by the hand and leads him to the door and to their bed chamber. By the morning Edward knows everything.

2

April has at first, thought she will try to lie her way out of trouble but sees it is too late for more fiction if her marriage is to be saved. She throws herself on her husband's mercy and prays he will not disown both her and their son. She leaves no part of the subterfuge untold; she confesses about May pretending to be her on that winter night. She tells everything in the hope he will not throw them overboard. She reasons quietly and calmly even though she has never been so terrified in her life. It is not just her life at stake it is also her son's. If Edward disowns his wife he may well disown his son too.

Her husband at first incredulous, then hurt beyond measure, cannot see a way ahead. 'It is as though a sea fret has fallen and I cannot find my way through the fog, I am lost'. April is trying to lead him through the murk yet he is resisting, not knowing whether she is leading him further off course.

'In my confusion I want to be led to safe harbour where everything will be as it was before the storm hit but I am shipwrecked and overwhelmed. I feel you have turned against me, did you never love me at all?'

'I did this for you – to give you the thing you wanted most, a baby – a son and heir. You know I did not love you in Whitby but then when we married I fell under your spell. You know I truly love you – why else would I risk everything otherwise!'

They are up all night long, until Edward begins to see the truth of the matter and knows what he must do.

♣

May is pacing and weeping. For once in her life she has no plan, no scheme, no way of steering the ship in the direction she wants it to go. The loss of control is of her own making. She sees this and is furious with herself for giving in to her need to satisfy her son. She has taken a grave risk and knows she might have lost him forever.

'I should go and see April, tell her what to say – she will not know what to do. I cannot think what to do, Dear Lord I am so mad with myself!' Flossie looks on but refrains from comment. 'If I go to her Edward might be there too and he will not want to see me! There is nothing to be done but wait and hope my sister as new captain of this sinking ship will think of some way of rescuing us.'

'The master has not been down this morning, he must be still with your sister.'

'I know not whether that is a good or a bad thing. Did you hear voices from their room?'

Flossie had been despatched on manoeuvres earlier. 'All was quiet Miss.'

It is mid-afternoon when a servant delivers the

message that Captain Driscoll awaits her presence in the library. May's stomach turns over. She has eaten nothing all day – nerves are making her feel sick.

Edward is standing with his back to her looking out of the window. A pale sun is streaming through the glass highlighting his fair hair. As he turns, May is shocked by the stern look on his usually kind face. He sits behind his desk, ashen faced but does not invite May to take a seat. He picks up an envelope in his hand and looks at it as if he has never seen it before.

'I am sorry this has come to pass but not as sorry as you I imagine?' He waits but May does not speak. She stands head held high; her hands folded one upon the other in front of her. She cannot defend herself for she does not know what April has said and she fears incriminating herself further. She judges it best to remain silent.

'Your sister has told me everything. I know she has not given birth to my – to Edward and I know why she was persuaded by you to carry out the deception. I know you swapped places with her and pretended to be my wife that night.'

May breathes deeply registering his remarks. 'April has confessed all it seems, but have you in turn, confessed your sins for we both know she and I are not the only ones who have lied,' May says.

She has nothing to lose now she thinks. How dare he sit there so sanctimoniously? Her sister it seems has deserted her too; May cannot believe she has been betrayed.

'What your sister has done,' Edward continues as if May has not spoken, 'she has done under your influence.

She is too soft hearted, too easily led and you have taken advantage of her good nature. You have plotted to insinuate yourself into my affections, into my bed, with little regard for your sister's well being. You are selfish and have thought only of your own needs. You wanted my money possibly. As for whether you wanted me – I am embarrassed to realise I have been made a fool of by both of you but it is you I blame the most. From the beginning you have stopped at nothing to get your own way. This plan of yours, this spectacular scheme, would have worked too had you not given in to impulse.' He passes the envelope through his fingers tapping it harder on the blotter.

The action is annoying May and she wants to rip it from his hypocritical fingers. May's temper is beginning to rise. She resents being made to stand while he sits as he promulgates the moral high ground. She feels like a servant waiting for orders. She speaks through clenched teeth trying her utmost to sound calm.

'You flatter yourself Edward – on the contrary. It is I who is the injured party. It is I who is the selfless one. Is it not I who offered up my body to you so that you could have your one wish? It is I who have laboured and borne you a son. It is I who have unselfishly given him up to April so that she can be a mother. I have repaid my debt to you for rescuing me from the brothel and housing me these last years. I felt it my duty to do for you what April could not.'

She pauses the better to get herself under control. Her face feels flushed with suppressed anger. 'April has not been pushed into doing something she was opposed to – she has done what she thought was right to make you happy. If you cannot see this then you are blind.' She moves towards the desk and leans across it. 'April loves you with all her heart. True, at first she was unwilling but then you treated her with nothing but kindness and she in turn, wanted you to have the one thing she could not give you – a son. I only sought to help her as I too loved you as a—'

'Love! You know nothing of love. You know only jealousy and spite.' He drops the envelope, stands and moves away from the desk and her proximity. She sees the anger in his eyes.

'I am not even sure you understand how you have hurt April, she is breaking her heart over this yet you stand here dry eyed still trying to save your own skin. Well it is too late May you have plotted and failed.' He sits down again and picks up the envelope once more. This time he pushes it towards May and leaves it, laying between them.

'I have discussed this with your sister and this is what is to happen. Today you are to leave this house for good. You are to order your maid to pack your belongings, all of them, I want nothing of you left in this house.' He says this with a look of distaste on his face. 'In this envelope is a cheque,' he continues. 'It is enough money to make you independent of us for the rest of your life. Where you go from here is entirely up to you. If I had my way you would book a one way passage and never come back. You have your sister to thank for this for I would have thrown you out this minute with nothing but what you have on your back.'

May's temper finally gets the better of her. 'You want nothing of me left in the house you say? Well then, have Lizzie pack Teddy's belongings, for where I go, my son goes too.' The words are spit at her former lover and her face is crimson with anger at his double standard. 'You were happy enough to take advantage of April's trusting nature while we romped in your bed when she was taking the waters. I don't remember you holding back from your pleasure then. Did you not stop to think of the hurt you would inflict on her if she found out?'

The door is flung open and April who has heard everything bursts into the room tears gushing. She strides over to her sister and slaps her twin a resounding thwack across the face.

'How dare you! I hate you,' April shouts, fury and pain show equally on her face. 'You are no better than a whore – you would have done well for yourself had you sought your fortune on your back! You have betrayed me – me of all people. Your sister, your twin, the only person in the world who loves you.' She sobs. 'Get out, I will never ever forgive you.'

The worm has turned!

'As for you,' she says turning to her husband, 'you are no better than one of Mrs Jansen's "gentlemen." I loved both of you and both of you have used me to your own ends and gone behind my back. Had I stayed at the brothel at least I would have known where I stood, known my attackers. How could you *both* deceive me?'

May tries again. 'He pushed me into an affair, he threatened to throw me out if I did not—'

'Stop it. Stop it both of you! I cannot tell truth from

fiction. Both of you are beneath contempt.' April paces up and down between her two betrayers. 'We are all to blame here. None of us is innocent in this mess. We have all sought to deceive for one reason or another. Yet at the heart of all this is a baby. Ted is the only innocent here; he is the only one without motive.' She sits on a sofa shaking. There is silence as each of the three protagonists thinks what to do next.

Eventually April speaks quietly but firmly, 'If May leaves this house with Ted then I shall go with her. They are both my blood and I cannot be without them.' She turns to Edward a look of hatred on her face. 'I know I agreed that May had to go yet I find I cannot let her. Despite everything she is my sister, my twin sister and we cannot be parted. We were together in the womb and will be together until death. Ted has my blood too, I trusted you and you let me down – with my own sister' April deathly white, looks exhausted after the long night of confession. 'I see what must be done.'

You weren't expecting that were you? Blood is thicker than water, apparently. Oh you were expecting that! You are cleverer than you look.

Edward strides across the room and holds his wife by the shoulders as May watches. 'You must see she cannot stay! She has come between us. The only way we can recover from this is by her going away – alone.'

April will not meet his gaze. 'Recover? I am not certain I want to recover! I have told you what we did and why. I have broken my heart over this yet it is only by listening at the door I find out the last piece of the jigsaw. We are not the only ones who lied Edward, you have lied to me and not confessed that you have been laying with my own sister: In our bed. When all is said and done there is blame to lie at your door too. I never thought you would prove deceitful especially after I have confessed my part in this, this – tragedy.'

April pulls away from her errant husband. The room falls silent again. April walks to the door. 'I am going to lie down. I cannot bear to look at either of you at this moment. Perhaps I am the one who should leave – am I not the outsider?' As she reaches the door Edward rushes to her side. 'Leave me alone Edward,' she pushes him away. The sound of Ted crying in the nursery reaches her ears and with a warning look not to follow her she instinctively goes to quieten the child.

In the nursery she picks him up, 'Where is everyone?' she mutters. She strokes Ted's black hair that is made darker from sweat with the effort of crying. She strokes the soft curls. He continues to writhe in her arms. He is strong and she feels weak. Ted's crying continues.

Black hair? May's hair so blonde, Edward's hair so fair. Kit Charterhouse's black curls. The thought wheedles its way into her brain like a bug burrowing in a bed. She remembers tea at the Blythswood. She sees her sister flirting with Kit. She sees his thick, dark, curls.

April rings for a servant. May arrives at the same moment as the wet nurse and April hands the bawling baby over to the nurse and nods to May to follow her. Once in her dressing room April looks hard at her sister.

'Tell me the truth. You have lied to me already and I will not have you lie again. You know no matter what you have done I will forgive you, fool that I am. It is not forgotten, never forgotten, but forgiven because you are my twin sister. You have nothing to lose now by owning up.'

'About what?' My love you are—' She knows what is coming next:

'Is Kit Charterhouse Ted's father?'

'April! Of course not. I know your opinion of me is low but please credit me with some morals. You know I have only ever had eyes for one man.' She attempts to look remorseful. 'I had my chance with Kit as well you know but I turned him down as I did not want second best.'

There is some truth in this statement but you have to be good at dissection to get to it. Truth or fiction, May has self preservation on her mind and she knows Edward would not raise another man's child even if her sister would. May has thought she might have to deny her son's dubious parentage and has already made her mind up to deny it.

'What you said to Edward – about leaving, you would not surely? You cannot leave us, our bond is too great to break.' May takes April in her arms and holds her tight, 'We have to get through this crisis. We can do it because we both want the same thing.'

'What! Edward do you mean?' Her sister pulls back in horror.

'No! A contented baby who is loved by all his family; let us leave here together, take Teddy and begin again – just the three of us.'

'You think Edward would let Ted go? He would not! He loves the boy to distraction. He has waited so long for a son he would sooner give me up than him.'

May has to think on her feet. She does not want to leave George Square and all its comforts. She thought to scare her sister into acting against Edward. She tries another tack. 'Let us try to talk Edward around together, it has always been us against the world, some compromise must be sought if we are to survive.' She pulls April back into an embrace and strokes her hair. May realises she still has rough waters to navigate but with April on her side she is sure she will reach dry land safely.

3

May has spent several sleepless nights and has kept to her room. She has seen no one except Flossie and has interrogated her each time she has brought her food.

'Mr Driscoll has issued orders that neither you nor your sister are to be alone with the baby; none of the servants including Lizzie and the wet nurse, can tell you apart he says. That is why his wife is watched too.'

'Or he fears one or other of us will kidnap him! How dare he – was it him that laboured to bring Teddy into this world? Of course not! He was just there for the enjoyable part!'And do not look like that. If I lose my home where do you think that leaves you? Get your ears to the door and she what you can find out.'

May is again summoned to the library but this time April is present too. Husband and wife stand behind the large oak desk. April's chin is held high, May is worried.

'We cannot go on like this. Edward and I have discussed the matter again and a new solution has been found which we hope will be agreeable to you.' May sees her sister swallow hard. 'Everyone is hurt and angry. We have to come to an agreement where Teddy's needs are put before our own,' April looks at her sister's identical face.

'All this pain, this anguish these lies have been to get a child and now we have him, I for one, intend to put his needs first.' April looks to her husband to carry on the speech they have rehearsed.

'April is right; you two becoming estranged will help no one. You have a bond that will never be broken and that no one, not even I it seems, can come between. We have another proposal.'

He outlines the plan. May sits listening with a look on her face that gives nothing away. 'My company owns a house, a town house nearby. It is not large but it is comfortable. We would make you an offer of this house for as long as you have need. Your bills will be met in full by me and you can take Flossie and appoint your own small household. You will be allowed to visit your sister if and when April chooses. In time if April allows it you can see the baby but only ever in the presence of your sister.'

Remember she is not one and twenty years old yet. She has lived a lot of life for one so young. Her future is before her. It is the best offer she's going to get, she is relieved.

May agrees but knows she is between a rock and a hard place. She thinks to stall for time and is already thinking of another scheme. It is plain to May that Edward is lost to her. She never fooled herself she could take him away from April but she had hoped to stay at George Square and share him.

Like most men, May thought, Edward could be manipulated while ever she lay with him. She knew how to keep his attention in that respect. Now she is forced to admit that if ever Edward cared for her just the tiniest bit then she is disabused of this fact now. He has used her like she were a two bob whore. A convenient distraction while his wife was indisposed. She despises him.

All he has offered her he has offered because April has insisted no doubt. She realises without her sister's help she would almost certainly be out on her ear by now.

Later she brushes her long blonde hair and looks at her reflection in the mirror. If she's not careful she thinks she will lose her looks. All this worry is not good for the skin. It will sag and the wrinkles will start to appear. With each stroke of the brush her resolve strengthens and her hatred grows. As yet she is unsure how the plan will manifest itself but she knows Captain Edward Driscoll will not come out of it well.

4

May is ensconced in a leafy street near to George Square but it is not George Square – nothing like George Square. Palatial it is not: it does not have large reception rooms or an up to date gas light and she does not have a carriage at her disposal. Her bedroom is smaller than she has grown used to and there is no water closet next door. The courtyard garden is shady and overgrown and the kitchen does not boast a chef. She feels like the poor relation.

She thinks about all she has done to get where she is – all the calculating and conniving, all the deception and the lies. Where has it got her? Nowhere very grand she decides. May has been cheated, let down. Again she is the jobbing actor and not the lead.

And who is it she asks herself who has let her down, who has brought her to this? There is only one answer: Captain Edward Driscoll.

She wishes she had never laid eyes on him. He has used both her and her twin shamefully. He has deceived them and yet April has forgiven his sin of adultery it seems, more fool her. May wonders if it is too late to convince her sister to leave him. She could try again. If she can come between husband and wife one more time it would be Edward moving out, not her. She could be happy at George Square with her sister and Teddy and the opulence. With the loathsome Edward gone, she cannot bear to think of him any other way, they could have a happy life. Just the three of them.

It is true the man she once idolised is sickening to her now. She sees he is spineless, selfish and disloyal. She cannot abide him but how to convince her sister? She smiles to herself. In the beginning she tried desperately to convince April to take him but now she wants April to disown him. The irony is not lost on her.

Can she seduce Edward again? Let her sister know of his weak will and show her how he can be manipulated? Even she cannot see how this is to be done, especially since he will not be in the same room with her since she left George Square. She will not hurt her sister again; she has to think of another way. She has to separate her sister from her husband.

♠

April, living apart from her sister for the very first time must be worried she has seen nothing of May since she moved out.

She writes to her:

"Dearest May, How I miss you. Have you been ill? I have called twice and been told you are not to be disturbed. Please send word when I might call upon you. We cannot become estranged; you are my sister – my other half. Please write to me at least and tell me how

you do."

It has been three weeks since May removed from George Square and her plan is in its infancy. May is distancing herself from April and Teddy even though it is hurting her more than she imagined. She has never been alone before, never lived alone and never had to fend for herself.

By "fending for herself" she means only having Flossie and three indoor servants at her beck and call. Not to mention a new cook and a gardener.

Despite the hardship she is determined to see this through and not see April and Teddy – yet.

She writes back:

"I have been indisposed – as you might imagine my nerves have been much stressed but I am feeling a little better now. I am mindful also that you and Edward need time to repair your marriage and I thought to give you both the time and the space to do this. I hope you and Teddy are well."

Next comes a letter from April outlining how lonely she is without her twin.

"I too have been in low spirits. Can you possibly imagine how lost I am without you, lost not having you to confide in – it is strange to me. I miss your support and guidance. Despite everything I miss you dreadfully. We need to talk my dear for the longer this rift lasts the more frightened I become. We need to mend this breach. Please come to lunch?"

May replies refusing.

"I think it best if I do not see your husband for a while. We might both say things we come to regret."

Along with the note she sends him her best wishes and a bottle of his favourite single malt whisky. It is she says, "A peace offering".

Another week passes. April again writes asking if they can meet alone. This time May relents and agrees. She sees the time is right.

'Oh May, I have missed you so much. We have only ever been apart once before when I was on honeymoon, I have been so dejected without you.' April embraces her sister warmly. May is thinking about the last time they were parted and who it was that parted them.

'I have missed you too! Living alone is so isolating, so lonely. I have no one to talk to except Flossie and she is dim witted at the best of times. At least you have Teddy… and your husband. I have no one.'

May knows how to turn the screw. She knows April will feel the guilt.

They sit in the morning room at George Square either side of the fire as they were wont to do when May lived there. It feels so long ago. There is a constraint between them, not a lack of warmth but a separation, a lack of trust on both sides. It has never been felt before.

May is desperate to go to Teddy but dare not ask to see him. They drink tea and try to ignore the tension in the air. At last April rings the bell and asks for the boy to be brought from the nursery. May has longed to see him and he will be a distraction she hopes. They have never needed one before.

'He has grown so much,' May says dying to grab the

boy from her sister's grasp. Her physical body as well as her heart yearns to hold him. He in turn smiles brightly at his birth mother.

'He is changing every day – he thrives,' April says as she hugs him possessively. After a few minutes she hands the wriggling boy over to her sister. Despite everything she cannot deny her twin. May is overcome as she looks at him. It is true – he has changed, his hair looks altogether lighter not so dark as when he was born.

Perhaps he is Edward's after all?

The twins pander and praise Teddy until he becomes fractious and hungry. Lizzie comes to take him to the wet nurse. May feels bereft when he leaves the room, the pull is still strong. Stronger even, now she has not seen him for weeks. She has ached for her son, she has missed him almost as much as she has missed April. She never imagined she would feel this way. She had thought when she devised this plan that she would think of him as a nephew but she does not; he is her son and to be without him is torture.

She tries to push him from her mind. 'I have so missed the garden since I left,' May says when they are alone again. She had taken to going to work in the garden most days when she lived at George Square. She has always liked the fresh air. The garden at her new abode is uninspiring. She has become quite knowledgeable whilst under the tutelage of Robins the head gardener.

'Might we take a walk in the sun so I can see how it has grown?' The sisters walk out to the walled garden and May inspects the plants. She exchanges words with Robins as she used to do most days. He is a stern, red headed Scotsman but like most gardeners he is keen to pass on his pearls of wisdom especially to a pretty girl. She has learnt a lot from him. During their talk April is called away on a domestic matter. May seizes her opportunity.

'I have such a slug problem in my new garden Robins, it is very damp and shady and they are thriving, unlike my poor plants.'

'Aye, they are pests if not kept under control. Wait here Miss and I'll get you some stuff to get rid of the wee beasties, if you don't keep on top of 'em you'll have no plants left at all.'

'Thank you Robins but would you mind sending it over this afternoon. I am not going straight home from here and don't wish to carry it with me.'

'Aye, that I'll do Miss May but you be careful, remember to keep it away from other animals and wash yer hands after you've used it.'

He chuckles. 'Funny to think the Driscoll's fortune is built on tobacco. The stuff in my concoction that kills the slimy devils is nicotine which is got from the tobacco leaf.'

'Is that so? Why is it then gentlemen who smoke aren't killed?'

'It is not present in such quantity in a cigar. They would have to smoke boxes of 'em to get poisoned. Nicotine is strong stuff though, as I told you – watch out how you use it.' May smiles and thanks the gardener as she makes her way back indoors.

♥

Over the coming weeks the sisters begin to meet often,

but always alone. Neither can imagine how things would be if Edward were present. They begin to feel as they always did in each other's company. The only time when tensions rise is when Edward Junior is present. Each twin feels an uncommon jealousy of the other.

Some little time later April eventually says, 'It is about time I think that you came to dinner. Alistair and Beatrice are to dine with us, please say you will come May. We cannot go on like this forever. You and Edward have to see each other sooner or later.'

May has been waiting for this invitation. She hums and haws and sounds like she will refuse but to April's delight she eventually agrees.

She is a cunning minx! She plays her part well.

The dinner passes as well as can be expected. As they are in company there is no chance of the conversation turning personal. May and Edward are politeness itself but only ever converse indirectly. May is surprised to see Edward looking pale and drawn. When the ladies leave the men to their port May broaches the subject.

'Is Edward unwell, you have not mentioned he is ailing?'

'I think he is working too hard, April shuffles in her seat uncomfortably, 'although he has had a stomach upset that has lingered longer than it should.'

'I thought he did not eat much at dinner,' Bea says, 'He usually has a good appetite like Alistair. Between them they would easily finish off the beef usually.'

'He has only been having a little chicken – light foods that are easy to digest. He has seen the doctor and he says he will give himself an ulcer if he hasn't already. He works so hard and will not slow down, he is so driven.'

May listens as the two women compare their husband's workloads and habits and is bored. She feels like a poor, spinster aunt.

'Like all men,' April continues, 'he only takes the parts of the doctor's advice which suit him. He has been told to cut down on his whisky consumption but of course he has overlooked that proposal!' May is pleased to hear this nugget of information.

The next day a dozen bottles of Edward's favourite single malt arrive at George Square from a patron.

♦

May is now seeing her sister most days. They often walk the baby together in the park or take luncheon or tea. On some days they do all three. Edward is about his business, he is still hard at work, though who knows why when he is so rich. May seldom has to see him.

'How is Edward today?' May asks feigning interest. Yesterday April had told her Edward had been up most of the night vomiting.

'He is a little better, he fasted all day and he slept well enough, he said.'

'Was the doctor called?' May asks all concern.

'He will not have him! He gave him some powders last time he was taken ill with his stomach. Edward swears they make him feel worse. I am sure he has an ulcer, I am trying to persuade him to see Doctor Stewart again but he can be so stubborn.'

'Perhaps if you leave off nagging him he will come around himself and get the doctor in. Perhaps he is trying to spare your feelings?'

'I do not nag him. I am trying to cajole him. Why are men so pig headed? As for sparing my feelings it is having the opposite effect. I am worried more than ever about his condition. He has lost more weight I think and hardly eats anything that is not plain boiled and bland; when he eats normally he suffers greatly.'

You will see April's kind nature has reasserted itself. She is trying to mend her broken marriage.

'Poor Edward,' May says wiping a dribble from her son's chin. It is mid afternoon and they have just returned back to George Square for tea. The footman is hovering and looking thin lipped.

'Good afternoon Mrs Driscoll. I am sorry to tell you the doctor is here. After you left this morning Captain Driscoll came back home from his meeting, he has been taken ill. We sent to Miss May's to let you know but you had both left and no one knew where you had gone.'

'The doctor is still here you say? Oh dear. We have been out longer than we intended perhaps,' she says as if she is accountable to the footman. 'He must be very bad if Stewart has been here all day?' She looks at the hall clock and is surprised to see the time.

'May, please wait while I go and see what is happening.' April's face is white as she goes to her husband's side.

When she has gone Teddy's nursemaid wants to take the boy to the nursery. May stops her. 'I will take him to my sister's sitting room to wait for news, Lizzie. I am sure she will want to see us both as soon as she has seen Captain Driscoll.' She smiles and gives the nursemaid a look that is not to be challenged. Lizzie dithers. She has had her instructions about Teddy not being left alone with either sister. 'Under the circumstances,' May reasons, I am sure you can make allowances.' She nods and leaves the boy alone with May.

It would seem May's scheme is working sooner and better than she had thought. Now she is not in the house to monitor his consumption she has been unaware how much whisky Edward has been drinking "to ease the pain". She has been worrying that he might have taken his doctor's advice and given up his favourite tipple. She need not have fretted; the dozen bottles of whisky have dwindled nicely it would seem.

Act 5

1

The funeral bell tolls as the Glaswegian sky pours rain in torrents on the mourners. The church is full with family, friends and business associates. Captain Edward Driscoll it seems was a popular man. Despite his extraordinary wealth he will be remembered as a fair and honest business man, a loyal brother and a good husband and father.

He was known to work hard. When the doctor pronounces he died of a stomach ulcer it is a salutary warning to others. He is young and his death has come as a shock to all Glasgow society. It has come as more than a shock to his wife.

By the graveside close family and friends stand with heads bowed. May, supporting her sister is grieving too. Despite everything she is remembering the man she had once loved. It is the memory of a love which was unrequited.

Effie Claire back from France is being held up by

Alistair on one side and Beatrice on the other. Alistair though grim faced, is trying to bear up for his sister's sake. They are a dour little group.

The wake is endless May thinks. The food and drink, quaffed at this sad event is of the finest quality as is expected by Glasgow society; April and May partake of nothing but hot, sweet tea.

May wishes the mourners, the hangers on, would leave them alone. She has of course moved back to George Square to help her sister grieve. They sit side by side in identical mourning, with identical looks of grief upon their identical, beautiful, faces. The mourners struggle to discern which of the two is the widow. They mutter their condolences to the dry eyed pair and move off to eat the lavish spread.

At last the family are left in peace, the crows having picked the carcass clean. May sighs as the last of them staggers off replete with meat and wine.

Effie is close to dropping. 'You equipped yourself well today my dear,' Alistair says to his sister,' but now the strain is altogether too much for you I think. Go to bed and see if you can get some sleep. You look done in.'

'I think I will – it has been as you say, an unbearably difficult day.'

Poor Effie, she was close to her brother. She was alarmed to receive the telegram in Paris to say he was dangerously ill and to come home immediately. He had passed by the time she returned. Effie has been berating herself ever since. She is devastated not to say goodbye to him.

'Here take this,' says Alistair, 'It is Edward's favourite

single malt. He always said it helped him sleep.' He swallows down the emotion that is welling. He feels his brother's loss keenly. 'He always swore a "wee dram" put him into the arms of Morpheus.' He tries to smile. Alistair pours a glug of the amber nectar into a glass.

'Hot milk would possibly do you more good,' May offers.

'Nonsense! We Scots know a snifter is the best cure.' Alistair hands the glass to Effie. 'Good night dearest heart, I shall come and see you tomorrow,' Alistair kisses the top of Effie's head.

Finally Alistair and Beatrice go leaving April and May alone. May takes it upon herself to ask that Teddy be brought to them.

She is already reaffirming her position you will notice. She is back where she belongs: in George Square with her sister and her son.

May takes Teddy from Lizzie. When April looks at him tears burst from her eyes and she sobs. Until now she has been in shock and has not shed a single tear.

'Poor Ted will never know his father,' she says between sobs. May is momentarily flummoxed. She is looking at the baby's hair and thinking it looks lighter still.

She can convince herself Edward is the father all she likes but no one will ever know for certain.

May was surprised earlier to see Kit with his fiancée at the church but thankfully he was not at the wake. That ship has sailed. Rekindling the affair is far from her mind at the moment although she would not rule out a little distraction in the future.

'You have been so brave April, it will do you good to

cry. Now the worst is over it may aid your sleep if you can let it out.'

'The worst is not over – how can you say that? The worst is yet to come. A lifetime without the man I loved more than life itself.' April breaks down again. She has forgotten her husband's betrayal. May puts Teddy on a blanket in front of the fire and tries to console her sister. 'Teddy is fatherless and I have lost my precious husband. Life is not worth living. He worked himself to death and for what? We already had all we could possibly need. If it were not for Teddy...'

May strokes her sister's hair as she sits on the arm of April's chair. She is watching her darling boy shake his hands as if he is trying to free them from some bond. She is thinking of their future. The three of them living here at George Square: happy, wealthy, respectable, wanting for nothing.

They will jointly share in Teddy's upbringing, loving him and guiding him. Effie will no doubt leave them soon to a good marriage and they will live by their own rules, untroubled by men. Unless of course they wish to take lovers. May thinks again of Kit and his handsome face. She should not like to remain celibate all her life. This new life will be perfect. A contented sigh passes her lips.

It has taken courage and cunning to get to this place but at last she has what she has always dreamed of – well almost.

◆

A knock on her bedroom door wakes May from a bad dream. In the nightmare Edward is offering her an overflowing glass of whisky and asking her to taste it. "Go on he says, it will put you in the arms of the law."

She sits up and shudders. 'Come in,' she says wiping sleep from her eyes. Flossie is standing in the doorway in her night shift. 'Can you come Miss, I didn't want to wake Mrs Driscoll, she's had such a time of it. It's Miss Effie that needs you.'

May throws a shawl about her shoulders. Flossie continues, 'She's been that sick, puked all over her bed she has.' The maid wrinkles her nose in distaste. May is halted.

'Sick you say? It is possibly the strain of the day catching up with her. Like the rest of us, she ate very little yesterday, or drink for that matter.' May is quick to account for this new travail.

You will notice even this late at night she has her wits about her.

May waits by the door to Effie's room as a maid cleans up the poor girl. The bed has been changed but the sour smell of vomit lingers. May wrinkles her nose and breathes through her mouth.

'Effie my dear, how are you feeling now?'

'Hold my hand please May, I am sorry you have been disturbed. I feel a little better I think for bringing it up – whatever it was. I just need to sleep now. Will you sit with me until I drop off?'

'Of course my dear, close your eyes and rest.'

'That is just it. I cannot, for every time I shut my eyes I see Edward's face calling to me. I should have been here, not gallivanting around Paris, I never got to say goodbye.' Tears flow down her pale as putty cheeks.

'You were not to know Edward would pass, how could you? None of us did.'

This is not strictly true is it? May can hardly confess to poisoning this distraught girl's brother now can she? She feels sorry for causing her pain. She is collateral damage. It cannot be helped.

'Can I get you anything? Some water perhaps?' Effie shakes her head and closes her eyes bravely. May is hoping Effie will drop off soon. She suspects the whisky given to Effie by Alistair is tainted, a leftover bottle from the dozen. She needs to retrieve it and dispose of it. Not that she poisoned every one of the twelve bottles – just some of them.

She has always known the only person in the house to favour whisky is Edward. He alone would drink it unless Effie was present and then she too would have a snifter with her brother. April and May hate the stuff and Alistair prefers brandy. Bea rarely touches spirits and Edward always kept a different brand for his guests. Not inferior, just a less mellow brand. May has known that with Effie in France she would hit her target. Randomly she has laced some of the bottles with an amount of slug killer that will not prove fatal if one glass is ingested; she has banked on the cumulative effect doing the damage.

She knew Edward's consumption had gone up and hoped he would work his way steadily through the consignment. She had not, of course, known how many bottles he already had in his cellar and so could not predict when he would start on the doctored bottles. She was prepared to wait. She smiles to herself at the phrase: he had certainly needed a doctor after he had drunk them! He has surpassed himself she thinks as she sits by the bed watching for Effie's breathing to slow.

After a while Effie is sleeping, if not peacefully, then fitfully. May makes her way down to the drawing room and looks to the small side table where she remembers Alistair put the near full bottle. It has gone. She knows the servants will have tidied up when they retired so May is not perturbed, she moves over to the drinks table thinking it has been placed with the brandy and port. It is not there either. A cold shiver runs down her back. She knows the staff well and cannot believe one of them has pilfered it. Why would they risk their jobs? Where can it be?

The next morning everyone, except May, are late risers. May goes to the butler's pantry and finds Tibbs. 'Is any of Captain Driscoll's single malt left Tibbs?' She does not say why. She is careful enough not to tell any unnecessary lies. Tibbs goes to the cellar and comes back with a full bottle.

'The captain did not order his usual quota this month, him being so poorly. This is all that is left.' It is an unopened bottle.

'Thank you, I will take it up. 'Miss Effie is the only member of the household to take whisky now so I expect the order will be much reduced; she only ever used to take a little with her brother,' she adds as if he didn't know. She reminds herself not to elaborate. She will incriminate herself if she is not careful.

'Would you like me to put it with the other bottles in the drawing room Miss.' Tibbs uses the title loosely as he is unsure which sister he is addressing.

'I will take it. It is just that yesterday Mr Alistair opened a bottle for Miss Effie to take a dram. That bottle seems to have gone.'

'Dear me, I cannot account for that Miss. I will of course investigate the matter.' Tibbs looks concerned and May knows he will not rest until he knows what has happened to it. He is diligent and heads will roll if he cannot get to the truth.

'I am sure there is nothing amiss but if you do find out where it has gone I would appreciate it if you would please let me know privately. Do not disturb Mrs Driscoll at this difficult time.'

At last he knows who he is talking to. 'I will Miss May, you leave it with me.'

May goes out to the garden and pours the contents of the whisky bottle over a rose bush. She hopes it is one of the doctored bottles; it will kill the green fly if it is. She takes the empty bottle and hides it in the compost heap.

The next few days sees the house in turmoil. Effie, unaccountably to some, is suffering the same symptoms as her brother. The doctor is suspicious. Is it possible that she too has an ulcer everyone is asking? Of course the answer comes back in the negative.

April still abed says: 'Doctor Stewart is of the opinion that the symptoms are the same as Edward's but how can that be?

'He is a fool,' May says,' 'She has never done a day's work in her life and stress is a strange concept to her. She has always had a carefree disposition. Until now she has been a typical, happy-go-lucky young woman with everything to live for. It must be her grief putting a strain on her system.'

'I expect so. As for myself I have no appetite at all.'

'The doctor has clearly misdiagnosed. I am sure I have smelt spirits on his breath.'

May is covering her tracks.

Poor Effie is reduced to bed rest with a high temperature, bilious attacks and abdominal pain. She can neither eat nor drink without vomiting. At first May is not concerned poison will be suspected; she knows one wee dram cannot account for these severe symptoms. She is sorry for Effie. She sits by her bed day and night. Then something occurs to shake May's confidence. She finds the missing whisky bottle. It is empty.

♣

May has always liked Effie Claire. When April was on honeymoon they spent much time together. Effie though younger and sillier, was good to May. She helped her to fit into her new life when she first came to Scotland. She helped her know how to behave in society and was never condescending; just pleased to have a new friend to go about with. She was like a younger sister. May is fond of her.

Since the funeral, April has been in no fit state to do much beyond sit in the nursery. May has been torn between looking after her sister and nursing her sister-in-law. She has not wanted to leave Effie, in case she says something incriminating, though May cannot think what she could say that would be detrimental. She is wary nonetheless.

May has left the room and taken some food whilst

Effie is having her bed changed. When she returns, one of the maids is bundling up the soiled bed sheets when May notices something nestling amongst the linen. It is the missing whisky bottle

'What is this?'

'I don't know Miss.' The maid is barefaced.

'This I mean,' May says taking up the bottle and holding it aloft.

'I never see'd it before Miss. It must have rolled under the bed.'

'Is under the bed not your province?' May challenges then thinks better of making a fuss. 'Very well, no matter You need to be more careful in future, off you go.' The maid scurries out of the room relieved not to be reported to the housekeeper.

May, still holding the bottle, sniffs it; she can smell nothing but whisky. She hides the bottle in her underwear drawer until she can safely dispose of it. Her head is swimming. Effie must have come back downstairs on the night of the funeral, perhaps she could not sleep. Had she drunk the whole bottle that night? Surely not! Perhaps she had been secretly imbibing over a few nights when May has dozed by her bed or when one of the maids has sat with her when she was with April?

Either way, May's findings could be catastrophic. She paces her room. Wringing hands is not usually May's style but that was before this horror. She is anxious and not just for herself. She goes back to Effie's room and sits by the bed willing her sister-in-law to recover.

The doctor is expected and Effie is awake but to May's consternation Effie is now delirious.

'Give me a wee dram,' she says her eyes rolling in her head, 'it will help me sleep.' She parrots the words Alistair said to her after the funeral. May tries to calm her. If she is ranting like this when the doctor comes Effie will lead him right to the cause of her troubles. She needs to make the girl sleep, but how? May knows the doctor has left sleeping draughts for Effie and so looks amongst the bottles on the night stand. She reads the labels quickly and finds the bottle she is looking for. It is empty. She utters an oath under her breath. There is a knock at the door and the doctor is announced. May composes herself.

'How is the patient today?' Doctor Stewart asks moving to the side of Effie's bed. The girl is quiet and smiles up at the doctor. 'It always makes me sleep,' she says dreamily. May thinks on her feet and taking Effie's hand to distract her, says to the doctor. 'I was just telling Miss Driscoll she hasn't any sleeping draught left Doctor Stewart. 'I just checked the bottle and it is empty.'

'Aye, that is one reason I have called this morning. I only left enough to last until today. I did not know if she would need anything stronger and thought to start her on the lowest dosage first. It seems from what she says it is doing its job.' He lifts Effie's limp wrist and takes her pulse. His face does not give away his thoughts.

'How has she been— Any more bilious attacks?'

'No doctor, not since the night before last,' May lies.'

'Good, that is something to be thankful for. Has she eaten anything? May shakes her head. 'I suggest some bone broth initially and let us hope Miss Effie can keep it down. Hopefully we are turning a corner,' he says looking at the patient who is slumped back on the pillows. At least, May thinks, she is quiet again.

The doctor takes medicines and the sleeping draught from his bag and puts them on the night stand. 'Very well I will call again tomorrow. I will order some tests to confirm my suspicions Miss May – it is Miss May is it not?' The doctor thinks he is on safe ground as he has already asked the butler how the mistress of the house does and has been told she is resting.

May nods. 'Your suspicions, doctor?'

'Aye, I had at first thought that Miss Effie might have an ulcer like her poor unfortunate brother but I have read an article in The Lancet which leads me to another conclusion. I think Miss Effie may be suffering from a viral attack. We shall see. When she is recovered a little I intend to do tests on her blood and liver function as well as test her stomach acids and spleen. I will do the tests in the morning. They will tell me what I need to know.'

May is stunned. If the doctor carries out these tests what will he find? Traces of nicotine in her blood no doubt! May cannot have him run the tests yet she cannot think how she is to prevent him.

To his face she smiles and says, 'Thank you doctor. It is good to know you are up to date with current medical practices. I am sure Effie will soon be on the road to recovery.

That night Effie Claire dies.

2

Holy Moses! The doctor has ordered a post mortem. April has taken to her bed and May, well May is wondering what to do for the best. The plan I think you will have to agree has gone awry.

May is in the nursery rocking Teddy in her arms. He is smiling and cooing contentedly. She has not slept for days. Between caring for April, who is brought even lower, May has been running the house which is now in double mourning. She also has to contend with Blasted Beatrice "helping out". If only the damned woman would go away.

Alistair has been at George Square every day. Of course he is grieving, both for his sister as well as his brother. He is organising another funeral as well as sorting his siblings' affairs.

In addition he is looking for someone to blame. It is after he has insulted the doctor by calling him a "Quack" that the post mortem is ordered. May wishes she had made a gift of whisky to Alistair too.

'Might as well be hung for a sheep as a lamb,' she

mutters when he finally leaves taking Bea home with him.

He has been poking about all day and upsetting the servants. Edith is in high dudgeon, 'I would have resigned my position Miss May, if it wasn't for the fact that I care for the mistress so much. I could not leave her in the state she's in but Mr Alistair goes too far. He has questioned me like I was a naughty school girl!'

It is only right Alistair is upset she thinks but he is now using the full force of his position as a wealthy man to get the police to act and act quickly. He has taken it upon himself to carry out his own investigation and now he has convinced the police there is foul play and ordered them to look into the matter.

May suspects Alistair is blaming the doctor, thinking him incapable. He has accused him in her hearing of treating his siblings with some unorthodox quackery. 'I want him struck off and hung for murder,' she heard him yell at the inspector who was called in yesterday.

May thinks to remove herself from George Square. Perhaps a little recuperation by the sea?

The Mediterranean Sea that is.

If Alistair cannot blame the doctor he will have someone else's neck in the noose. No one it seems is safe. Flossie, making herself useful in the servants' quarters reported to her mistress she heard him interrogating the below stairs staff.

'He asked if anyone had seen anything suspicious.'

'Oh, did he indeed and had anyone?'

'The maid with red hair, the dim one – she said she found a whisky bottle under Miss Effie's bed! She told him about it straight away – he terrified her by saying her cap was askew! She's frightened of her own shadow that one so him towering over her was a threat and a torment she couldn't tolerate.

May's stomach plummets. 'She told him about a bottle she found under the bed?' May asks trying to keep the worry from her voice. Flossie shrugs. 'She possibly thought to confess before he sees into her soul and accuses her again of being slovenly.' Flossie laughs unsympathetically. 'She's a right little sniveller. When Mr Driscoll said she should have told the housekeeper what she had found I thought she was going to pee her pants.'

May is worried. 'What else did she say?'

'She told him that you took it from her. Said she was that relieved you weren't going to report her for not cleaning the room proper, that's why she never told anyone about it. Her tongue right ran away with her silly little tart, she looked terrified she would be let go.'

May says calmly. 'He is beside himself with grief no doubt, poor man.'

'He might be but he tore a strip off her anyway. Told her she should have kept a better eye on his sister when she was so ill. Mixing alcohol and medicine can be dangerous, he said. You have been remiss in your work young lady. She burst into tears at that point.' Flossie laughs heartlessly.

'Then he says – Did you say Miss May knew about this empty bottle? She told him you took it from her.' Flossie grins 'Then she suddenly goes bright red and says that at least she thinks it was Miss May – who knows, she says,

I can't tell 'em apart.' Flossie chuckles to herself. 'Well I suppose she was singing like a canary hoping she wasn't going to be let go.'

'And were her fears warranted?'

Flossie laughs. 'He sacked her on the spot.'

♠

Alistair marches into the sitting room and confronts May. He knows April has barely risen from her bed since his brother's death so thinks he can be sure who took the bottle from the maid.

'Why did you not tell anyone about the whisky bottle in Effie's room?' he says brusquely.'

May is relieved to have been forewarned no doubt.

'Good evening Alistair,' May replies pleasantly. She is cucumber cool. She smiles benignly up at him from her chair by the fire. How could she ever have considered joining with him she wonders? The deaths have aged him. His face is grey and his hair is in need of attention she notices. He is behaving in a most ungracious manner.

You have to hand it to May, she is unflappable. Beneath her composed exterior she has to be, well, extremely worried, shall we say. Yet to all around her she is calmness itself. She has spent the day following in Alistair's wake and pacifying the servants. They think her a saint.

'I had no idea it was pertinent, how is it relevant do you think?' She wants to know which way his mind is heading but is soon relieved when he says. 'I don't know but it may not have helped her condition if she was mixing alcohol with the medication that fool of a doctor prescribed. Did you tell him she had taken whisky?' he barks.

'I did not, I was unaware she had been drinking. In fact I came to the conclusion she had drunk little or none of it.' May smiles a reassuring smile. She knows the effect a smile from her can have on men. Alistair is no different to the rest of them.

'Then how do you account for the bottle being empty?' May sees he is uncertain.

'When the maid left I noticed a damp patch on the carpet by the bed. At first I assumed it was where Effie had been sick and where subsequently the maid had cleaned it up. Yet I had not seen Effie be sick on the floor. A bowl had always been offered – excepting for one time on the night of Edward's funeral, when she vomited on the bed covers. I got down and smelt the carpet,' she wrinkles her nose prettily, 'it smelled of spirits. I presumed Effie had indeed tried to take a drink but had dropped the bottle and it had emptied and rolled under the bed. She was far too debilitated to recover it. She was very weak; I had to lift her in my arms when she had a sip of water as I'm sure you remember.'

Alistair is subdued. May suspects he has no idea what point he is trying to make and now he feels foolish.

'I am exhausted.' He slumps in the chair opposite his sister-in-law with his head in his hands. 'I am sorry May, please forgive me – the strain is beginning to tell. I have slept little since all this began. I know you nursed my little sister determinedly, the servants have all said so and now I feel mean spirited. Forgive me.'

'Think nothing of it Alistair. It is the strain of waiting for the funeral while the medics do their infernal tests. I hate to think of Effie above ground for a day longer than is necessary.'

We of course, know why don't we? May must be on tenter hooks waiting for the knock on the door. She surely knows that it will come. Why would it not?

The post mortem will show traces of nicotine present in Effie's body. May fears the police will become even more suspicious and exhume Edward's body. They will follow the trail from the head gardener, Robins, to her door. She will be accused. There will be little point in denying the facts. She will hang. She is certain of it.

May resolves to convince her sister they must get away for the benefit of their health. They must escape and quickly.

May's health, that is.

She cannot go without her sister and son; that would look callous but April not only refuses to leave her home she refuses to leave the bed. May begins to feel cornered. She has tried, in vain, to convince April to take a rest cure. May feels panic begin to rise and admits to herself she needs another scheme, one where she puts distance between herself and the law.

She goes to April's room and sighs as she looks at the wreck that is her sister. April's nerves have never been strong but now she is a pale imitation of May.

'My love – how are you? Is the nerve tonic Dr Stewart gave you helping,' May sits on the bed.

'I don't think so it just makes me drowsy. I cannot sleep without the draught he has given me but then I have bad dreams and think I would sooner lay awake. Have you been to see Teddy this morning? I was just about to go to the nursery.' She has clearly not been out of bed yet; her hair is unbrushed and her face pale and waxy.

'He is fed and is in the garden with Lizzie. Do not trouble yourself. Have you given any more thought to what I said about a rest cure? An Italian or Swiss spa resort would be lovely at this time of year. Just the tonic you need to perk you up. Remember how well you felt when you took the waters at Whitby. It would be a distraction, a diversion for you. I can organise it all, you should have nothing to do but enjoy it. We can take Teddy, Lizzie and Edith. We will manage easily.' May stokes her sister's hair.

'I cannot. How can I go anywhere until after Effie's funeral?'

May assumes a voice she would use if she were addressing a troubled child, 'You would be going under your doctor's orders. Of course you can go. You can do anything you like. I will ask him for a recommendation for where to go so you should get the best possible care.'

'It would be nice to get away from all this.' her twin agrees, It would be pleasant to be outdoors in warm sunshine. The Scottish weather is so dreary. My mood feels as grey as the weather.' May is pleased at this turn of events. With luck they could be gone by the end of the week.

'Very well if you are sure you can arrange it,' April says smiling wanly, but only of course if you promise to come with me.' .

3

It is too late. All May has thought comes to pass. The knock on the door she has been waiting for comes before her travel plans are completed.

April, still weak, her nerves in shreds, had relapsed and could not be prevailed upon to leave. May could not find it in herself to leave her sister or her son. Now it is too late.

April does not know the police are at the door. She is sedated and sleeping.

May is with Teddy in the morning room. She is showing him the garden through the window. She does not make a scene when the police are shown in. She takes Teddy in her arms and holds him close before kissing his sweet, plump cheek. She rings for Lizzie to take him to the nursery and is led away to the police cells. The servants are stunned and would all gladly vouch for her if only they were asked. They are not asked.

April, alerted to what is happening by Tibbs, is barely capable of getting out of bed but with help from Edith she manages to get dressed and follows in her sister's wake to the police station.

'What is happening? I do not understand, she asks Inspector Fraser who is in charge of the case. 'Your sister has confessed to murdering your husband and Effie Claire Driscoll.' April faints clean away.

When she comes round she is told she is not allowed to see May. April is stunned at this turn of events. 'No! Why are you saying this, my husband had an ulcer, Dr Stewart said so. Ask him, he will tell you. It says so on his death certificate.' April looks frantically at the Inspector.

'I am sorry to cause you further pain Mrs Driscoll but we, the police, will have to exhume your husband's body – I am very sorry for the distress this will cause. Tests will show he was killed with poison, of that I am certain. The same poison that killed your husband also killed your sister-in-law. We suspect Nicotine.'

April becomes incoherent. She cannot understand what she is hearing. First she loses her husband then Effie, now she is to lose the one person in all the world she cannot live without; her twin.

♥

The Chief Inspector sits behind his mahogany desk and glares at Inspector Fraser. 'Come on man, what you say is fanciful at the very least. These are important people, they are rich and have influence.' The Inspector has just told him of the latest turn of events in the Driscoll's murder enquiry.

'It is true, Mrs April Driscoll has also confessed to the murder. She says she has just as strong a motive as her sister and I am inclined to believe her. The fact the ladies are identical is not helping matters. We aren't even sure we arrested the correct twin in the first place!'

The inspector, under the gaze of his Chief shuffles uncomfortably.

'When their servants were interviewed it soon became apparent they never seemed to know one sister from the other. The only way to tell them apart was Mrs Driscoll's wedding band but she took to leaving it off when she was with child as her fingers swelled. Now they wear mourning black not even their clothes can tell them apart!'

'You say there are no distinguishing marks – nothing that can identify one from the other?'

'Not that we are aware of or that they are confessing.' The Chief Inspector shakes his head. 'Perhaps there is some other way to identify them?'

'It seems one of the sisters, April Driscoll, was unable to have a baby so the other twin, May, provided the couple with a child. I am hoping a doctor can examine them both to determine the one who has given birth.'

'Ah, now that should be conclusive.'

'It seems Captain Driscoll was kept in ignorance about the birth, then the truth came out and there was a rift. That seems to be the cause of his demise.'

'I should expect there was a rift! Dear God what the rich get up to these days.' The Chief Inspector rubs his mutton chops with his finger and thumb. 'So the crux of the matter is placing the murderer at the scene as it were. I can see the difficulty. If, as we suspect, it was nicotine in the slug killer that did for them then it could conceivably have been administered at a distance – if it were premeditated.'

'By way of the single malt we suspect. What a waste of good whisky,' Inspector Fraser says mournfully.

'There is an Aunt it seems. She is coming from London. She might be able to say which is which? She is on her way north. If she cannot tell them apart then what hope have we got? We shall have to have a double hanging!'

'We need to get this right. Imagine the repercussions if it later comes to pass we have convicted the wrong sister. We will be a laughing stock.

♦

April sits in her cell waiting to be interviewed by Inspector Fraser. She is at her wits end. She misses May and Ted. When Edward died she had thought life could not get any worse. Now this!

She has always known May has a ruthless streak – a self protection to shield herself from life's troubles. Since they were children she has always been the stronger one, the one who protected them both. When they were at the brothel it was May who had plotted to get them away but she never thought her twin could kill, especially not Edward. There must be some other explanation but April cannot think what.

April has chosen to put herself in this position, confessing to murder to cover for her sister; she does not regret it. That is not to say she is not frightened. She is terrified. April tells herself that May deserves to have a chance of happiness, to raise her own son, she has been selfless in giving him up. This is the way to repay her.

Now Edward is gone she wants to go to be with him.

April knows herself to be too broken, too lost, to live without Edward, she would rather die than spend the rest of her life without him. Even the thought of Ted is not enough to deter her from this path; after all he is not of her body. If only she can convince the Inspector she is the guilty party. She must save May at all costs – after all she cannot live without her twin.

They say love is blind but April seems to have given up the ghost. She is able to delude herself it seems. Grief and guilt are a heady combination.

April is taken to an interview room where the bearded Inspector is waiting.

'Good morning Mrs Driscoll.' She sits opposite him. 'I hope you are as well as can be expected under the circumstances?' He remembers his Chief's warning. These people are prominent in Glasgow society, he needs to tread carefully.

April looks down at her hands neatly folded in her lap and says nothing. 'You know you are entitled to a lawyer. I see you still have no one to represent you. Are you sure it is wise?'

April, mute, continues to stare at her hands for some minutes then looks up at the Inspector and stares hard at him with her ocean blue eyes. Fraser, for a few seconds, is dazzled by her beauty. Most women he interviews are pathetic, raggedy things: whores, petty thieves, poor, hapless creatures brought low through poverty and misuse. He cannot believe either of these fine looking twins can have committed double murder.

'I do not need representation. I did it. I killed them.

I have already confessed. Why have I not been charged and been brought before the court? I hope my sister has been released, Ted needs his mother.' The words gush from her lips but she is perfectly composed.

'As I said yesterday Mrs Driscoll, we need proof. Your sister has also confessed to the murders. I cannot simply take your word for it – or hers for that matter. I urge you to think carefully. Perhaps you are shielding your twin? The bond between you makes you do this perhaps? It is possible she is doing the same thing to protect you. If convicted you will hang by the neck, have you thought of that? What of your son? Should you want to leave him an orphan?' He pauses and looks keenly at the woman's beguiling face.

'The baby is not mine. May is the mother and my husband the father. When I found that my husband had impregnated my sister I was devastated. Then he cast May aside and made her leave our home. I could not tolerate him near me after what he has done. He was a monster.'

It is breaking her heart to speak of Edward this way yet she has to save May. 'I wanted my sister more than I wanted him. Is that so hard to understand? Blood is thicker than water they say. I said all this yesterday Inspector Fraser why do you not believe me? I cannot think any woman would want a husband who has betrayed her in such a way, especially when he has been false with her own twin sister!'

'Yes, I remember clearly what you said Mrs Driscoll, but you have to realise your sister also says she murdered your husband and also has a compelling reason for murdering him.'

He shuffles in his chair and changes his line of questioning. 'I understand you have a strong motive for killing Edward Driscoll,' he moves papers in front of him, 'but why would you want to kill your sister-in-law? By all accounts you were on friendly terms with her. She was Godmother to your son. You did not elaborate on this point yesterday.'

'May's son, Inspector – not mine. I can explain Effie's death. It was sheer misadventure, and I regret it most sincerely. She accidentally took some of the poison meant for Edward. I had no intention of murdering her, as you say I had no reason. I was very fond of her and regret her death immensely. She is an innocent victim and I deserve to die.'

'How did she come to accidentally take the poison Mrs Driscoll? You were not altogether clear how you administered the toxicant to either of the victims?' Fraser hopes to trick her here. April, though flustered, gives him her most beautiful smile.

She has not spoken to May remember, so is uncertain exactly what her sister has used to kill them or how.

She has deduced it must have been poison and she is almost certain it was administered via the whisky. She remembers May being angry that Alistair had quizzed her about a whisky bottle that had gone missing. She also knows, even when Edward was refusing food, he was still taking whisky. She had given it to him herself as he had pleaded with her saying it helped with the pain. Technically she has poisoned him even though it was inadvertently she tells herself. She struggles to keep her emotions in check. She feels exhaustion weighing her down

She also struggles with reality it seems. Has she forgotten he was bedding her own sister?

'I thought we had gone over this point yesterday Inspector. I put the poison in my husband's favourite single malt. He partook of it most days, sometimes he drank too much of it. I knew if I wanted to kill him that was the best way as no one else in the house touched the stuff. I put in small amounts so he would not taste it. He had a good palette and would notice if a large amount had been added. Effie Claire, the only other person to like it was in France. Guests were never offered his favourite brand.' She realises she has hit upon the method when she sees the look on Inspector Fraser's face. It was a gamble which has paid off.

♦

The Inspector is becoming frustrated. He seems no further on with his investigation. He was hoping a night in the cells would have brought reason to Mrs Driscoll. It appears not.

The inspector puts the same questions to May. She too is intransigent and sticking to her story, refusing to budge. The only concrete fact he has in her favour is how she got the poison. The head gardener has said he sent a bottle of slug killer to May's house after she complained of an infestation. She therefore had the means at her disposal and she clearly had motive. April also had the means but closer to hand, he tells himself but is her motive as strong? He sighs in frustration.

He returns to his office and puts his head in his hands. He is under pressure to convict the right twin yet still he cannot decide which of them has done the deed.

Maybe they planned it together. Are they both in on it he wonders? Knowing they are caught what if they have both confessed to put the cat amongst the pigeons? Is it a cover to confuse and add uncertainty? He remembers seeing a play where a type of fog was pumped onto the stage. It had the effect of concealing and adding to the mystery. He feels he is being blinded in an attempt to cover up the crime.

'Can I prove they are both guilty?' he mutters to himself. He knows his own neck is on the line; whichever twin did it, he must be able to prove it beyond reasonable doubt. If they both admit to the murders will it introduce an element of doubt in the minds of the jurors or will it strengthen his case? He imagines for a moment, twelve good men and true being faced with sentencing one or both of the ravishingly beautiful twins. He fears, men being men, one smile from their comely, rosebud lips will see his conviction quashed. All his hard work will be for nothing. He rubs his whiskers irritably. He looks at his notes to try to find clarity.

Just as he is pondering his next move his Sergeant announces Lady Elizabeth Vennor. The aunt has arrived. He stands, offers her first his hand and then a seat. She is an attractive woman. God save me from beautiful women he thinks to himself pityingly. They are causing him to question his own judgement!

Such is the lot with men. Show them a beautiful face and their wits move location.

The more he thinks about the case the more inclined he is to let them both off as he cannot envisage either of them committing even a minor infringement of the law. Now here comes the aunt to cast even more uncertainty.

Lady Vennor must be in her early forties he guesses, yet she is still a comely looking woman. She has the same blonde hair and the identical, penetrating, ocean blue eyes. He is captivated.

The inspector has only ever seen the grey sea of Glasgow harbour, you would think he were a poet not a police officer.

When they have been introduced he begins questioning her. He has never had to question a Lady of rank before. Gently and kindly he probes, hoping she will be able to shed some light on the situation. He notes her fine clothes and reserved demeanour. She looks out of place here in the police station.

'Thank you for travelling to Scotland, Lady Vennor. I am sorry it is under such tragic circumstances. Can I offer you some refreshment? Though sadly it will be poor fare I am afraid.'

Elizabeth is playing the role of Aunt to the injured parties. She is altogether a Lady of means, with manners and affectations to match. Her accent would cut glass. Anyone watching the performance would believe she is to the manor born. She looks from under her lashes at the unfortunate detective.

'Could you please tell me are there any differences between your nieces which are not evident by just looking at their general appearance? Does either one of them have a birth mark or a mole perhaps? Some distinctive mark on their, er, person, I wonder.' The Inspector is flustered under Elizabeth's gaze at having to allude to the beautiful bodies of his suspects.

'They are identical twins Inspector Fraser. Identical in every way. They have nothing, so far as I am aware, which you or anyone else could see to tell them apart.'

Her demeanour is positively aristocratic; no one would believe she is the daughter of a fish gutter and a whaler.

'Yet you say you can separate them? How so, if there is no discernible difference I venture to ask?' he smiles hoping to disarm her.

'Je ne sais quoi Inspector.' Elizabeth says tossing her blonde curls causing further disquiet to the policeman. 'It is hard to put into words, yet it is something that I, and I alone, have been able to do. Since their mother, my dear sister died of course. Obviously she knew them apart. I can only suppose it is because we are related and I have known them since the moment they were born that I am able to recognise one from the other.'

Well that part is certainly true. Elizabeth has known them since the moment they were delivered of course.

She carefully mis-remembers that one twin has a mole near her left buttock. She is as yet not cognisant of the whole of the facts of the case against her "nieces" and so does not want to say too much in case she incriminates one or the other of them. She may not always have been a good mother but she has no wish to see either of her daughters hang.

'Am I allowed to see my nieces Inspector? I have been distraught as you may well imagine, wondering how this ghastly situation has come about.' She flutters a pale hand in front of her face, the white lace touches the corner of a dry eye.

'I would be happy to let you see them for the purpose of identification but I am afraid you will not be allowed to converse with either of them.'

'You say they have both confessed to the crime? Could it be that they are both innocent and covering for a third person Inspector?' Elizabeth smiles sweetly and flutters her lashes. The Inspector's defences slip a little further.

'Who, for instance, Lady Vennor? We have no reason to suspect anyone else is involved in the case. Your nieces are the only suspects. There is no one else with motive.'

Elizabeth acts downcast. Before she can cause him more disquiet he shows her through to the interview room where May is seated and staring at the wall in front of her.

'If you could confirm for me which of your nieces this is please.'

She looks through the grille in the door. 'That is May,' she says shocked to see her niece wearing prison clothes. The last time she saw her she looked very grand. 'Is she arrested? Is no one representing either of them? Who is acting as their defence.' She gives the policeman a withering look. 'They are both extremely wealthy young ladies and are used to the better things in life. Must she wear those rags? You must be aware the Driscolls are probably the richest family in Scotland Inspector Fraser. I hope you know what you are about. Mr Alistair Driscoll will not take kindly to his sisters-in-law being mistreated!' Fraser's heart sinks further.

'I am indeed aware. The press too, now that the story is leaked, are alert to the fact they are being questioned.

Neither is yet arrested and both are declining lawyers, which in my humble opinion is madness, under the circumstances. Murder is a hanging offence, double murder would mean there would be no reprieve. However, Mr Alistair Driscoll has not, as yet, been to see me regarding his sisters-in-law.' The Inspector is of the opinion Alistair suspects one or other of the twins and does not want to jeopardise the enquiry.

Next Elizabeth is shown April, to be certain she has picked the correct twin. She is in no doubt and is then taken back to the Inspector's office from where she prepares to take her leave. She has confirmed what he thought he already knew. At least he has had it established he has arrested the right woman. He is relieved. Almost.

'I shall today engage representation for both my nieces, whether they consent or not. I have already made enquires and aim to find the very best man in the country. I advise you Inspector, to be certain of your facts. Any loopholes will be exposed. If my nieces are charged and when, as I expect they are cleared, you in turn, will be charged with defamation of character – twice over if necessary.' She smiles seductively at him as though she were inviting him to kiss her not threatening him. She makes her exit with a flourish.

4

Inspector Fraser is at Alistair Driscoll's office waiting to interview him. He is interested to get a brother's perspective on the murders.

'I am sorry to keep you waiting Fraser,' Alistair says as he enters the office. 'Can I get you something to drink?' The inspector declines, though he could well do with a tot of something. He notices the strain on Alistair's face.

'Sir, you will be aware I now have two confessions to the murder of your brother and sister.'

'If you have any sense you will release April. She is grief stricken and has undoubtedly confessed as a result of the strain, she is near breaking point I imagine. She could not hurt a fly. She is the most gentle of women and a most attentive mother. She would not wish to orphan her son. It is grief which has temporarily unhinged her I am sure of it. Her sister is manipulative, a cunning minx in my opinion.'

'Thank you sir, I will bear your comments in mind. I am sorry to have to share details, delicate, em, details sir, that ordinarily you may not have been aware of regarding your brother's marriage. Details that perhaps you would never have been privy to had this tragedy not occurred.'

'Inspector, my brother and I were very close. I am sure there is nothing you can tell me I do not already know.' Alistair pours himself a brandy.

'You are aware then sir that Edward Junior's rightful mother is May and not April?' Fraser waits for the point to sink in. 'Your brother fathered the boy and May gave birth to him. April is the child's aunt – rightfully speaking.'

Alistair's eyes open wide. 'Don't be ridiculous man!' The inspector sees the brothers weren't as close as Alistair thought. The Inspector reiterates his point adding more detail.

'It seems when Mrs Driscoll could not have children the sisters devised a plan to give your brother the heir he wanted.'

'This is madness! He would have told me! Who has told you this scurrilous lie?'

'Both your sisters-in-law, sir. I am sorry but it seems it is the truth. April used padding to make her look like she was expecting a baby, while May went to England to give birth away from prying eyes.'

It takes time for Alistair to recover his senses. The Inspector waits patiently to ask the questions he hopes will help him piece together this mystery.

'On the night of the funeral when only family were present I understand you offered Miss Driscoll some of your brother's favourite single malt before she retired.'

'Yes that is correct.'

'Can you tell me where you got the bottle from please

sir?'

He thinks for a moment. 'I asked Tibbs if there was any in the cellar. I thought it apt to toast Edward with his best loved tipple. Tibbs said there was a newly opened bottle in the library and brought it to me.'

'Did anyone else partake of the whisky?'

'Just Effie. She took a sip then took the rest of the glass to bed with her.'

'The rest of the glass or the rest of the bottle sir?'

'Just the glass. I put the bottle down, on a side table I think. Or I could have put it on the drinks tray, who knows? I cannot remember, why is it important?'

'The nicotine which killed your brother and sister was administered in the single malt. We believe several bottles had been doctored with the result that they both died after ingesting the malt whisky. Effie, must have gotten hold of, or was given, the rest of the bottle from the library. That is what killed her.'

'Are you certain? So the incompetent doctor is not to blame?'

'No sir, although he was in error suggesting your brother had an ulcer – the post mortem proves otherwise. Had he known he was being poisoned—'

'He might have been saved! I'll have his head for this. Not only have I lost my brother, I have also lost my sister. The fault is his in part for mis-diagnosing the ulcer. I shall prosecute and see him in hell.' The Inspector leaves Alistair none the wiser but certain that Alistair Driscoll is not a man he wants to cross.

♣

A female warder takes May to the hospital wing where she is examined by a doctor.'

When did you give birth to your child?' he asks. May tells him the date of the birth. 'The birth was normal?'

'It was,' she answers. 'Although he was premature I think.' How different this experience from her pre-natal visits to Dr Sinclair she thinks as the doctor examines her intimately.

April suffers a similar invasion. 'You are unable to conceive?'The doctor asks.

'I can conceive but not bring a baby to term.'

'You have had several pregnancies?'

'Several miscarriages, yes.'

'No live births,' he says without an ounce of feeling.

'Sadly no,' she murmurs feeling the humiliation of the examination. What they are hoping to ascertain from the probing she is unsure. They are told nothing and are taken back to the cells.

Later Inspector Fraser reads the doctor's report. The results are inconclusive. Either of the women could be the boy's mother. Fraser had not known Mrs Driscoll had suffered miscarriages. He thought to prove which woman was the boy's mother by discounting the one who had not given birth. He is working on the assumption, falsely as it happens, that a mother would not put her head in the noose and leave her offspring orphaned.

He does not know May's character does he?

♠

The expensive lawyer argues the case against his clients cannot be proven as their identity is called into question.

He contests the fact the police cannot provide evidence that either one of them killed Edward and Effie Driscoll and so insists his clients be set free.

He can argue all he likes. Fraser is not about to let either twin off the hook.

Inspector Fraser is hauled back to report to his Chief Inspector.

'We are no further forward than when last we met as I understand it Fraser?'

'No Sir,' the Inspector admits looking at his size eleven boots.

'Although we are certain now which twin is which, we still cannot prove which one is a killer? Of course Lady Vennor could be lying but why would she?'

'Exactly Sir. Someone, separately or together administered the poison. We have to decide who to charge with the crime. Do we charge Mrs Driscoll who has motive and opportunity or do we charge May who likewise, also has motive and opportunity and an empty bottle in her unmentionables drawer. Are they in it together and playing a long game hoping to confuse and cast doubt? Whichever way you look at it the evidence is circumstantial. No one can vouch for seeing either twin administer poison but one of them did. Unless the butler did it,' he laughs.

'What of the twelve bottles? They are reputed to have been a gift from a client?'

'Yes Sir. We looked into that. The bottles were ordered and paid for at the wine merchants in cash. He does not remember who placed the order. I banked on the fact the wine merchant would remember a beautiful lady making the order. He says the order was placed, as far as he can remember, by a man, says he does not have ladies buy from him directly. He has lady clients of course; ladies usually have staff to order their wines and spirits he says. I checked with Tibbs, the Driscoll's butler, who would normally do the ordering and he said no one at George Square had ordered the bottles. They did not come from their usual wine merchant'. All this talk of whisky is giving him a thirst.

'I checked his records and the last order for that particular brand of single malt had been for two dozen bottles. His records showed all those were accounted for. When bottles come back to his pantry empty he makes a note so the cellar does not run dry! How the other half live!'

'You have been unable to trace the person ordering the whisky but what of the client, what does he say?'

'He says he did not send any such gift. His name is Crocker. We have checked him out and can find nothing to link him with the alcohol. He is a Methodist so would be unlikely to send whisky anyway!'

'The poison was definitely in the whisky bottle that was found in May's dressing table drawer?'

'It was – remiss of her to have kept it. It is incriminating and the only bit of concrete evidence we have though her lawyer would say it had been planted! Possibly she had not had chance to dispose of it or she forgot about it. Apparently she was by her sister-in-law's bed night and day over the last few days before the girl died and also looking after her widowed sister.'

'We are at stalemate then Fraser?' The Chief raises his

eyebrows.

'Usually we are eager to make criminals confess yet here we are hoping someone will retract their confession so we might at least hang the correct lady!'

'So it would seem Sir.'

'I know you are not a betting man, but if you were to put money on it who would you go for Fraser?'

The Inspector looks pained. 'Can we just charge Robins the head gardener? That would make life simple. Seriously though Sir, I would still plump for May. She seems the most likely to me. She had the most to gain, while April had the most to lose.'

Again the Chief raises a bushy eyebrow. 'In what way does May have most to gain?'

'May had been separated from her son, she had been ousted from George Square and she had been thrown over by her lover, the father of her child, in what she must have thought, a callous and cruel manner. We only have the twins' accounts of course, as to why the rift occurred but safe to say May's circumstances and prospects were reduced. George Square is a magnificent place, riches beyond my ken. The mansion has every luxury and modern convenience. Gas light, heating, servants who glide about inconspicuously! Even indoor water closets! The best of everything! Whilst May's new address is hardly a tenement block, it is less grand shall we say? Less well appointed and the address not so prestigious, which matters to people like them. She would certainly feel the reduction in her circumstances. She seems a self confident, opinionated woman who would not take kindly to being ordered to leave all she holds dear. Her loss of position and the loss of a sister and son would be galling I would imagine.' He scratches his head as he asks, 'Where does your gut lead you Sir, if you don't mind me asking?'

'If I were to speculate, and I am by no means sure, I would go for both twins working in tandem. It is as you say; May has the most to gain. She had already moved back to George Square to her son and her sister, it is evident there is a strong bond between them. If April had acted alone she would have had to show tremendous courage and from what you have told me and from her confession, I don't believe she is brave enough to work on her own.

May seems the schemer here to my mind. I would venture she put the weapon, as it were, in April's hands, in the form of the whisky bottles. All April had to do was make sure Driscoll drank them. Granted May had procured the slug killer but it could quite as easily have been put in the bottles at George Square. Unlike the butler, the head gardener was lax with his records, not really knowing how much of the stuff he had at any one time. It was a preparation of his own devising. He made it up as and when he needed it. He did not throw away any surplus but kept it in an unlocked shed. It is common practice for gardeners to use Nicotine. I use it myself to spray greenfly,' he added as an afterthought.

The Chief Inspector takes two tumblers from his desk drawer and pours blended whisky into both and hands one to Fraser.

'April also had a lot to lose. Her sister being the most important amongst all the riches you listed. She had her longed for son but she also had a husband who was unfaithful. Ladies of any rank do not want to be cheated on, especially under their own roof and by their own flesh and blood.' He stops and adds a little levity to the proceedings. 'Had I been in Mrs Driscoll's place I would have been tempted to bump off May. After all, it was she who had caused the rift in the first place it seems. Firstly by having an affair with Driscoll and then by giving birth to a son. April Driscoll must have felt the pain keenly when she could not have a child of her own. She would no doubt blame herself.' The Chief sighs. 'All this speculation gets us nowhere. Without concrete evidence we might as well toss a coin to decide whose confession to believe!'

5

The case is over. The accused has been tried and the defence has failed. May is convicted of the murder of Captain Edward Driscoll and his sister Effie Claire.

There has been much interest in the case, especially since the press unearthed the twins' sordid past. Far from them being ladies of rank they are found to be "Ladies of the night". Headlines splashed across the papers such as "Whitby Whores: Which Twin Killed Wealthy Husband." and "Twin Whores, Double Killing" have graced news-stands both in Scotland and England.

To Inspector Fraser their past had put a whole new light on the matter. 'I had imagined they were gentlewomen!' He tells his superior. He now sees they are both nothing more than common harlots. 'Aye they swapped a brothel for a mansion but they are still whores,' the chief agrees.

'We were duped by Lady Vennor as well! She was just a common actress before her marriage, just one step up from a tart, the title paid for by laying on her back.' It has been a salutary lesson for him; never judge a book by its cover.

♥

After heart searching missives back and forth the sisters finally agree it will be April who withdraws her confession. Their QC conveys the messages that convince April to retract:

April my love none of this is of your doing. I need to atone for all I have done. If I had listened to you in the first place we should not be sitting here now facing death.

She writes from her prison cell:

It was my jealousy and greed that has brought us here. You are guilty of nothing but loving and trusting me too much. I am ashamed and sorry for all the pain I have caused you.

Of course there are hurdles to jump before April is freed; the police need to be sure they have the right murderer after all the media attention they do not want to end up with egg on their faces.

Their QC Jonathan Wetherly, an astute, clever man makes sure April is released. It seems money can wash sheets clean of any stain.

May is sentenced to hang. Ironically she is to hang on the morning of her birthday; she is still so young. She should have all her life before her.

Wetherly continues working to commute the death sentence to life imprisonment and assures April he can spare May the noose. He is arrogant and experienced but it is proving more difficult than he imagined.

He tells April as kindly as he can. 'After all the speculation the police and the judicial service are determined to have their pound of flesh I am afraid.'

April looks ready to drop. 'A double murder has been committed and she will hang for them I am afraid.'

It seems everyone agrees May deserves to die. Effie Claire's death has been particularly mourned by the public as she was a beautiful, young heiress cut down when she had everything to live for. It is said the girl befriended the treacherous twins and was murdered because she knew too much. The newspapers made much of contrasting her with the manipulative, murderous May.

During her short life April has learnt not to trust anyone except her sister. For a while she did begin to trust Edward but sees now this was a grievous error. She is determined to see her sister before she hangs.

'I have to see my sister one last time,' she tells Wetherly, 'I cannot live the rest of my life without one last...' The tears stream down her pale cheeks. She does not trust the QC at all. He is arrogant and sure of himself. The case has raised his profile and it has gone to his head she thinks.

'I will do all I can of course to arrange for you to see Miss May but the police are—'

'You will be amply rewarded for your trouble sir. I am sure the police need not be bothered with this matter. Surely you know which palms to grease!'

For two weeks he is unsuccessful. Eventually at the eleventh hour a meeting is scheduled for the day before the hanging. April is thankful and relieved but does not know how she will get through the visit.

♦

Mrs April Driscoll waits in an antechamber. The female warder is to conduct a body search. This is in case April is trying to smuggle in a weapon so May can cheat the hangman she presumes.

May might well still be scheming but she is not planning to stab herself. You would bet she will think of something more audacious than that if she can summon the strength.

The trial, the loss and the hardship of gaol have all taken their toll on her. Not that you would know it to look at her. Her skin glows; no prison pallor for her. Her blonde hair still silky, is dressed simply yet elegantly in a chignon. Even the prison garb she wears looks understated and demure.

♥

The warder looks at April, she is the spitting image of the prisoner in the condemned cell she thinks. It is disconcerting. She has never met identical twins before. The warder begins the body search.

'Please excuse the intrusion Madam.'

She runs her hands over the finest wool she has ever touched, so soft it feels like silk. Mrs Driscoll is not wearing stays, she notices and is surprised. The warder expects to feel whale bone. Most women wear a corset. Often wives trying to smuggle in a sharp knife do so in their stays hoping the warden will mistake the feel of steel for whalebone.

She notes, and admires, the new smaller, fashionable bustle. She lifts up the petticoats to check there is nothing concealed under the bustle's cage. 'Sorry Madam but I have my orders.' Mrs Driscoll, glowing like a furnace at the intimate intrusion, smoothes her grey, day dress back in place as the warder steps away. The search has revealed nothing untoward.

'You are allowed thirty minutes,' the warder says, her voice matter of fact. 'You can't take your reticule in there I'm afraid – leave it with me please.' From a bunch of clanging keys hanging from a chain at her waist, she selects one. After looking through the grille in the heavy cell door she unlocks it and stands back to let April in. The door bangs shut and the warder relocks the door.

This will be the last time the twins will see each other. The last time they will look at each other, face to identical face.

After exactly half an hour, the warder once again looks through the grille and sees the two sisters sitting side by side on the bed, their hands entwined and their heads together. The warder, untypically for her profession, has a soft heart. She too has a sister with whom she is close. She cannot imagine how the twins must be feeling now. She has read in the papers that twins have a particular bond that stays with them all their lives. She wishes she could give them more time together but she knows if her superior finds out she will be for the high jump. She has already broken the rules by not staying in the cell with them.

She unlocks the door and tells the twins their time is up. She watches as they embrace for the last time and her heart goes out to them. They are so beautiful she thinks. How will one live without the other?

A tender hearted gaoler! Who would have thought it? She has been paid well to stay outside the cell. She knows she should not leave them alone yet, when she is offered the amount of money Mrs Driscoll's QC suggests she is keen to turn a blind eye. She has given the condemned prisoner her last wish she thinks. And besides from what she has read in the paper they can afford it.

In the antechamber the warder returns the reticule back to its owner. She sees the look of abject grief upon the young woman's face. She has been crying and is now trying hard to compose herself. The warder marvels again at the likeness of the twins. They are like "two peas in a pod" she thinks. A pin has come loose from the young woman's blonde chignon and a stray wisp of hair falls in front of the almond, shaped eyes. The warder notices the eyes are as blue as the ocean on a summer's day. Her small bonnet is a little askew, as is her bustle. She is a little more ruffled than when she went into the cell to say her goodbyes. Hardly surprising under the circumstances. She had witnessed the two ladies clinging to one another. The warder imagines it is the least of the young woman's worries. The gaoler unlocks the door of the ante chamber where the attorney is waiting to escort the poor lady home.

♣

The clock ticks, the hands move irrevocably towards the hour. The warder looks at the young woman sitting before her and feels moved. It is hard to believe this lovely creature is capable of double murder. She shivers. 'Are there any other items to go to your next of kin?' She is predisposed to be kind to this beautiful creature in her last moments.

'I don't think so. There is just the book I have been

reading. I never will know the ending now shall I?' She smiles and raises an eyebrow. I have not had the patience to read of late. You can have it if you would like it. My sister has read it and found it entertaining.' She smiles weakly. 'You have been kind, thank you.'

They are both waiting for the turn of the key which will signal the end.

The warder suddenly looks at the prisoner's hand. 'Oh but you are still wearing your wedding band. That will need to go with your possessions.' The warder's eyes widen as the ring is removed, a flicker of confusion on her face. She takes the gold band and places it on the book.

'Why are you—' The door clanks open making them both jump. The hangman enters the cell.

♠

She sits by the fire as she has done so many times before but feels no warmth from the blaze. It is the evening of her birthday and she thinks of the celebration she imagined she and her twin would share. Now her sister has been hung by the neck until she is dead. She shudders.

It is as though an axe has cleaved through her body and half of her has gone. The fraction she has lost is her better half. She is exposed and alone.

All day Teddy has cried in his nursery, he is usually such a docile little boy. At almost two years of age he does not often cry, being spoilt he has nothing much to cry about.

Lizzie is struggling to keep a hold of the squirming, distressed boy. She is red in the face and sweating.

'Put him to bed, I will look to him while you have a break. Go and have some tea, it has been a trying day.' Her voice is calm and impassive as she moves towards the boy. Tiredness weighs upon her like a stone. Strange, she thinks, I should feel so heavy when there is only half of me left in the world.

'He just won't settle ma'am, perhaps he is sickening for something?' The nursemaid drops a curtsy and is relieved to escape.

'I will ring when I need you.'

Teddy stops his fretting and smiles. Her presence has calmed him, it always has. His tears stop as he holds out his arms and says: 'Mama.' Standing over Teddy she eases the soft, downy pillow from under his head and strokes his damp, dark curls from his forehead. She plants a kiss on his plump cheek. 'Ssh now, you should be sleeping it is past your bedtime young man.' She holds the pillow to her face and breathes in the scent of him.

Powder soft, like a cloud. She sits by his bed and he is soothed. Almost at once he begins to slumber.

'Goodnight my darling boy, sweet dreams.' She lowers the pillow over his face and gently, but firmly, holds it in place until his arms and legs are limp. May lifts the pillow and replaces it under his dark curls. 'Sleep well my darling son, I will see you soon.'

She takes the bottle from the pocket of her dress and sits heavily on the nursing chair. After all has been said and done she is so very tired. The dose, she has made sure, will be instantly fatal. She does not want to linger, April and Teddy will be waiting for her. Perhaps even Edward? She drinks and closes her eyes to wait.

Epilogue

Lady Vennor has taken to her bed. The news a stay of execution has been denied her daughter and the news that the best QC money can buy has not been able to save her has shocked Elizabeth. Money after all cannot buy everything she thinks as she lays back against her feather pillow and closes her long-lashed eyes. She sighs deeply. She cannot imagine how this state of affairs has come to pass. It is like a melodrama or a tawdry penny romance.

Having her name associated with the case in the newspapers has of course been vexing. Only yesterday she was approached by an old associate offering her a role. It just goes to show the adage is true; all publicity is good publicity.

Not that she intends to tread the boards ever again. She has not the need. Her star has risen and now she can rest. She has had her time in the limelight, enjoyed the standing ovations and the warm applause. A wan smile curls her rosebud lips at the memories.

There is a knock on her boudoir door and her maid

moves noiselessly to her bedside. 'This came in the post for you Milady.'

Elizabeth is about to wave the maid away until she sees an elegantly wrapped box in the girl's hand. She notices the box is from her favourite Chocolatier. Elizabeth takes the chocolates, unties the silky ribbons and lays aside the tissue to reveal the dark, luscious, violet creams.

Whoever has sent them must be acquainted as the sender knows her tastes. They are her favourites.

Who is her admirer she wonders? There is a card she notices as she bites into the fragile chocolate shell. As it cracks open she tastes the fragrant, sweet, fondant cream. Languidly, she opens the card. It is unsigned but written in a beautiful cursive hand that she vaguely recognises. She takes another of the delicious treats and eats it greedily.

The card reads:

Yours has been the performance of a lifetime. Bravo! You have been word perfect. Prepare to take your final applause. No more playing to the gallery for you, Mother Dearest. Time to exit the stage, take a bow, this is your final curtain call.

The End

Acknowledgements

The author would like to thank her early readers for wielding their red pens with alacrity without whom this book would never have come to fruition. Also thanks to Chris Kershaw for his IT expertise and Jill Craig and Sheila Kershaw for their endless patience and input. In addition, my thanks to Charlotte Mouncey for her interpretation of my ideas for the book cover.

On some occasions I may have fictionalised or blurred some details for the sake of the story. In such places, the errors belong to me alone.

Before You Go

Look out for **My Constant Lady** by Jane Fenwick coming early in 2020